PROMPOSAL

PROM

POSAL

RaeChell Garrett

POPPY
LITTLE, BROWN AND COMPANY
New York Boston

Poppy
Hachette Book Group
1290 Avenue of the Americas, New York, NY 10104
Visit us at LBYR.com

First Edition: April 2023

Poppy is an imprint of Little, Brown and Company. The Poppy name and logo are trademarks of Hachette Book Group, Inc.

The publisher is not responsible for websites (or their content) that are not owned by the publisher.

Confetti vector copyright © form and form/Shutterstock.com
Rose vector copyright © Naddya/Shutterstock.com

Library of Congress Cataloging-in-Publication Data
Names: Garrett, RaeChell, author.
Title: Promposal / RaeChell Garrett.
Description: First edition. | New York : Little, Brown and Company, 2023. | Audience: Ages 12 & up. | Summary: "When the school of her dreams puts her on the wait list, Autumn enlists the help of a former crush turned rival to form a promposal service in hopes of impressing the admissions committee." —Provided by publisher.
Identifiers: LCCN 2022004088 | ISBN 9780316371704 (hardcover) | ISBN 9780316372046 (ebook)
Subjects: CYAC: Proms—Fiction. | Schools—Fiction. | Interpersonal relations—Fiction. | African Americans—Fiction. | LCGFT: Romance fiction.
Classification: LCC PZ7.1.G3763 Pr 2023 | DDC [E]—dc23
LC record available at https://lccn.loc.gov/2022004088

ISBNs: 978-0-316-37170-4 (hardcover), 978-0-316-37204-6 (ebook)

Printed in the United States of America

LSC-C

Printing 1, 2023

For Granny

Chapter One

From: Admissions, Mercer School of Business, Great Lakes University
To: Autumn Reeves
Subject: Admissions Decision

Dear Autumn:

Thank you for your application to Mercer School of Business, Great Lakes University. After a thorough review of your qualifications, we cannot offer acceptance at this time. However, based on the strength of your application, we would like to offer you a place on our waiting list.

Our waiting list is not ranked. If an opening becomes available, the entire pool of waiting list candidates will be reconsidered for admission.

Please <u>accept</u> or <u>decline</u> your spot as soon as possible.

Sincerely,
Valerie Ferrer
Dean of Admissions
Mercer School of Business, Great Lakes University

From: Autumn Reeves
To: Admissions, Mercer School of Business, Great Lakes University
Subject: You've Been Compromised!

Dear Valerie Ferrer:

This morning, I received the email (now pasted below) with many red flags that cause me to question its authenticity. After careful analysis, I think you may have been hacked. I'd be happy to provide any further information you might need to help determine who might be responsible.

In the meantime, I look forward to receiving an official letter regarding my application to Mercer School of Business.

Sincerely,
Autumn Reeves
Mercer BIPOC Summer Program *Innovations in Business* Scholarship Recipient

From: Admissions, Mercer School of Business, Great Lakes University
To: Autumn Reeves
Subject: Re: You've Been Compromised!

Dear Autumn,

Thanks so much for bringing your suspicions to our attention. After our own investigation, I can assure you the email you received is official and reflects the decision of our esteemed admissions committee. Your qualifications show great promise, and for that reason, if space becomes available, we'll reconsider you for admission as part of this year's incoming class.

Best of luck,
Jeannie Gutierrez
Office of Admissions
Mercer School of Business, Great Lakes University

I stare at the screen, willing the words to change, until my eyes glaze over and I have to squeeze them shut.

I don't believe Jeannie Gutierrez.

Just because the email is official doesn't mean I'm the one who's supposed to get it.

How, in the midst of performing a thorough investigation of a breach of their security, could the Great Lakes University Office of Admissions possibly find time to verify or confirm the status of my application? It's only been a little over three hours since I let them know my suspicions.

And I'm sorry, but is Jeannie No-Title-Worth-Mentioning Gutierrez trying to be funny? Great promise?

I promise she'll be the first to know when I find out where the error is.

It's easy to get distracted. Maybe someone transposed numbers, or left one out, or added too few or too many zeros. Obviously, there's been a data entry problem. All I have to do is bring it to Mercer's attention.

First, I pull up my confirmation of application email and compare the applicant number to the one in the wait-list email. I read the numbers aloud, backward and forward. I look away, then repeat the process again.

They match.

I check my name, address, and school information the same way.

Then I open the transcript posted to my account. My name isn't exactly original. And I'm sure there are places other than southeastern Michigan with a LeBeau High School. Maybe the wait-listed Autumn Reeves lives *there*.

I compare what's uploaded to my file to a printed copy of what's on LeBeau's student portal. There must be *something* that doesn't match up.

But from the line breaks to the class titles, everything there looks good. My grade point average—4.0—looks stellar. And my test scores are in the ninetieth percentile.

I'm real with myself. Those stats wouldn't get me into an Ivy League, but Mercer isn't Harvard. My scores line up against the averages of Mercer students admitted in past years. And last year I was the Mercer BIPOC Summer Program *Innovations in Business* Scholarship Recipient.

The scholarship itself would maybe pay for two semesters of books. But when it comes to solidifying my potential as a student, I thought its value was limitless. I was chosen out of fifty super-talented people of color from five states. I hadn't expected to win the scholarship, but since I did, I at least expected to be admitted to the school. The official award letter clearly states the scholarship is contingent upon acceptance to Mercer, but I figured that was just a formality. It's not like I've somehow fallen off since then.

Next, I pull up the three letters of recommendation I received. They're glowing. Maybe my references could've honed in on my weaknesses a little more, but I didn't pick anyone who's more aware of those than necessary.

The only error I manage to find is a typo in my personal essay. I had two people proof it and I read it aloud to myself several times. A typo legit shouldn't have happened. I have no one to blame but myself. But is that enough to keep me out of where I'm trying to be?

I read the wait-list email again.

I verify the identifying information again.

It's all me, down to the tragically silent and unnecessary *I* in my middle name. Aniyiah.

I fall facedown onto my pillow. The air whooshes from my lungs with the sudden impact. I imagine it's my dreams leaving me to find a more promising subject to inhabit. There's no other way to look at this.

I've been wait-listed.

Chapter Two

I roll around on my bed, wrapping myself in my blankets. Some people pray. Some journal or run. I swaddle. Being tucked in tight feels like a force field around me. Nothing gets in. I can focus.

Usually, I can focus. But the phone notifications are out of control. And apparently, I like punishing myself by reading acceptance posts from what feels like all 441 members of LeBeau High's graduating class. The announcements started popping up weeks ago. Until now, I was proud of everybody living their dream. Now I'm tempted to shatter my phone and make it look like an accident.

But my curiosity about a new post in the MBSP group chat wins out.

The fifty of us were close during the three-week program,

promising to stay in touch after it ended. We did, for a few months. Now, nobody posts unless they're humble-bragging about some new accomplishment. I've visualized being the first to announce getting accepted to Mercer the way athletes imagine scoring at the last second to win a national championship.

Except getting into Mercer is even bigger than that. No other school in the state has an entrepreneurial studies program, let alone a senior capstone course that churns out actual viable businesses. No other school has as many students working for themselves within two years of graduation.

All I need to hear is the MBSP notification chime and I know: Someone has stolen my shine.

> **Maisy:** Am I the first to post? They want me!

> **Varesh:** I'm in.

> **James:** I got in, but I'm still waiting to hear from a few other places.

> **Lauryn A:** Issa yes for me!

> **DM from Lauryn A:** You better request me as a roommate and want to stay on west campus.

DM from Tayo: You notice who hasn't posted yet? Julian! Is it too much to hope he got rejected?

Then Tayo makes a separate group chat with just me, him, and Lauryn called *Mercer Knows Best* and proceeds to speculate on why Julian may have been rejected.

I seriously doubt Julian didn't get in. He's the reason I thought there was no way I'd receive any sort of recognition at the MBSP camp. He was always on top of everything. He also loved to bring attention to my mistakes. I didn't realize this was because he viewed me as his biggest competition until I won that scholarship.

His exact words were: "I knew it would be someone like you."

As happy as I was to be recognized, I spent weeks trying to figure out what his comment was supposed to mean.

And *I* haven't posted yet either. But because of the scholarship, they all assume I'm in. Just like I did. How could I not be? How is it possible that me and Lauryn sharing a room just like we did last summer might not happen?

Suddenly my swaddle feels like it's cutting off my circulation. I whip off the blankets. I need to talk to my boyfriend, Brandon. The way he says my name, like my very existence enchants him, is guaranteed to boost my ego.

Before the notes of the first ring are finished, his face fills my screen. A millisecond later, a melody alerts me that he's paused his gaming console.

He does not disappoint. He says my name, all breathy and deep like the sight of me is a relief.

Being the person someone else can't wait to hear from causes an instant uptick in my mood. I'm a little breathless too. "Hey. What are you doing?"

"Waiting for you to call me when you finished with Margo's promposal like you said you would. Took you long enough."

If six months of being with Brandon have taught me anything, it's that this boy likes his attention. He complains about me not calling exactly when I say I'm going to. He pouts about being left on Delivered. It's like he can't believe I'd be thinking about anything more than I'm thinking about him. And I kind of like it. He wants to be on my mind all the time because I'm on his mind all the time.

The idea is enough to bring a smile to my face in spite of everything.

The success of the promposal I did for my neighbor, Margo, also lightens my mood. It's the high I was dropped from when I got Mercer's decision. I've been setting up scavenger hunt clues all week. Today, we finally reached the promposal punch line.

"You should've seen them." My voice squeaks with the excitement of the memory. "Everything turned out cute."

Slowly he licks his lips as if it's all he can do to stomach my self-satisfaction. "I know. I saw the video. A lot of people did."

Did they? I'm the one who posted it, but between MBSP notifications and Mercer, I haven't gone back to look at it.

I swipe my phone's screen to check. A lot of people *did* see the video. There are more comments on the promposal than new *Look Ma I Made It* posts...for now.

"I was waiting for you to call because I want to come pick you up."

There's a shift in his tone when he says this. His speech is distorted like he has a mouth full of marbles.

I frown. "You're not mad at me, are you?"

"You know I can't get mad at you." His voice is softer and he's already walking through his house on his way to me, so I believe him. Still, he's different somehow. I don't think his eyes have landed directly on mine once since I called. I decide to let it go. I want to see him too.

I don't plan on shouting my failure from the rooftops, but Brandon knows how much I want Mercer. Being together and talking about the wait list will hopefully take some of the sting out of being told I'm not good enough. The sooner that happens the better.

"I'll be there in a little bit. Dress comfortable."

When he says that, I know exactly where we're going: the first place he ever tried to talk to me as anything other than a cool girl from class—Touch the Sky trampoline park. I was there on a Saturday afternoon with my little sister, Peyton, aka Baby. Brandon had seen me come in. When toddler hour ended, I was surprised to find him waiting for me by the lockers with a thin sheen of sweat on his deep brown skin and a shy smile.

We talked right there on a bench until Baby got tired of her favorite toy, had blown through all the snacks I brought, and started on her nap. Brandon made me laugh. And it didn't hurt that he had thick, long lashes framing his eyes like two passes of precision-tip eyeliner and volumizing mascara.

Touch the Sky is only sentimental to me, though. Brandon swears he'd been trying to get my attention since junior year. I'm not the best at picking up on clues about stuff like that when it comes to myself.

Now, other people's chemistry? I can spot that a mile away.

A trip to Touch the Sky is just a release of all the energy he has. Either that or maybe he has something on his mind too. He sounded...nervous. It's not an emotion I'm used to seeing on him. That's why it was so hard for me to name.

Wait.

Hold up.

Maybe this is about to be my promposal. Maybe he felt inspired when he saw my post about Margo.

I don't want to get my hopes up or anything, but a promposal would *definitely* make my day better. It would also be the sweetest thing Brandon has ever done for me.

Twenty minutes later, Brandon is here. He rings the doorbell instead of waiting in the car.

Mom's on the fourth day of her twelve-hour nursing shifts and Dad isn't home from work yet—he's picking up Baby from daycare. But Brandon learned the hard way—if you're taking Preston Reeves's daughter somewhere, you come to the door or Preston Reeves comes to you. He's not out to intimidate anybody, he just needs it known somebody loves me and will come looking if things don't go right.

Brandon is wearing the sweatshirt he wore to school today, but he's traded jogging pants for basketball shorts. This is one of the few times we look like we're going to the same place. He is the king of athleisure that's too expensive to just lounge around in, and I prefer jeans, a sweater, and boots.

I like that about us. We're complementary opposites.

I try to sound extra chill when I greet him. If this is my promposal and it's supposed to be a surprise, I don't want to ruin it by letting him know I'm onto him. I get up on my tiptoes for a quick kiss. At the exact same time, Brandon turns back toward the driveway, and my kiss lands on his ear.

I always find a way to sneak a kiss when I see him. He expects it. Sometimes he waits for it before he says anything. But not today.

I duck my head to hide my smile. He's definitely planning something.

When we're in the car, I get another notification about someone and their dream school.

I swear I can be happy for other people, but it hurts not having a story of my own to share. I release a heavy sigh and turn off my notifications.

Brandon glances my way as he pulls out of the driveway. "What's that all about?"

I don't want my wait-list situation to ruin whatever he has planned, but the angst is building. Getting it out of my system might make what happens next even better.

"You won't believe it, but Mercer wait-listed me. It's hard to see everyone out here all proud of themselves. I'm"—at a loss for words, I shrug and put my palms up—"in shock, I guess."

He glances at me again, surprise on his face. "Really?"

Knowing I'm not the only one who thinks this whole wait-list thing is some BS is like him blowing cool air on a fresh cut. Talking about this right now is a good thing. "It's crazy, right?"

"No, I mean, you get As but..."

I watch him, waiting. I need him to finish the thought. Nothing I can come up with makes sense as a way to finish that sentence. "But what?"

He shrugs and shakes his head. "But you take classes like Interpersonal Communication and Personal Growth Workshop."

I jerk my head back. "And? Those are electives."

"Electives anybody can get an A in."

I shift in my seat, turning my whole body toward him. I have to see as much of his face as I can to make sure he's serious. Even though I don't know how he can be. He sees how hard I work. There are plenty of times I want to be with him but do homework instead. I don't think *anybody* can do that.

His lips are set in a fine line. He *is* serious about this.

My chest goes hollow. It's like the reassurance he gave me earlier just by saying my name has left my body.

I swallow hard. "Not everybody can do well in those classes. Personal Growth Workshop taught me a lot about myself. It was hard."

"If you say so."

"And I took Spanish, which I'm now fluent enough in to earn college credit."

He knits his eyebrows as if the flaw in my logic perplexes him. "It's not like you're trying to be an interpreter, though. You applied to a top-ten business school. They want rigor."

He pauses to look both ways before turning out of my neighborhood. The only reason that pause isn't filled by my counterargument is…I'm not ready. He's supposed to be supporting me, not asking me to prove myself or defend my transcript. I've never missed a chance to tell him how special *he* is. He should do the same for me.

"And plus," he—ill-advisedly and without prompting—continues, "everybody knows you only stay in Spanish for the trips, which are mostly vacations."

"I learned a lot on those trips." There's so much force behind my words, actual spittle comes out with them. "And all of my core classes are either honors or AP. *And* don't forget, I won their summer program award."

Not to mention, his own record pales in comparison to mine. His dream school has a 70 percent acceptance rate. Mercer's is 15 percent. He knows that.

I could bring that up, but why? I don't want the idea of inadequacy to flood his brain the way it has mine. Deflating his ego won't build me back up. And I would never want to hurt him that way.

"I bet pretty much everyone who applied to Mercer can say all that. People are out here with awards we've never even heard of." He raises his eyebrows as if he's having a revelation. "Maybe they're doing you a favor. Why would you go to school for four years and spend all that money to be an event planner?"

Those words reverberate through me like a slap across the face. It actually burns with embarrassment. Brandon— my boyfriend of six months—thinks I'm average. Average. And oh yeah, my career goals aren't worth the investment it takes to achieve them.

"Believe it or not, there are qualifications for event-planning professionals. I can't go out right now and get a job whether you think anybody can do it or not."

There are random pauses between my words as if there are misplaced commas and periods everywhere. But speaking slowly and precisely is the only way I can get this all out without the quiver of hurt creeping into my voice.

"And can you please explain to me why you think it's okay to say all this to somebody you supposedly care about? How am I supposed to look at you now and not think about how average you think I am?"

"You don't have to," he mumbles, without even a glance in my direction.

I look out at the road and blankly back at him. "How can I not think about it?"

He doesn't answer. He sits there biting his bottom lip. I resist the urge to repeat my question. Instead, I let the tink of the car's blinker fill the silence. The sound acting as a countdown to something explosive. I don't want to do anything to speed up the clock.

After a while, Brandon clears his throat. "I'm saying, you don't have to look at me."

His telling me not to look at him, as confusing as it is, makes me eye him more intently than I ever have. I see the boy I think I could love. The dark eyes. The dense, spiky kinks of his hair. "How am I supposed to not look at my boyfriend?"

Brandon keeps his face forward but shifts his eyes slowly toward me and frowns. The rise and fall of his chest is way more than what's required for sitting at a stoplight. Could it be he's realized his words have ruined whatever he has planned? I don't know what to think.

When it's our chance to make the left turn, he grips

the steering wheel but keeps his foot on the brake. A horn sounds from behind us.

Slowly the words seep out. "You don't have to look at me as your boyfriend."

Several people behind us are laying on the horn now. The arrow flashes yellow and suddenly, Brandon speeds off. He barely makes the light, leaving no time for anyone to turn behind us. My phone flies to the floor as I let it go in favor of the door handle.

But even with all the chaos he's creating, I don't miss his point.

This isn't a promposal. This is a breakup. I squeeze my eyes shut, hoping to shock myself out of whatever alternate reality I'm in. But when I open them, I'm still here. This is real life.

"Why?" It's a question born out of weakness. I should be thanking him for breaking up with me. After everything he's just said, *I* should be breaking up with *him*.

The car might be careening on two wheels when he blows out a gust of air. "If you think about it, it's better for both of us if we do this now, tie up loose ends. I can hang out with my boys these last couple months, and you can keep doing you. It's not like it would work with us being hundreds of miles apart anyway."

I want to tell him I think about the future of our relation-ship every single time I hear about someone breaking up because they'll eventually have to. Like it's on some senior year checklist. Or when someone refuses a crush because *what's the point.* The difference between me and Brandon is when I think about breaking up, I see how stupid it would be.

Why stop kissing him if I don't have to? Why not go to prom together? Why miss out on daily good morning texts or the way he says my name? Why would I choose that?

Our breakup should be something unavoidable. It should be because long distance is unrealistic and I can't inhale the scent of his leave-in or sneak a kiss through video chats. Not because I'm an average loose end.

But because of everything else he's said, my pride won't let me say any of this. How can I make a case for staying together when he's already decided I'm not worth the energy?

"Let me out. Now," I say, surprised at how steady my voice is.

"No." His voice goes high with disbelief and what I think is supposed to be concern.

He can't believe I'd want anything to do with him. Especially after dropping all these bombs on a day my skin is thinner than I even knew it could get. But somehow, Brandon is still driving toward Touch the Sky like we're about to go all out on some trampolines.

"Not in the middle of the street," I spit out. "You haven't driven me to that, you egomaniac. Pull over."

He exhales deeply through his mouth. I think it's a behavior I'm supposed to model. But I just twist my lips and roll my eyes. If he tells me to calm down, all the ego protecting I did a few minutes ago is going out the window.

"I know you're mad, but I don't think walking six miles back to your house is the way you want to prove that point."

"Ultra Fresh is right there." I slice my hand through the air as if splitting it, pointing directly in front of us. "Reese is working. I'm good."

He takes another deep breath. This one, however, is for his benefit.

"What? You don't want me to tell my best friend you tried to take me to the very first place you told me I was cute and break up with me for no reason after telling me I'm average?"

As we pass Ultra Fresh, Brandon's jaw works. Reese is actually a Brandon fan, but we all know it's provisional. They're good as long as he's good to me. And Reese's bad side is a bad spot to be in.

"I know you're mad, but I don't think refusing to let me out of your car is the way you want to prove that point." I try my best to imitate his arrogance.

To the dismay of many a driver, Brandon makes a skidding U-turn. I hold a full breath until I'm sure we're going to live through him acting like he's the one with a reason to be mad.

Even though I've made Brandon this angry, I don't feel vindicated. His anger isn't about us. It's about him. And that makes me wish he had let me get out and walk. Taunting him might not be able to cover my hurt for as long as I need it to.

I look out the window, focusing on a single pile of snow that's too packed together to melt even though spring starts next week.

Before I'm out of the car good, Brandon is speeding back out to the road. No goodbye. No nothing.

When I walk into the fluorescent yellow-and-green café, my eyes start to well. This is where I should've come in the first place. If anyone can help me see things more clearly, it's Reese.

Chapter Three

"I got wait-listed."

I don't have to say by what school. Just like I know playing Division I basketball is everything to Reese, she knows going to Mercer is everything to me.

She's also the only person who knows I didn't apply to any other schools.

Across from me, she slumps in the tiny, mostly plastic chair. We're at a table in the back, as private as we can get in this tiny space at the center of a strip mall.

Reese and I have known each other since middle school, when I tried out for the basketball team. I thought the only reason I wasn't athletic was because my parents never put me in sports. But things didn't work out. My athletic talent is limited to warming a bench while cheering on others—that is, if I can even make the team.

Reese hasn't always been the person I call in times like these.

We became closer in the middle of freshman year, right around the time the person who previously filled the role decided we couldn't be friends anymore. And I one hundred percent deserved that verdict.

Reese coughs out a laugh, but there's no humor in it. No trace of her broad, gummy smile. It's more like a sound of disbelief. She sticks a finger underneath the cap she's forced to wear and scratches at the base of her low ponytail. "I figured at least one of us would be happy and I was okay if it was you."

Before I can tell her that one of us being happy is not enough, she slams both of her latex-glove-covered palms on the table. "What is wrong with these people? You did all that AP stuff, everything they say you should. They gave you that scholarship, and you have to wait? This is just like when coaches said I wasn't strong enough and I got stronger. Then they said five nine is short for a small forward. I grew an inch and now there's nothing special about me. I'm just average. I mean, what do they want us to do?"

There's that word again. *Average.*

I fill my cheeks with air and blow it out slowly. Reese's question isn't rhetorical. It's one she's been asking herself since State—*her* dream school—used all their available scholarships before offering one to her. And when other players from her AAU basketball team started getting DI offers and she didn't, she felt like she'd earned an aha moment.

Now it's my question to turn over in my brain. What could I have done differently? What could have made me better than average?

I feel the pressure building behind my eyes again. I'm not even sure which part of today is making me like this. Everything has gone left. And the more Brandon's words sink in, the more I think he could be right. There's nothing I've done that everyone else hasn't.

Reese uses a fingernail to pick at something stuck to the table until it gives and sails to the floor. "My mom's been talking about me taking up a skilled trade. Probably electrical. I can apprentice under my granddad."

I side-eye her. "What about basketball?"

"Advancing from Division II or junior college to Division I is just as hard as getting into DI right out of high school. What's the point?" She pulls lip balm out of her apron and pops the top off. She stares at it long enough that I'm convinced she only took it out to have something to look at as she drops this bomb. "Everybody knows if it wasn't for basketball, I would've tried to get my GED back in middle school. I'm not going to college just to go. I'd never even finish."

I nod. Reese is a B-minus, C-plus student who doesn't like learning anything she can't use practically. Basketball made school worth it, though.

"You're saying that now, but you might not feel like that in a few months."

She shakes her head. "I don't want to play and get my hopes up again for something that's not going to happen. Then I'll get to feel all this failure shit twice. Once is enough."

I shake my head right back at her and with just as much conviction. "But what if it's not a failure? What if you could work your way to Division I and then whatever's after that?"

"I'ma need a job, Autumn, not a what-if. My mom made that very clear. She's already sacrificed a lot so I can play basketball. I can't keep asking her to sacrifice more."

"I'm so—"

She makes a quick zip noise with her mouth, cutting me off. "Don't say that. Nobody's dead."

Reese made me the mystery mix smoothie she knew I needed the minute she saw me. I take a sip of it and swallow all the sympathy I want to give my friend. "Since we're dropping bombs, Brandon broke up with me."

She goes from slumped to straight-backed, like a transition in a TikTok routine. Next thing I know she stands up and unties her apron.

"Wait for me outside," she whispers. "I'm about to call in sick so we can go to your house and see what your dad is cooking because this is too much."

Chapter Four

I don't sleep all night. Instead, I stare up at my bedroom ceiling. The teal I spent hours picking out is dotted with traces of moonlight filtering through the spaces where the window blinds don't meet.

Even switching my phone off doesn't stop my mind from replaying the day's events. Nothing is turning out the way I thought it would. The way I planned it. The way I worked for.

There's no Brandon. There's no acceptance.

Before I force myself out of bed and get ready for school, I log in to my Mercer Applicant Status Page. The decision hasn't changed. I'm still wait-listed.

Wait-listed. Dumped. Average.

My cursor inches toward Accept, the button that would

make Mercer's decision official. When I get too close it lights up like it's a thing I should want in my life. I pull the cursor away. Not because there's any chance I won't click it. I don't have much of a choice. The problem is, once I do, I can't be in denial or keep looking for loopholes and mistakes. Accepting is admitting I'm not good enough to make it in on the first try. Maybe even at all.

I move the cursor again and force myself to click Accept. When I do, my status changes from *Waiting List: Pending* to *Waiting List: Accepted.* And there's a new link—Submit Additional Materials.

I sit up.

I click on the new link and am taken to a simple page with a text box, as well as an upload button. Above the text box, it says, *Please submit any additional information you believe may strengthen your candidacy.*

Additional information?

I look around the room, settling on separate piles of clutter as if the answer to the *additional information* riddle is hidden under one.

I need something to fill that box with. But I mean, I've told them everything good there is to know about me. If that's not enough, I don't know what is.

I'm going to have to come up with something new and better than average.

I stare at the text box, willing a new, innovative idea to come to me. Whatever it is has to be the polar opposite of anything I've already told the admissions committee about myself. I have to prove I'm worthy of a chance.

But how?

The answer isn't in this room, but there is an answer. At least that's what I try to convince myself as I email my counselor, Mrs. Tanner, and ask if we can meet before first bell.

I pull myself out of the tangle of blankets and head to the shower. When I open the bathroom door dressed and ready to go, Baby is standing there buck naked and holding her wet diaper out to me.

She's the cutest kid. She has these huge brown eyes that make you think she's already seen more of the world than the rest of us, and full cheeks that must be smooched on sight. Jury is still out on which of my parents she looks like, but no one wants credit for her already well-developed knack for shenanigans.

She says "No" as a question and laughs when I tickle her belly. I throw her over my shoulder, angling her so the diaper doesn't touch me.

Someone who's not late is going to have to take care of her situation.

Dad's downstairs at the kitchen counter in boxer briefs and dress socks. He's eating one of the breakfast quiches Mom bulk-bakes and looking at his phone. Must've been on his way to the laundry room to look for something clean and got sidetracked by hunger. This is a common occurrence in the Reeves household.

Mom is standing in front of the coffee machine pulling her locs up in a ponytail. Except for these, and the self-described "fluffiness" where I'm lean and tight, she's basically the older version of me—narrow eyes, high cheekbones, and medium-brown skin with layers of yellow underneath.

My parents eye me cautiously.

I was a little emotional last night when I told them about Mercer and eventually Brandon. They're probably wondering if I'm in that same volatile headspace. I'm going to go with yes. How could my head be anywhere else?

I hand Baby over to Dad. In a high-pitched voice he teases her about being ready to be potty-trained; then he tells her to give the dirty diaper to me. She laughs as she drops it on the wood floor. I ball it up and tape it closed.

"Get me a clean one and a wipe too," Dad instructs over his shoulder.

"I don't have time for this." I shake my head as if he's just given me the most complex task. "I have an appointment with Mrs. Tanner. I can get off this wait list. I just have to prove to Mercer I'm good enough."

From the breezeway, I toss the diaper toward the trash can. If the sound of its landing is any indication, I miss my target.

"You're plenty good enough." Mom's words carry the weight of an afterthought, like my comment is so absurd it barely deserves a response.

"Is that attitude why you guys didn't stop me from taking

so many apparently useless classes? Or point out that I need a lot more sparkle to get into the college of my dreams?"

I mean, they should know how to navigate higher learning. Mom's a labor and delivery nurse and dad's a safety engineer. I dash past them and take the steps two at a time to get the diaper and wipe from Baby's room. After handing everything off to Dad, I wash my hands.

"We don't dictate what classes you take or your extracurriculars because you've known who you are since the day you were born. You're ahead of the game on that." Mom wets a dish towel, wrings it out, and starts to wipe down the counter. "Don't let Mercer convince you you're behind. We went over this last night. If one place doesn't want you the next one will. Start taking the other schools you applied to seriously."

"I ca—" I trip over my own words, coming this close to letting slip the reason I can't take her advice. The whole situation has me so frustrated, I'm fighting an impulse to stomp my foot. "That's not what you're supposed to say. You're supposed to tell me to buck up. Work harder. Never give up."

Mom rolls her eyes. "Doing nothing at all is giving up. Choosing option B isn't."

I groan. There is no option B. Even if I had applied to other schools there wouldn't be an option B.

"What do you want me to say?" Mom sticks out a finger, preparing to tick off her points as she makes them. "You're a great student, you have goals, you respect yourself and other people, you believe in something greater than yourself. I feel like we're batting a thousand. The rest is just growing up."

She looks at Dad for assistance. He jumps in like he's been patiently awaiting his turn.

"Just do the pros and cons of all the schools you're considering. If you need to make a visit somewhere, we can do that."

Mom goes back to her morning chores as if Dad has just said the words that will forever put an end to this conversation.

"There's no point. I'm not going to do well somewhere I don't want to be," I spit out, anger and exasperation flowing through my hands just before I ball them into fists. I let everything I feel settle there, otherwise the tears I held back yesterday are going to force their way out.

If I cry, Mom's going to keep sermonizing in that matter-of-fact tone as if she has biblical backup, and Dad's going to keep making it sound easy to give up on what I see for myself.

Mom points toward the back door, my exit, with both hands. "Please. Go to school. There's no point in this conversation that *you* started if you can't listen."

"Whatever. Let me go, then, learn how to think small and scale back my hopes and dreams," I say with fake enthusiasm.

"Sounds like a solid strategy. Goodbye." Mom turns

away as if it's the end of the conversation whether I like it or not.

And I don't like it, but I'm not mad at my mom. I *am* everything she's proud of, but I can't put any of that on a transcript.

Chapter Five

I take in the organized chaos of Mrs. Tanner's office. There are no fewer than twenty perfectly lined-up stacks of paper in various spots around the room. And—through no fault of her own—a section of chipped paint on the wall reveals a layer of color for each of the four decades LeBeau High has been around.

Her office is normally a place where I'm relaxed. Not just because she's super laid-back, with leggings she tries to pass off as actual pants, and a haphazard blond ponytail at the crown of her head, but because she tells me all the time, I'm one of the kids who makes her job easy. It's a no-pressure zone for both of us.

I hate to shatter expectations, but today is about to be different.

We still have our jackets on. It takes the building until at least second period to warm up, if at all. At the same time, everything that comes in contact with my skin suffocates me. And as annoying as I find the sound, I can't stop the tip of my boot from bouncing rhythmically against her desk.

Mrs. Tanner gives the winning smile that always makes me wonder what I've done to deserve it. "Your email was a little worrisome. The first thing we need to do is take a breath."

I pin my lips between my teeth to make sure the depth of my disappointment doesn't seep out. She thinks we have time for a breath. We do not. If not for the risk of passing out, I'd suspend my breathing altogether to prove the point.

"National College Decision Day is May 1. That's six weeks away."

She nods slowly. "I'm aware."

"Well, when the lucky people who got accepted the first go-round start declining, I need to be the obvious choice." I wrap my arms around myself and grab fistfuls of my sweater. "For all I know someone already has declined, and the admissions committee is preparing to give my spot to someone else on the wait list right now."

She frowns. "I understand the pressure you're under. But...maybe this is an opportunity for you to focus on some of the other colleges you've applied to."

I swear, the next person who says that is going to get the truth.

I stretch my fingers out and tap the chair's armrest. How can I say what I mean without it leading to another anecdote I've heard at least ten other times?

Giving up on being anything other than cutthroat honest, I sigh. "I'm sorry, Mrs. Tanner, but Mercer is the place I want to be. I need them to want me too."

She taps her chin thoughtfully. "There are groups around school that I'm sure would love to have you help with some of their end-of-the-year projects. So many of them don't have enough hands for all the things they dream up."

"I've already done all that. I always have your back when you ask me to volunteer for things no one else wants to help with. And I like doing that"—I lean back in my seat, frustrated—"but you already put that stuff in my recommendation letter."

"What about Women's—"

I shake my head. "I need something more. A statement."

Her pale white fingers glide across the keyboard before she nods and says, "Yeah, that's what I thought. You've taken one of our women's study capstones. You didn't find it challenging and rewarding, something you could expand on?"

"Yes, I did find it rewarding," I admit. "But the admissions committee already knows that about me. I need to show them something different, show them I'm well-rounded."

To be honest, I'm kind of irritated. We met every spring in this very office to discuss my curriculum. Mrs. Tanner never once mentioned that something like this could happen.

Yes, we talked about what colleges like to see, but she never got specific. She never said the classes I chose would limit me. She never asked me if any particular class was a direct reflection of my goals or suggested a more impressive way to explore my passions. It was all *Autumn, you'll do well in that course.*

"Okay." She presses her pointer finger to lines I'm pretty sure I caused to form on her forehead and massages a tight circle. "Where do you see yourself after college? Let's try and make a connection there."

"I want to major in entrepreneurial studies. To be an event planner. I see myself working for a couple places at first and then branching out on my own." I nod approval of my ability to articulate exactly what I want. "Not that many schools have the specialization. Mercer is the perfect fit."

I keep talking because I suddenly feel the need to justify applying to such a competitive school. "I got a small scholarship from their summer BIPOC program. And yes, I knew I still had to be admitted, but I thought that was just a formality or whatever. I mean, you had to apply to the program itself."

My voice fades on the last few words. I realize if I hadn't had that one tiny bit of recognition, I would've spent more than two weeks prepping my application.

Mrs. Tanner's eyes do the same thing mine did earlier this morning, flit around the room looking for answers.

That's when I know she's thinking big, outside the box. I lean in.

"Mr. Richmond, the junior advisor, has a student involved with Young Black Entrepreneurs and he's always talking about the great things she does with them."

She scrunches her nose and looks out across her office as if it's all coming together in her mind.

"If you're interested in entrepreneurship that's where you need to be. They're very exclusive and only work with a limited number of the most dedicated students, but let me make some calls."

All I hear is "very exclusive" and "limited number" and I know YBE is something I have to at least try.

Before I can get out a proper thank-you, the senior class president comes over the PA system. Senior Superlatives are being announced today.

I forgot.

Immediately, my mind goes to my hair. I haven't twisted it in three days. Calling it frizzy is a compliment at this point. This morning I gelled it all up into a moon-shaped bun and tied my scarf around it. I'd hoped there was enough time for the process to tame my edges before I walked into school. As my luck goes, there wasn't.

Even though my clothes have all the telltale signs of being plucked from the floor in my rush to get out the door this morning, I'm at least dressed in my normal uniform of a sweater and jeans. Still, I look like I've been wait-listed and lost sleep over it.

I'm going to go down as the most disheveled *Most Likely to Succeed* ever.

Or maybe not.

The first couple of Senior Superlative awards go as expected. Reese, of course, gets Most Athletic.

But Most Likely to Succeed goes all wrong.

It's not me.

And when all the other *Most Likelies* that fit me, like Most Likely to Be a Billionaire or President or My Boss's Boss, sail by and go to other people, I stop listening. Why did I ever think my name would be called? There's no superlative for Most Likely to Continue to Be Average.

I make eye contact with Mrs. Tanner so I can thank her and get to class. She shushes me.

"Most Likely to Brighten Someone's Day, Stanton Rimmer and Autumn Reeves," comes over the PA system.

I look up at the speaker in the corner of the ceiling expecting a correction.

Mrs. Tanner directs a soft clap and big smile my way.

"They said Autumn Reeves," I practically spit out.

"Yes." Her smile gets even bigger. "Doesn't it feel good to be recognized by your peers?"

My shoulders slump and I let my head fall back against the chair. It's like she hasn't been listening to me. It's like my whole high school career I've failed to properly give the energy of who I am.

"No." I shake my head slowly, trying to pick my words just right so this woman will get me. "If I can't convince my class I'm worthy of more than recognition for my personality, there's no way I'm convincing anybody's admissions office."

"Oh, Autumn…" Her voice trails off and she sputters as if she means to say more but can't figure out exactly what.

When the tips of her ears go pink I decide to take some of the pressure off by thanking her and showing myself out.

Chapter Six

I almost hit my counterpart Stanton with the door on my way out of the counseling center. I'm not entirely sure I'm on my way to the media center to have my picture taken for the yearbook until I see him. He's all smiles.

He totally and completely deserves this recognition. I force a smile back.

He flips fine brown hair out of his eye with a toss of his head. "This is cool. We can bring double the joy into the room."

"Do we have to?" I cross my arms and look down at the scuffed floor as we make our way along it.

In this dim hall, it's easy to imagine that everyone here could use some light. I just don't get why I have to be the source. Why haven't I done something more productive with my time?

"I didn't expect to have to start my uplifting with you." He stands a little taller like he's just had a great idea. "I voted for you."

I know he's trying to raise my spirits, but my side eye has a mind of its own. This was a write-in ballot, not multiple choice. He had to come up with my name all on his own and we haven't had a class together in two years.

"Wow. Thanks."

His "You're welcome" tells me my sarcasm game is weak today.

When we reach the media center, he holds the door open for me. It's packed with seniors already, who for some reason are bottlenecked at the entrance. At least I don't have to worry about seeing Brandon. He wasn't nominated for anything.

I can't help but wonder if he missed something this morning, though. Six months straight he walked me to first period every single morning and stood in the hall with me until the very last minute. To this day, I have no idea how he ever made it on time to his class on the other side of the building.

What did he do this morning instead?

Not that I want him to walk me anywhere. I absolutely do not. But it says a lot about our relationship if he doesn't at least notice my absence as much as I notice his. Did everything about us matter more to me than it did to him? Is this really easier for him?

Stanton brings me back to the present. "I wanted to talk to you anyway. I saw Margo's promposal. I need you to help me do something like that for Luca."

I look up at him, surprised. A real smile creeps up.

I loved seeing the look on Margo's face as things came together. It made her happy to see Will happy. And being close to their happiness made me happy.

"Make sure I'm the next person on your list to help."

Confusion must show on my face because he hands me his phone.

"I guess you haven't seen Margo's post thanking you. Look."

He reaches over my shoulder and scrolls down to the comments. And there are *a lot* of them. Some are saying the promposal bar is high. Others are saying the promposal looks too much like work. And others are flat-out asking for my help. I hand his phone back.

I'm not going to act like I didn't like working on the promposal, because I did. I just don't have time for more. My focus has to be on Mercer. Stanton and Luca are cute together. I hate to say no, but that's how it's going to have to be.

"That was something I did for *her*," I say. "It's not, like, a thing I do. The only reason it worked out the way it did is because she and Will have been together forever. I know what's cute about them. I've known Margo since before all the Black kids started sitting together in one corner of the cafeteria."

He presses his hand to his chest as if my words have ripped out his heart. "But you're good at it. It was so sweet, and not generic, like everyone else's. There's no way those clues would've worked for any other couple."

I squeeze farther into the room as more people get here. "That's because I've given Margo rides to and from school a billion times and she tells me everything about her and Will on the way."

"I'm an open book. What do you need to know about me and Luca?"

Thinking out loud, I use my fingers to tick off questions as they come to me.

"Where you met? How you met? What you guys like about each other? What you don't like about each other? What you fight about? How you make up and who initiates it? What are your inside jokes? What's his favorite color? Basically everything."

He covers my hands with one of his. "Those are all my favorite things to talk about. Think about it and let me know. I want to do it soon."

It must be all his enthusiasm that makes "Sure" come out of my mouth.

He thanks me and excuses his way through the crowd. Somehow, I get more pressed into it. Normally that wouldn't bother me, but closeness leads to conversation. And I am not in the mood for a conversation that flows into talking about what I'm doing after graduation.

"Don't give your ideas away."

I flinch at the low and deep voice that creeps up from behind me.

I don't even have to look.

That voice belongs to Mekhi Winston—aka Most Likely to Be a Billionaire.

The feeling that he's snuck up on me is one I'm used to. He's the boy you don't notice at first because he's drawing the least attention to himself. Never talking just to fill silence or speaking loud enough to be heard by anyone his words aren't expressly meant for. And he's never dressed in anything more or less than jeans, a T-shirt or sweatshirt, and a gold chain—no pendant.

But once the dark amber skin with a smattering of freckles catches your eye, it's kind of hard to get him off your mind. The boy will have you doing things like Googling the proper name of the little indentation above your top lip. I'm not sure if it's the way his slightly bigger top lip sits over his bottom one or what, but every single time I look at him my eyes go straight to the *philtrum*. And I won't even mention the number of articles I've read with titles like "Here's What the Shape of Your Philtrum Says About You" and "Are Pouty Lips Really More Attractive?"

Admittedly, I knew the answer to that last question before

I even read the articles. The answer is definitely yes. Mekhi Winston's lips are more attractive than just about anybody's.

I look past all of that, searching for the person he's talking to, because I know he's not talking to me. We haven't spoken directly to each other since freshman year. I was supposed to be hooking him up with my then–best friend, Jordyn, but everything went sideways.

Mekhi kissed me. I kissed him back.

I was one hundred percent wrong. He didn't know Jordyn lost her train of thought when she saw him. *I did*. I deserved to lose my best friend and have her never speak to me again no matter how hard I tried.

What I didn't deserve is him telling me straight to my face with an audience that our kiss didn't mean anything to him. That I didn't mean anything to him.

It's fine if he didn't like me like that, but he didn't have to make it seem like I repulse him.

We're not friends. We're not even acquaintances.

There are obviously people we both know around us, but none of them are looking at Mekhi. He's not looking at me either, though.

I'd like to keep it that way. I go right back to minding my business until another soft mumble comes from his direction.

I deep-sigh and prep myself to step around whatever trap he's setting for me.

Then again, I'd rather have him go ahead and try me so I can clap back in all the ways I was too hurt to do before.

"What?" I say, low enough that if he doesn't respond I can play it off like I'm talking to myself.

I don't know what he would get out of pretending to speak to me, but it's not like I've ever understood his logic.

"Huh?" It's almost as if he's as surprised to hear *my* voice as I was to hear *his*. Like he's just now realizing he spoke out loud.

"Nothing." I add a note of breeziness to my tone.

If there's no conversation here, I'm not interested in starting one. Mekhi and I have zero to say to each other.

The bottleneck finally starts flowing as the yearbook advisor tells us when we'll be called and asks that we go back to class once our picture has been taken. A grumble goes around the room telling me the last part is probably not happening for most people. Senioritis is real.

Suddenly, Mekhi says, "When you were talking to Stanton it seemed like you might give your ideas away. I was thinking, it's cool to do promposals for your girl, but you should get paid for your time and energy for anybody else. From what I hear, a lot of people are interested. You can probably make a lot of cash."

I look up at him. He's peeking down at me now. There's no mistaking this. He's trying to have a conversation. With me.

I raise one eyebrow and suck my teeth.

Mekhi Winston offering me advice is where this string of bad luck and unexpected experiences ends. Life can't keep setting me up for failure and embarrassment without me taking some sort of action.

"Thank you for your concern," I deadpan. "But you don't have to look out for me. I don't let people take advantage of me anymore."

He jerks his head back and scrunches his nose like he can't believe I've said what I said. Then a grin spreads slowly across his face and he laughs. Out loud. At first, it's little whimpers, and then it takes off.

So much for the clapback I looked forward to. All I can do is clench my jaw.

I'm about to let him have it when I spot Jordyn, of all people, through a small break in the crowd. She's sitting at a table, hunched over a textbook, and staring at me and Mekhi. His bellowing laughter must have caught her attention.

I rarely see her. LeBeau is a big school, but it's also like Jordyn and I repel each other. How is it that the one time I say two words to Mekhi in over three years she's here to witness it?

I pull my hands into the sleeves of my sweater and wrap my arms tightly around myself. Just a few seconds ago I was hot with anger, but with her eyes on me—on us—I feel a shiver of shame. Even after three years, it still feels the way it did all those times I tried to talk to her about what happened. I never even figured out how she knew something *had* happened between me and Mekhi, but she did. I stopped existing to her after that.

When she realizes I'm staring back at her she tosses her long box braids over her shoulder and smirks before she goes back to using the media center for its actual purpose.

My train of thought is interrupted by AJ, Mekhi's best friend. He pokes his smiling face right between us. "What y'all over here laughing at?"

The question is enough to draw my eyes away, but it takes a little longer for my mind. I want to leave the whole scene, but regardless of all the similarities between AJ and Mekhi—height, complexion, low fades with curly tops— their personalities couldn't be more different. AJ can be a clown sometimes, but in the best way. And he's a nice person. We'd be friends if not for Mekhi. I don't have any reason to ignore him.

I'm sure it's not a secret to AJ that me and Mekhi don't speak. He probably thinks he's entered some type of alternate universe seeing us standing here next to each other and Mekhi looking like he's having a good time. An alternate universe would at least explain the last twenty-four hours.

"She thinks I'm concerned about her," Mekhi says with the raise of an eyebrow. Laughter lingers in his voice.

"And he's just being himself. An asshole," I grind out.

"Whoa. Whoa. Whoa." AJ puts his hands up between us as if he's holding us both back. "This is supposed to be a joyous occasion. You're not sitting in class. People have love for you."

"Love isn't supposed to hurt." I pointedly direct my comment only at AJ. I'm done acknowledging Mekhi. I do note he's suddenly gone quiet. *Asshole* must be his Off button. I'll keep that in mind should I have the misfortune of him speaking to me again. "I rebuke anyone who voted for me."

AJ puts his hands up defensively. "Don't look at me. I didn't do it."

Reese pushes her way into our vapid party. This is my first time seeing her today, but she obviously remembered her picture might be taken. Her bone-straight, shoulder-length hair is free of her trademark ponytail. She has on a pushup bra too. I only know because I am well versed in Reese's breasts or lack thereof. She spends a lot of time telling me what she'd do if she had what I have. It's like she honestly believes a C cup is a superpower.

And instead of her usual sweatshirt and leggings she's wearing a cropped button-down blouse and jeans. It somehow makes her legs look even longer than usual.

She focuses her attention on AJ but not for the same reasons as me. Regardless of what I've told her about Mekhi, she continues to think he's a nice guy.

"Why you always lying? I was sitting right next to you when you filled out your ballot. AUTUMN REEVES. All caps like you meant it."

AJ's mouth drops open, and he cocks his head. "I was copying you. That's your girl. I figured you would know."

I gasp, like a for-real sharp intake of air. She's supposed to be my friend. "How could you play me like that?"

Reese's eyes look like they're about to pop out of her head, but she doesn't deny what she's been accused of. "Why are you even in here? No one voted you anything," she says to AJ as she pulls me toward the media center doors.

"I'm supporting my boy," he yells after us, but she shushes him as if she's suddenly interested in abiding by media center rules.

"How are you even friends with him?" she yells back.

She's talking to Mekhi now. He doesn't answer. He's too busy eyeing me like I've swindled him out of his first million. I give him the same look right back. I said what I said. If he feels called out he needs to ask himself why that might be.

Before we make it back out of the door to "freshen" me up, I look to the table where I spotted Jordyn earlier. If she'd been present for the whole scene she'd know that Mekhi and I are still barely on speaking terms. But this alternate universe won't rest until it's poked every sore spot. So, of course, she's gone.

Chapter Seven

I have to take a deep breath before I walk into room 207 of LeBeau's community center for the YBE meeting. I'm supposed to be looking for a junior from LeBeau named Maddie. There are literally five Black Maddies in the junior class, and I don't know one from the other even with a last name. When I walk in, about twenty people are pushing chairs into a circle and sitting down. I want to figure out who among them has been accepted to Mercer.

After school, Mrs. Tanner called me into her office to give me the details about YBE. She told me at least three members have been accepted. She also told me about the projects some of them are working on, like project management tools to help streamline health care billing systems and creating new cryptocurrencies. Then there are the past success stories, like full rides to Mercer. She was trying to sell me on YBE, but all she did was prove how super inadequate I am.

"Autumn, right?"

I look up to see a girl who can best be described as statuesque. I've seen this Maddie around a lot. She's hard to miss. I mean, I'm pretty put together on most days, but I can be kind of basic about it. I'm not turning heads all day every day with my very presence. Maddie, on the other hand, is the hair did, nails did, everything did type. And that's not a dig. She's . . . aspirational.

"I don't mean *right* like are you Autumn. I know who you are. I mean . . . never mind." She shrugs and motions for me to follow her. "I saved you a seat."

I follow her, searching the now fully assembled circle face by face for anyone else I recognize. I shift my gaze quickly, trying to make a connection, and then I do.

Mekhi.

His arms are folded, and he's in a very intense conversation with a light-skinned guy. I swear. He's always trying to look important. I'm sure whatever they're talking about can't be that serious.

Of all the gatherings of Black people doing worthwhile things, I had to walk into this one.

I don't realize I've stopped dead in front of him until he looks up. We both jerk our heads back, but I'm quick to correct myself. I don't want to be doing anything at the same time he's doing it.

Maddie gracefully sits down, *right* next to him. I don't break our eye contact. I want him to know that whatever he thinks about me being here is irrelevant. If anything going on in this room can help me get into Mercer, there's no way Mekhi Winston can keep me from it.

He narrows his eyes. I sashay two steps to the lone empty chair on the other side of Maddie. Then I make a show of sitting down and getting comfortable. Mekhi doesn't miss any of it. When I turn back to him, he's leaning forward on his forearms, zeroed in on me.

I smirk. He scoffs and turns back to his friend.

I win and I don't even care if I get a prize.

Maddie pulls my attention back to her by clearing her throat. "So, basically, David is our advisor. He helps all the worker bee prodigies assist the dreamer prodigies as they turn their business ideas into realities."

I tilt my head and study her. "Are you not a prodigy?"

She shakes her head quickly as if she can't believe I would even suggest it. "My parents force me to be here because they don't believe in the concept of social media influencer as a career. I just do whatever David tells me to. But you'll fit in perfect."

I smile. I'm not sure if it's a compliment but fitting in here is exactly what I want.

She reaches forward and presses my shoulders down. "You have to relax, though. People shouldn't be able to tell you're nervous."

There's a clap at the top of the circle. A guy with a bright smile and gleaming white teeth, made even more obscene by the contrast to his dark skin, calls the room to attention.

"Hello, Autumn," he says, looking right at me. "I'm David, the group advisor. I can see you're already getting acquainted."

That almost makes me laugh. I don't think *acquainted* is the word. It takes everything I have not to glare at Mekhi.

David turns his attention to the rest of the room. "Everyone, Autumn is a senior from LeBeau. And from what I've heard she has some of those intangible skills that make a good businessperson that I'm always trying to pull out of you all."

I don't know what Mrs. Tanner told David to get me into this group, but she might have exaggerated a little. I'm good with people, but I don't know about the rest of it. Also, I'm not here to focus on what everyone *already* sees.

"I hear you have some great ideas. What are you working on?"

"I'm sorry, what? What am I...what?"

I swear, I can string together full sentences. But that's a very specific question. And based on what Mrs. Tanner told me about the kinds of people they let into this room, it requires a very specific answer. *I need something to make myself stand out to Mercer's admissions committee, and I was hoping you'd tell me what that might be* isn't going to cut it.

My eyes dart around the room, willing someone to get tired of the silence and fill it. Maybe if I can maintain eye contact for longer than a second one of them will pick up on my distress and help me.

Are they always so respectful, attentive, and on the edge of their seat waiting for each other to be brilliant?

"Sorry to put you on the spot, but Julia told me you have some great ideas you need help developing," David says. "The way we work is you give us your idea and we brainstorm to help you flesh it out, test its viability."

It takes me a second to realize he's talking about Mrs. Tanner when he says Julia. It takes me another to realize he's still talking to me. Not only do I have intangible skills, but I have ideas. If I could find out what they are so I can make them tangible, that would be great. This is nothing like the Mercer summer program where we were given sandbox projects. This is real.

"You mean you want to know my business idea since this is, like, a place to explore that kind of thing?"

There's soft laughter around me, not teasing necessarily, but that doesn't stop a bead of sweat from making its way around my armpit. These people are my competition. These people have already beaten me. And I got nothing.

"Yes, I mean business ideas. They can be ideas you plan to carry out or innovative ways to help others execute their plans."

I look away from David's kind smile. It's not helping. Instead of strength and competence, I'm giving baby-bird energy.

There's movement next to me. I whip around, hoping

someone has raised their hand to speak. But no, it's Mekhi leaning in again as if my predicament is bingeable. Lucky for him, I don't have time to scorch him with my side eye. And unluckily for me, I still don't have anything to say.

I'm about to continue my gaze into nothingness when what Mekhi said earlier about not giving away my ideas flashes in my mind.

Was he onto something?

I did like coming up with Margo's promposal. Stanton seemed for real about wanting my help. And there *are* a lot of comments. If any of those people are serious, promposal planning could be a thing. There's a chance I could be good at it. I think.

I sit forward in my chair. I have to do *something* to get some *additional information.*

I also have to speak before everyone here loses faith in my ability to do so. And if the idea sucks, they can all help me come up with something else...I hope.

"Well, and I don't know how innovative this is, it's not like high-level or anything—but I like organizing and planning things." I look up at David, who nods for me to continue. "I organized this promposal for my neighbor and now people keep asking me to do the same for them."

There are murmurs around the room—positive or negative, I'm not sure.

One of the girls I don't know says, "Why would you pitch your idea that way? Like you don't even like it?"

My skin burns with the possible answers to that question. Am I embarrassed of my idea altogether because it's not innovative or requiring any special skills worthy of Mercer acceptance?

Or am I embarrassed because I will happily get carried away doing something as frivolous as helping one person ask another out in a special way?

"Good question." David smiles sympathetically in my direction. "No one will buy it if you don't think it's worth selling. But no worries. We've got plenty of ego in this room. It'll rub off on you."

There's another murmur of laughter.

"I think it's a great idea. Everybody wants to be different, get likes and shares. People always want to feel special," the guy next to Mekhi says. "But if you haven't started on it yet, it might be kind of a rush to get it going. A lot of people already have dates."

I deflate with disappointment at his last comment as easily as I expanded with hope at his first.

"That's true." David nods, pacing at the front of the circle. "But it's not something I'd give up on that easily. If she's a go-getter and has a little help, I think she can get it off the ground quickly."

"Mercer capstone in a day," someone says from the other side of the room.

David nods as if he likes the connection. I kind of love it. Following the principles of Mercer's senior capstone course and getting a business up and running by May 1 has to be enough to get me off that wait list.

My stomach roils and I shift in my seat. I have six weeks to do what Mercer allows an entire semester and beyond to complete.

I know a promposal service is nowhere near the level of what I'd be expected to develop as an actual student, but it's more than Jeannie Gutierrez's possibility of promise. It's a promise realized.

"As we all know, some believe Mercer's capstone plan to be infallible. It'll be a challenge. Autumn, what do you need?"

"I don't even know where to start." I laugh at myself as I take out my phone to do more research on the specifics of Mercer's senior capstone plan. Of course, I know what it is, but not what makes it so bulletproof.

"That's okay. This will be a good exercise for you," David says. "Spend some time getting to know everyone. Determining strengths and weaknesses and temperaments. Decide who you think would be a good asset to your team and go from there."

David claps once, signifying everything is all set, and moves on to reports from other groups. Once he's finished with me, the rest of the circle portion of the meeting takes less than ten minutes. When it's over, everyone splits up into their business teams.

Maddie goes with Mekhi. I'm done following her if she's

attached to his hip. Instead, I walk around listening and learning. I stop at a girl named Sydney's group. She's like the polar opposite of Maddie, with a tapered natural haircut that I love but have never had the confidence to do. She's going to Mercer and is kind of brilliant.

She's an entrepreneurial prodigy and has been working on a line of hair care products specifically for natural hair for two years.

I want to be exactly like her, but on a way-faster time-table. Today would be ideal.

Every time anyone sounds like they know what they're doing and would be a good addition to my team, I put them on my list of people to ask for help.

Later, Maddie tells me everyone is going to Lane by Lane after the meeting. Bowling isn't my favorite thing to do, but I need to have something locked down before the night is over. I don't have time to waste.

Chapter Eight

I sit out in the parking lot doing all the research I can before I go inside the bowling alley. With my limited knowledge of the capstone, I thought time would be my biggest obstacle.

But now that I know more, the thing that worries me the most is the area where the majority of the Mercer students fail: providing evidence that a business idea can be profitable. And since I'm actually starting my business, I have to take things a step further. I have to actually *show* profitability.

One of the most significant markers of profitability is the ability to maintain a payroll of at least two employees. If a business can pay its bills but not its employees, it's not viable.

I have no idea how much I'll even charge for promposals, let alone if I can pay an employee. It's not like I have start-up money other than my weekly allowance from my parents.

Luckily, business owners can be considered employees. That means I only need to find one person to work with me and pray that somehow at the end of all this, I can offer something in return and fill the line item on my budget. And since YBE members help each other out simply for the experience, no one needs to know the whole of my situation. In the end, if I can't pay it'll be my own personal fail.

Though when this magical person finds out all the things I need help with—like starting with creating an entire "well-developed" business plan from scratch—they may feel owed in the end. Providing a "thorough analysis" of the service and how I'll carry it out is about the only part of the business plan I feel qualified to do. The rest of it definitely falls into the worker bee prodigy category. I have to find my worker bee.

By the time I get inside the bowling alley everyone is already in their bowling shoes and assigned to three lanes in a row. It isn't a league night, so it's not super packed, but you still have to yell a little to be heard over the blaring top-one-hundred pop hits.

Lane by Lane is the oldest bowling alley in the city. It's been updated at least once since I've been alive, but it still has a dank smell to it that my mom attributes to when it was legal to smoke in public places in Michigan. But people keep coming because it has pretty good food.

My list of potentials, starting with three people who've been admitted to Mercer, are spread out over all three lanes. I start at the first one and pitch my ideas with a little more detail and confidence than I showed in the meeting. Everyone I talk to thinks the idea is great, but as if there's a glitch in their system, they all go on to tell me how swamped they are with everything on their plate.

A lot of them also mention Mekhi, who's "looking for a project" and is "excellent at helping people get projects off the ground" and "really detail-minded." I nod as if I'm taking it under advisement, but if I'm going to work with somebody, I have to trust them, and I don't trust Mekhi Winston. After the way he glared at me during the meeting, I'm pretty sure it goes both ways.

Once I get through all the names I've written down and am still employeeless, I'm asking anyone who makes eye contact. But there aren't any takers.

With a basket of fries for comfort, I hover in the space between the lanes and the pool tables, trying to figure out my next move.

Ben, the guy who sat next to Mekhi in the meeting earlier, and a tall, wiry boy from Sydney's group are in the middle of a loud, heated pool match. My favorite kind. I've asked them both to be on my team. Ben because he's going to Mercer and the other because I'm running out of options.

Ben takes a deep, sobering breath before waltzing around the table and sinking his last three balls. He takes his time, posing on the table, deciding where the eight will go. I laugh.

"Promposal Queen," he yells over the table, "where should I put it in?"

I smirk at the innuendo but give him a serious answer. "Right corner."

"Do you know how hard that's going to be?"

"Hard for some people, I guess."

"Ben. Dude. Why do you always have to drag stuff out? I'm about to go find something to eat," the other guy says.

"No. Don't go. What if I miss?"

Without waiting for an answer, Ben takes the shot and makes it, as if it's the easiest on the table, which it is.

"I am the champion of this table." Ben hoists his cue in the air like a WWE belt.

"I got next," I yell.

There's an echo from a bar-height table near the wall where Mekhi is sitting with Maddie. He's halfway off the stool. When our eyes meet, we both come to a stop. My skin goes numb like I've just been unexpectedly pushed out into the icy cold of the night. Sometime during the meeting I'd convinced myself Mekhi and I have an understanding to avoid each other. But maybe that's how neither of us saw the other coming.

"Oh. Y'all go 'head," Ben says.

"That's okay." I wave him away. "I didn't know he was already...that you guys had a plan."

"There's no plan. I beat him all the time." Ben shrugs as he lays his cue across the table. "I'ma eat too. I'm already the king. I can't do much more."

I'm about to follow him and ask some poor excuse for a YBE member question—anything to gracefully get away from this situation—when Mekhi says, "You scared to play me?"

"No." My tone registers somewhere between annoyance and righteous indignation.

I would like to have been cooler. I don't want him thinking I care enough to let him get to me. Yes, the sound of his voice directed at me for the second time in one day puts me in a mood, but I'm not scared.

His lips twist at one corner as if my protest was too much. I can't wait to see the look on his face when I run him off this table.

I brush past him and make my way to where the cues are lined up on a wall. He comes up behind me—too close. Invading my personal space must be an intimidation move. I wonder if I could poke him in the ribs with one of these cues and pretend not to have known he's there.

The thought of it brings a smile to my face and I glance back at him. His eyebrows furrow. Yeah, he should be worried.

Winning cue in hand, I approach the table at the same time Maddie does.

"Wish I knew how to play," she mumbles.

I nod encouragingly. "Why don't you ask Mekhi to teach

you?" I can't imagine she needs *my* help with a guy, but somehow Mekhi doesn't notice her, like at all. Yet it's super clear to me her parents aren't the only reason she comes to YBE meetings.

"I was planning on it. You didn't give me the chance."

She tilts her head innocently, but something in her eyes says she's not having innocent thoughts about me.

"Oh. Ooh." I wince. I had no idea. But I can't back out now. It'll take him about two seconds to decide I'm backing out in fear. "It won't take me long to beat him."

"Too bad you don't sound that confident when you pitch your projects," Mekhi says.

Once again, he's snuck up on me.

And with a below-the-belt comment. But it's also true. I let him have that battle. The table will be the war.

As he racks the balls, Maddie pulls a barstool over to us and sits down. I swear she strikes a pose that accentuates every curve of her body. It's definitely an incentive for Mekhi to finish the game quickly.

Mekhi makes a sweeping motion across the length of the table. "Ladies first."

"I don't need all that. You go 'head." I don't want my win to be because of some perceived advantage.

He ducks his head a little. I think it's to hide a smile because when he looks up again, he's biting his bottom lip. It's like he thinks he's already won.

He lifts an eyebrow. "You sure?"

I puff my cheeks with air and let it out, exasperated.

He shrugs, leans lazily over the table, and strikes the cue ball. Solids and stripes shoot across the table. He looks collected, like either he doesn't care about winning or losing, or he's just that confident. Whatever this swagger is all about, I can do without it.

He pockets a solid. On the next strike he pockets my stripe.

"Thank you. You are so sweet." I aggressively bat my eyelashes, and call my first shot, which I sink.

"Oh, so you like to talk shit." He nods slowly. "I should've told Ben to stay and play you."

I back away from the table. "I thought I was the one who's supposed to be scared. It's not too late to back out."

"Nah. Take your shot." His words carry the same nonchalant air as every move he makes.

I take my shot and miss.

He doesn't say anything about my fail. Doesn't even smile. He sinks his next shot, though.

"You know, the more shit people talk, the faster I beat them," he says.

"I don't remember asking. And if you're not talking shit, I'ma need a new definition for it."

"I can see how you would take it like that, but I'm just giving advice."

He sinks another.

"Didn't ask for that either."

"Okay. I'll shut up."

He sinks another, and then finally misses, but the ball he struck is sitting right on the edge of a pocket.

I don't want to do him any favors. He obviously doesn't need my help. But steering clear of that pocket doesn't make my next shot any easier. As I walk the length of the table, looking for something better, he follows me shadow-like. At first, I'm not sure it's happening so I walk slower, hunched down so I'm eye level with the table. Every step I take, he takes one behind me. He even hunches down with me, zeroing in on every spot I do.

I turn around suddenly. He miscalculates the movement as another step forward and we end up mouth to chest. Finally, I catch *him* off guard. He can't deny his surprise even if he wants to because for the second we're pressed together, I feel his furious heartbeat against my face. Other than me beating him at his own game, I don't know what else would cause his heart to do that.

I take a step back. "Is this supposed to be some type of intimidation thing? So you can beat me?"

He leans in and looks at me seriously, as if he's breaking bad news. "I don't have to intimidate you to beat you, Autumn."

I put my free hand on my hip and give him the same look. "It's not over yet."

He looks from me to the table and back, then lets out a tinkle of laughter. Not like this morning in the media center.

This morning it was incredulous laughter. Tonight, he's really amused. If not for the fact that's he's laughing at me, I might not mind the sound of it. It's kind of melodic.

I roll my eyes and start to turn away.

"Wait. Listen," he says. "I was going to help you, but you started stomping around, studying the table like it's a chemical equation."

He does this walk that looks like slithering while standing. I guess it's supposed to be an imitation of me. I glare at him. He laughs, then clears his throat and tries to put on a serious face.

"I'm sorry. Can I give you some advice?"

"You can try. Doesn't mean I'm going to take it."

Keeping his eyes on mine, he nods toward something behind me. It takes a minute before I realize he's expecting something from me other than noticing how dark his eyes are and how that darkness makes them seem unending.

Mistaking my immobility for distrust, he nudges me with his knee.

"I won't steer you wrong."

"Yes, you will," I say, but I shuffle backward the way he directs with little nods because it doesn't matter anyway. Giving me bad advice at a pool table isn't the steering me wrong I'm talking about.

Mekhi leads me to things that feel good now but I regret later.

"Stop."

I follow his direction.

"You can get the nine and fifteen from there." He tilts his head from side to side as if analyzing the probability of his own advice. "You do that and maybe it's not over."

I'm still looking at him and not the table, but when our eyes meet again I nod, pretending to know exactly what he's talking about.

It isn't until I pull my eyes from his and take a step back that I realize Maddie is gone. I don't think Mekhi's recognized it either. I hope she didn't *leave*, leave. He seems primed and ready to show a girl how to do something.

I don't take his advice exactly, but I do get the nine and then the fifteen.

"Look at 'er, back in it." He grins at me mischievously. "But sorry. That's all you're going to get."

I guffaw. But he isn't wrong. In a few minutes he's down to the eight ball and I still have two left.

He puts both hands over his cue and rests his chin there, pensive. The best position for his next shot is where I'm standing. He tries to get in his stance next to me.

He tries on one side of me and then the other before saying, "Can you give me a little room?"

Straight-faced, I shake my head. I'm not going to help him beat me. If this spot on the table is my only advantage, I'm not giving it up.

He imitates my head shake. "What does that mean?"

"It means no. I will not move. I like this spot."

"You can have it back when I'm finished."

I cross my arms over my chest.

"Please." He stares at me intently, studying every part of my face. I think it's supposed to pull me in, but I know him. He's looking for a weakness.

I can't even believe he's trying it. This is not freshman year. I'm not going to hop into action because he gives me soft eyes.

I'm not saying the way he's looking at me can't work. I'm saying I'd have to want it to.

It's my turn to laugh in his face, and I do. "Save that look for somebody else. Not going to work on me."

We stare each other down, and he makes a noise that can only be described as a judgmental harrumph. Then, behind me, he waltzes to my other side, analyzes his shot from there, decides against it, and comes back. When I don't give even an inch, he sighs and starts his trip all over again, except on his way from one side to the other he blows a quick puff of air at the very base of my neck. It sends a tickle throughout my whole body. I definitely don't want that. Not if he's the cause.

I squirm out of his reach. That's all it takes. He's in my space and sending the eight ball into a side pocket just like he's called it.

"You have to learn how to play fair," he says.

I point at my own chest. "Me? I don't play fair?"

"Nope. Never have."

"What did *I* do? When?"

Mekhi glances at me from top to bottom and then back up. I don't know what he's looking for, but I feel everywhere his eyes land as he searches for it. I cross my arms over my belly.

He focuses on something else across the room and pulls his shirt back and forth away from his body, creating a personal fan. "You're really not going to ask me?"

I raise an eyebrow.

He tilts his head to the side and exhales loudly as if I'm supposed to know where this conversation is going. Did I not just ask him a question?

"You're going to ask everyone in YBE to help you except me."

I nod slowly. It's all coming together. That's what this little friendly competition was about? The promposals?

Well, not the promposals. His feelings. I should've known there'd have to be a reason for him to allow me in his space for this long. He would never be nice to me just for the sake of it.

"Aw. Is the big boy feeling left out?" I say in a voice I wouldn't degrade my little sister with.

"I'm not feeling anything. I'm just asking a question. I don't care what you do."

He shrugs one shoulder to sell it, but his voice is almost too butter-smooth, like he's making an effort to keep it even. He's also turned tossing his cue from one hand to the other into a competitive sport. Compared to the way he acted during pool, this is forced. "It *was* kind of my idea, but whatever."

Without a second's hesitation, I give him both fingers. I can't call him a liar, but he doesn't have to rub it in my face. He doesn't have to make it seem like, without him, we'd still be back at the community center waiting for me to stop sputtering and come up with an idea. And even if that *is* the case, it's rude to say.

I make my way back over to the rack and slide my cue into place. Before I turn back to him, I press a smirk on my face that bleeds superiority and disgust. At least I hope it does. If nothing else, I hope it hides the heat of embarrassment building in my chest. The business I'm trying to build from nothing in the hopes of being better than average isn't even my idea.

In my peripheral, Mekhi's propped on the edge of the pool table, lips pressed into a thin line, watching me. When I get to the opposite end of the table, he pulls a sweatshirt over his head.

I freeze, giving him my full attention. Right across his chest in gold block letters against a black background is MERCER.

Now, I can't go a day without seeing at least ten people in GLU paraphernalia. It's one of the biggest schools in the state and the football team has a long legacy. But you don't represent the business school unless you go there...or are about to.

I shake my head slowly. I can't be seeing this right. "*You* got into Mercer?"

Even if I want to, I can't hide the disbelief and surprise in my voice. I'm ranked nineteenth in a class of four hundred. He's maybe top fifty. How could he have gotten into Mercer over me?

A smile that's broad, genuine, but also a little embarrassed crosses his face as he nods. That particular smile—where he tucks his bottom lip between his teeth and barely meets my eyes—is one of the first things that caught my attention about him. It's the sort of smile that makes you want to smile back. I'm not a hater, but I do not allow a smile to happen.

"I was kind of surprised, too, but David says I'm the type they're looking for." He presses his hands into his back pockets. "I don't know."

Mekhi probably has experience with YBE that he can easily weave into his essay. Something that makes him special.

I can't believe I let this happen. I can't believe I didn't see something as obvious as being wait-listed coming. I haven't been doing enough. Meanwhile, people like Mekhi have been quietly making moves.

I'm not as smart as I think I am.

But that was before. I'm going to do things differently now. Better.

Instead of wallowing, I need to be picking his brain. If he's what Mercer is looking for, I need to be more like him.

Everything that happened freshman year hurt me enough. I won't let it get in the way of me getting closer to what I want, the way I let it get between me and Jordyn. I bet no other YBE member lets personal stuff get in the way of their success. Their projects wouldn't look so professional and well thought out if they did.

Just because I don't like Mekhi doesn't mean I don't have anything to learn from him. I'll count that as my first lesson in being Mercer-worthy.

But I can't let him know how important this is to me. He'd use it against me.

"What would you do first? If you were trying to start this promposal thing quick?" I ask.

He looks over his shoulder slowly. Not comically, but like he genuinely expects to see another person who "you" could be besides him.

"You want to know what I would do?"

"You seem to think you're the one I should be asking."

He looks at me thoughtfully. "I would do more of a business-plan-as-I-go kind of thing because of the time crunch, and because the momentum from the first promposal is already dying down." His eyes dart suspiciously around the space, and he lowers his voice. "But don't tell David I said that. He will ask you one hundred questions and get real testy if he finds out you're doing anything without a plan. In all the meetings from now on, you'll be an example of what not to do."

"What else?" I make sure to keep judgment in my tone, even though I want to laugh at the way he delivers his warning.

"You'd probably want to reply to all the comments mentioning they want your help and say something about you offering up your services soon," he says. "But make sure you don't do it under your personal accounts. Create a logo so you can build your brand recognition."

He *is* good at this. "I need a name first."

"PROMposal Queen," he says, as if it's obvious.

"Ha. Ha."

He looks toward the ceiling and nods as if he's replaying the name in his head and finding it meets the mark. "I'm for real. I like it. Ben always jokes around like that, then when you sit back and think, you realize he has a great idea."

I shrug. It definitely has the ego David talked about built into it. I can go with it.

"And then?"

"Build a form where you collect people's basic information and get answers to all those questions you asked Stanton earlier. And you have to get all your fine print together. That's probably the most important part." He's speaking quickly as if the ideas are coming at him so fast he's afraid he'll miss one. "Make sure you say you don't promise results. You need refund and cancellation policies. Oh, and a statement about all information being confidential. People might not want all their business in the street."

That is a list, and it doesn't even include all the stuff

Mercer requires. If I want to keep the momentum going and start a business the Mercer way, I can't take a week to find someone to help me start checking things off.

"Fine print's something you can do?" My voice is high and hopeful instead of low and commanding like I'm going for.

He nods. "We have a couple templates. They're good, but they're more product than service focused. You'll have to fix that."

I could fall asleep thinking about fixing it, while he shrugs like it would be nothing. It's possible Mekhi can be the prototype of a good business partner without being the prototype of a guy I would ever let near my heart again. Both things can be true.

I try again for an authoritative tone when I say, "No. I mean, that's something you can put on your to-do list while I work on the other stuff."

"Really?" His entire face scrunches in surprise and confusion.

I look up at the ceiling and sigh. I can't believe it either. I'm about to commit myself to working with Mekhi Winston.

"You seem excited about the idea and about things I have no desire to do—like write fine print." I let my eyes connect with his again so he knows this isn't a game to me. "You obviously know what you're talking about."

"You're saying you want me to be your last-resort operations manager?"

"You can call yourself whatever you want, but you have

to help with the business plan, and all of the promposal ideas are mine."

"Look at you negotiating. David is right. We will rub off on you." He presses his lips together in thought. "If I'm helping with the business plan, then I'm moving up to vice president."

I don't necessarily love the sound of it, but he's already been accepted to Mercer. It can't hurt me to have his help.

I put my hand out.

He stares at it a minute before he nods to himself. Then he puts his hand in mine.

We shake on it.

I hope I don't regret this.

Chapter Nine

The next morning, I open the door to my little blue Ford and fall in, breathless. A blast of dry winter air burns as it goes down. It was nearly sixty degrees yesterday. Today we seem to be in the middle of a polar vortex. Perpetually changing weather makes the concept of seasonally storing clothes laughable in Michigan.

My rarely dependable overhead light is on for no reason and super bright in the still-dark morning. I'm blinded by it almost the entire way to school.

I need to get there early to work on the questionnaire in peace without Baby hitting me in the head with a diaper, or Mom and Dad very obviously tiptoeing around me. Every time I think I'm done with it, I come up with something else

I'll need to know to create dream promposals. Even if the form is ready, what if I post it and nothing happens?

When I turn into the student lot, I come to a screeching stop. Mekhi's in my way. He doesn't look at me as he crosses in front of my car. I have this feeling he's purposely not making eye contact. Like he knows if he looks, he'll see me. And then what? I'll wave? Or smile? Or pretend to be looking anywhere but in his direction? Maybe that's why he doesn't look at me. He's as clueless about what my response should be as I am.

Just because we decided to work together doesn't mean we're suddenly friends. He's the same guy he was yesterday and all the days before when we refused to acknowledge each other's existence. We're just two people taking advantage of an opportunity.

Me, to make my dreams come true. Him...I'm not sure why, but I *am* curious. If this is just busywork or all about his ego, will he take it seriously?

I keep him in my peripheral, instead of staring directly at him. As soon as there's enough room for me to pass, I do. LeBeau High student parking is at a premium, so I pull into the first open spot I see.

My phone chimes. The only reason I look at it is to see if anyone else has responded to the hints I dropped in the comments last night. I have five likes. If I were in this for instant internet fame I'd be disappointed, but I have to think long-term. If a little over a month can be called that.

Unfortunately, the notification is just a reminder for an appointment with a seamstress about my prom dress. With everything else going on, I had completely forgotten about that. A dress probably would've stayed more top of mind if my date hadn't dumped me.

Prom. Yet another thing I have to get used to the idea of doing without Brandon.

As I tuck my phone away, a shadow comes over me. I look up and shriek when I see Mekhi staring at me with one eyebrow raised.

"What?" I yell through the window, my warm breath making a small cloud of condensation.

He motions for me to let the window down.

I press the control and wait. When it's cold, the glass is on its own time. Neither of us drops our stare as it squeals its way down. I want to look away—Mekhi looking in my eyes has never meant what I think it does—but if he's dishing out challenges, I'm meeting them. Even if it reminds me of last night and the way he looked at me just before he inexplicably told me I've never played fair. And just like last night, I want to cover myself.

"Why are you on ten, instead of your normal eight?" he says once there's no obstacle between us.

"Eight?" I twist my lips at his miscalculation. "I consistently operate on nine."

"And a half. But I was hoping the power of suggestion might simmer you down some." He leans into the window a little more. I inch back. He's way too close. "So...what's up? I thought you would be excited. You got the logo done. It looks good. You got likes. By the end of the day, you're going to be running a small business."

I groan, cover my face with both hands, and take a deep breath. Is this how someone who's been admitted to Mercer is supposed to sound? All upbeat and ready to handle whatever comes along? Maybe this is why I didn't get in.

His smile, the way his voice goes higher and he speaks faster when he's talking about PROMposal Queen—those are all polar opposites of what I can make my face and voice do.

This is my last chance to prove myself to Mercer. And I could fall on my face. Becoming an entrepreneur when all my dreams are on the line might be bad timing.

And why does Mekhi have to be around to witness this bout of insecurity? Having an audience intensifies the feeling.

"Don't say that again," I mutter from behind my hands.

He blinks. "What'd I say?"

I do not want to get into this with him. I'm no Sydney, or any other YBE member, for that matter. They're not rubbing off on me. Plus, I'm tired.

I grab my backpack off the passenger seat and motion for him to move away from the car so I can get out. This is a lot.

"Seriously. What did I say?" There's a hint of a smile on his face as if he thinks there's a joke hidden somewhere in what I've said.

"Move. Please."

He doesn't move. "Wait. I did my part. I finished the fine print. Do you want me to add it to the form, or should I send it to you?"

"There is no form." I motion for him to move again. If he doesn't get out of my way, I'm going out the passenger side.

His eyebrows bunch together, and I swear I see all that excited energy he brought over here draining from his body.

On the other hand, I don't want it to seem like I have no follow-through. I don't want to give him anything to judge. "There's a form. It's just not ready. I need the questions to be right."

His face brightens again as if this is a manageable issue. "Can I see?"

"The bell's going to ring."

He doesn't say anything. Instead, he stands there looking at me, calling me out on my flimsy excuse. Yes, we have fifteen minutes to first bell. And no, I don't think a tardy will hurt my chances with Mercer. I just don't want this boy critiquing my work, especially when I'm not even a hundred percent about it.

Then again, his help is literally what I signed up for last night.

With an inner sigh of defeat, I motion for him to get in the car. It's cold out. Keeping the window down to talk to him has me shivering.

It's hard not to laugh at how he trots to the passenger door. It's like he thinks I've made a limited-time offer.

For heat, I turn the car back on. As we sit at attention watching the window make its snaggy climb back into place, the parking lot gets even busier with everything from brand-new cars to hand-me-downs like mine. The quiet is closer to what it's been like between us the last three years, as opposed to the way we've been in the last twelve hours.

It's hard to decide which is more comfortable.

I take out my laptop, open the form, and hand him my computer. Leaning over the center console, I try to pinpoint what question he's focused on and when. I can probably trust his facial expressions more than any words coming out of his mouth. I think he's on question three when he slowly turns to me. Our eyes meet for a second. And then another. And another. I look away. This close, I'm no match for a staring contest with row after row of dark, feathery eyelashes.

He stutters through a lot of words that never amount to a complete thought before he pulls his phone from his sweatshirt pocket, swipes, taps, and hands it to me. I guess reviewing what he put together would be a better use of my time than staring over his shoulder waiting for him to find errors.

I try to focus on the screen in front of me, but every time he shifts in the seat or scrolls, I look up. Twice he's caught a typo. These are small mistakes, but they add up. If I'm lucky, this form is something Mercer will see. It has to be perfect.

I'm rereading a line of the fine print because I didn't focus long enough to know what it meant the first time, when he says, "This looks good to me. And if you come up with any other questions, you can ask them when a request is made, right?"

"I mean...I *could*."

It's not like I haven't known that the whole time. I just want the questionnaire to be perfect *now*.

"Cool." He nods to his phone. "If everything is good over there, we can add it to the form and sit back and wait for the requests to roll in."

I almost laugh at his confidence. "That might not happen."

He presses himself back against the passenger door, taking a long look at me. "Are you scared? Is that what this is?"

"No," I snap.

"Is that a yes?"

I smack my lips in real annoyance. Mekhi critiquing *me* is about the only thing worse than him critiquing my work. He doesn't even know me like that.

He chuckles.

I reach for my laptop. I'm done with him.

"Wait. Hold up." He maintains his grip on my computer

but can't cover his smile. "If you don't get any requests—which won't happen—then we'll figure out why and fix it."

" 'Cause I'm sure it'll be that easy."

"Easy or not, we'll fix it."

I hate how nonchalant he is about everything.

At the same time, if I don't let him add that fine print now, I will talk myself out of it later. And like he said, going live doesn't mean I can't make updates if I need to.

After he sends his document to my computer it only takes a few clicks and my password before he's pointing the cursor at Publish.

The reluctance must be all over my face because he says, "I shouldn't have laughed. I just never thought of you as being scared of anything. It kind of surprised me."

I look at him, surprised myself. Was that a compliment from Mekhi Winston? He thinks I'm unshakable?

"What exactly is making you scared?"

There's curiosity in his voice but also a note of concern that sounds genuine. It kind of makes me feel like I can tell him about Mercer. But that's Mekhi. He has this way of pulling you in and then leaving you hanging.

He's pulled me in that way before and I forgot myself. Or maybe I only thought of myself.

However I look at it, I forgot about my best friend. Letting him in, even just this much, might cost me something else. And the last thing I want to hear is how easy this should be. I don't think I can take that coming from Mekhi, someone who got into the school of my dreams all on his own. It makes me never want to tell him my secrets. No matter how kindly he asks or how deep his worry brow gets.

Mekhi has somehow cracked Mercer's code and gotten himself exactly where I want to be. I want some of that to rub off on me. But I don't need to bare my soul to him for that to happen.

Admitting I'm afraid already feels like too much.

I try to sound as lighthearted as I can. "Everybody's afraid the first time they do something."

Mekhi nods as if he's expecting more or doesn't believe my simple explanation.

And maybe he's right not to. Generally, I don't scare easily. Mercer aside, I'm just not a big fan of things deviating from what I've planned. It never leads to anything good. Going to a YBE meeting and leaving with a business to start wasn't in the plans. All that considered, PROMposal Queen has the potential to go sideways.

"I'm not trying to make you more scared. I'm just worried about keeping the momentum. Like I said before, it's important."

He's not wrong. The longer I sit on this, the more likely what I don't want to happen will happen. There won't be anyone left without prom plans to make requests. And the sooner I get this part finished, the sooner I can start the business plan.

I reach out and he hands over the laptop. With a deep

breath, I publish the form and then place a few links in the comments.

He rubs his hands together. "PROMposal Queen is officially open for business."

My stomach clenches with nerves, and I squeeze my eyes shut. "You have got to stop saying stuff like that."

There's a popping noise, like the sound of a top being pulled off something. We look in the direction it came from. Confetti wafts to the ground on the sidewalk in front of us as Luca unzips his jacket to reveal a T-shirt asking Stanton to prom.

I guess it's true. Momentum is everything. If I don't get started, Stanton won't be the only client to slip through my fingers.

Chapter Ten

I'm standing outside my seamstress's apartment, waiting for her to answer the door. With everything going on in my head, I should've canceled. But regardless of the Mercer situation, I'm going to prom. That means I'm going to need a dress.

Reese has to work, so I'm solo.

When she opens the door, Kamia, the seamstress, is on the phone telling someone she's too old for games. Before the person has a chance to respond, she ends the call and pushes the phone into her back pocket.

Based on the music she likes and slang she uses, I've guesstimated Kamia to be thirtyish. She loves to give her opinion about my high school life and tell me about her rendezvous. I've only been here once and I know all her business. It took her twenty minutes to measure my waist last time because she kept stopping to relay an important part of a story.

Somehow, she's still one of the best and most well-known seamstresses in the area. She can take the ideas her client has and sketch up something nice. Unfortunately, I don't have any ideas. When I made the first appointment I thought I did, but what I had in mind isn't doing anything for me now.

"What he's going to do is call me right back at least five times, knowing I'm busy with clients and can't answer, just so he can say he called me and I didn't pick up," Kamia says. "He stay trying to find something to be mad at me about because he's always wrong. You know what I'm saying?"

I get the concept but not why anyone would think it would work. Still, I nod and verbalize my solidarity with an emphatic "Girl."

"Did you come with some ideas this time? I've been saving a space for you, but if you're not going to do anything I'm going to book someone else."

"Um…no. I don't have a dress idea yet," I admit. "I haven't had time to think about it."

She sighs impatiently. "Show me something you like on someone else, and we can go from there. Google is your friend. Or, I mean, what's your boyfriend's style, even? I'll start there if I have to."

"I'm probably going stag."

This is the first time I've taken that in. I don't mind going alone—plenty of people are—it's just that I've imagined

Brandon by my side. He'd be more handsome than I've ever seen and unable to take his eyes off me.

But that's not going to happen. I need to imagine something different. I have no clue where to start. I do know it will be Reese and me unless she decides to take someone.

"Going stag doesn't mean you can't poke people's eyes out with how fine you are," Kamia says.

I smile. "I want to be cute. Trust me, I don't want to look back at my pictures and be sad because I look busted. I just haven't had time to think about it."

"You have time now while I finish up with a client." She points to the couch. "Take a seat and find some pictures. I should have her wrapped up in a second."

"Autumn?" a voice I know so well, but have heard so little of, calls from the doorway of the bedroom Kamia uses as an office. I stand up straight, trying to act normal even though I'm not sure what normal would be in this situation. Other than scowl at me in the media center the other day, Jordyn hasn't had anything to do with me in three years. And I tried until I ran out of ways.

But here she is now, pinned into a muslin mock-up of her dress and saying my name like we're cool. Like she can stand the sight of me.

Of all the times to be speechless, I am.

Kamia looks from Jordyn to me. "I thought y'all might know each other, but everybody likes to keep their designs on the hush, so I didn't say nothing."

"We know each other," Jordyn says, and in those words is a bit of irritation.

But it's okay. I'm used to trying to connect with Jordyn and her pretending not to notice. These few words from her are an accomplishment.

If I could get her to listen to me after all this time, we might be able to salvage something. I know we won't ever be as close as before, but I'd love to be able to talk to her, know what's going on in her life.

I clear my throat. "Is it going to be pink?"

A lot of things have changed about my ex-BFF, but I'd bet her love of every shade of pink isn't one of them. I don't mind letting her know I still remember.

"True pink. A chiffon. It's going to be lovely," Kamia says.

"I can see it," I say. Not that it's hard. In 90 percent of the pictures of us, Jordyn is wearing pink. She's also always looking at me instead of the camera. Like she's expecting me to do something to make her smile brighter.

Not today, though.

She doesn't need the reassurance from me. A ton of her light skin will show, and every curve will be on display. It's her dream dress. Perfect for the girl who came up with creative nicknames for people so we could talk about them without anyone knowing.

"You go back in there and let's get this mock-up off. Y'all not my last appointments for tonight," Kamia says as if *we're* the reason she's behind schedule.

Once they're back in the room and Kamia instructs Jordyn to get up on the pedestal again, I know it's going to be a minute.

My mind goes back and forth between pictures of people on red carpets and Jordyn. She definitely felt some type of way when she saw me and Mekhi together. Her face told me that. But what way? Was she just annoyed by Mekhi's loud interruption or did her feelings transport her back to ninth grade the way mine did?

Not all of those feelings are bad. Up until the day I betrayed her, freshman year was great.

Or maybe it was great until she met Mekhi. Or until I did.

Either way, I can't believe she spoke to me.

After a while, Kamia comes out of her office and goes into her actual bedroom. Yelling from there, she brings me mentally back to the present. "I'm thinking I might have the perfect fabric for you. It's a blue silk organza. I bought it for myself but haven't gotten around to using it."

I have no idea what silk organza means, but I'll take her word for it. This is her business.

Jordyn comes out of the room dressed in her own clothes. "I saw your promposal thing."

I pause, completely caught off guard that she would be up on anything I'm doing.

"I can see you being good at it." She leans on the kitchen counter, keeping enough distance between us that anyone walking in would assume we don't know each other. "I might even make a request."

Not going to lie, I'm so shocked Jordyn is A, speaking to me again and B, maybe hinting at telling me something private, that my vocabulary is becoming extremely limited. My response ends up being about ten beats too late.

"Who do you want to ask?" I don't even hide my excitement over maybe getting some juicy information, and Jordyn confiding in me like she used to.

"I want to be asked," she says, "but he's taking all day. I might have to do it myself."

I giggle. "Who?"

She tilts her head from side to side as if she's weighing whether or not to tell me. I hope what happened freshman year doesn't factor into the decision.

"I can't say, but if somebody requests something for me, tell me before you do it." She smiles a little. "I would do something big for him, but I don't want that for myself, you know?"

I do know. That sounds like Jordyn. It's one of the biggest differences between us. I don't mind being seen. Jordyn doesn't like having the attention on her.

"But who is it, though?"

She smiles even bigger. Big enough to let me know, whoever he is, she likes him a lot. That's all I get to know. Jordyn will never tell me anything that sacred again.

"You're going to get a lot of requests. Mekhi was talking

about it in first period. A few people said they were going to check it out."

I jerk my head back at the mention of *that* name. The last time Jordyn and I spoke the name Mekhi in each other's presence was coincidentally the last time we spoke at all.

And I can't help but think her bringing him up right after I ask her to tell me something private is her version of *Don't even think about it, Autumn.* Mentioning that name means she's never going to tell me anything again.

"I didn't believe it at first about you working with him on something. All that stuff went down a while ago, but I wouldn't be able to work with somebody who treated me the way he treated you." She raises an eyebrow. "Then again, you've never been one to hold grudges. That's me."

Damn. You'd think she's been waiting all day to say that to me or maybe even three years. There's shade laced in her tone and disapproval in the way her body leans away from me. As if unworthiness and the inability to judge character are contagious. I deserve it. But I want her to have a clearer picture of my partnership with Mekhi.

"It's not like we're friends. I don't trust him or anything like that. I'm only doing this with him because I need it to work and he's my best option to help make sure it does."

I hate the pleading in my voice but I mean, what else can I do? My ex–best friend, who hasn't talked to me in three years, is finally speaking to me, but it's only to set the expectation that it'll never happen again.

I probably should be happy Kamia chooses this moment to come back in with fabric draped over her arm. She could be my convenient excuse to change the subject to something less explosive. But instead I wish she would go back in the room. I want to ask Jordyn privately if she thinks she'll ever accept my apology. Will we ever be okay? Will we ever not repel each other in the halls?

"Losing you hurt more than anything he said about me," I blurt.

I want to get those last words in no matter who hears them.

"Why are you lying to yourself like that?" She pushes herself off the counter. Shutting me out again. Just like that. All because of Mekhi.

If he and I weren't working together, if she hadn't seen us huddled up in the media center, or maybe even sitting in my car together today, would we be having a different conversation right now?

And is she right? Am I lying to myself? Was Mekhi more important than she was? Even if it was only while I kissed him.

"So y'all know each other intimately then, huh?" Kamia says.

Neither me nor Jordyn responds to that. Jordyn just says her goodbyes. None of them are meant for me. If she waves or anything I wouldn't know because I'm not looking at her. I don't want to see the disgust in her eyes.

"I'ma have to burn my herbs. I can't have all that negative energy in here," Kamia says.

She can burn herbs or anything else; it won't change what's going on between me and Jordyn.

After Kamia sees Jordyn to the door, I follow her into her office, where she points at the pedestal in front of the mirror and I stand on it.

"It's expensive, but it'll be worth it. This blue will make your skin pop." She holds the fabric up to my face, then drapes it over my shoulders. "See that? This is why I could never find anything good enough for it. It's not for me. It's for you."

I stare at my reflection. She isn't wrong. I hold up my phone to show her a screenshot of a look I like. I've edited it, adding a few dots of sparkle here and there.

"Will this work?"

"It's definitely going to show off your figure," Kamia says, sliding her fingers across the screen to enlarge the image. "But it's so simple. Not that simple is bad. Less is more and everything."

"I like it," I say.

"Then you're going to have it. It'll work well with the fabric. That won't be a problem," Kamia says, and then chuckles. "But you better tell your parents the price before we move forward. There are no take-backs once I cut into this."

Chapter Eleven

By the time I get home from Kamia's, PROMposal Queen has five requests.

I won't lie, I'm kind of surprised, and with every notification, my confidence in my ability to plan promposals fades. I *have* to be good at it. Not only because of Mercer, but because people crush on each other in the cutest ways, and somehow, they make me feel it too. I don't want to be responsible for screwing that up. People are putting their faith in me to make their romantic dreams come true.

I spend the night sitting on my bed clicking between open internet tabs. There are the million I opened with searches like *unique proposals* or *best proposals*, and then there's Snapchat, TikTok, Instagram, YouTube, and even Pinterest.

I'm looking for anything to catapult me into the part of my brain that generates creative ideas.

Anything I think of doesn't seem good enough. Knowing my name will forever be attached to someone's happiness or unhappiness makes me doubt everything.

For example, Eliana, a super-quiet girl who I've had in maybe one class over the last four years, has a crush on a guy named Chris.

I guess, on the white social hierarchy of things at LeBeau High, Chris is considered popular. I've never said a word to the kid so I can't speak to who he is as a person. But Eliana can fill up a text box with her devotion. And these aren't observations from afar. She's gotten to know him.

Apparently, his gamer tag is similar to someone's she's played with a few times. Thinking Chris was that person, she invited him to her world in *Guardians of Liberty*. They didn't talk much at first, and it took hours of playing together before she realized who he was. From the sound of it—though she never comes right out and says it—he has no idea who *she* is.

They never talk in school, but he's the only person she'll play Xbox with, and because she sometimes gets harassed, Chris goes offline to only play with her. And they "really talk" and he's "super funny" and "laughs at himself." I think it's special because it's private, but at the same time, it does scare me that it's a secret.

I don't want anyone to get their feelings hurt. And I don't want to ruin them either.

I texted Eliana a few questions at about two in the morning. She answered quickly and had way more to say via electronic means than she does in person. I sensed the excitement, and I don't want to disappoint her, but all my ideas are, like, grand. The world of gaming itself is grand. And our budget is tiny. I'm charging just enough to be profitable, according to Mercer, and I'm not down for any out-of-pocket expenses other than my time.

The next morning, I have one foot out of my car in the student parking lot when Mekhi comes out of nowhere saying, "I knew this was a good idea."

I screech. Then he laughs, and his lazy, flirty grin transforms into a huge smile. Again, with that smile I refuse to be affected by. Again, with that excitement. Nobody can live up to the expectation of it.

He backs out of the way so I can get out of the car. "You're so jumpy."

"You're so sneaky." I mean that literally and figuratively.

I start toward the building, forcing him into a trot to catch up. Since the mere mention of his name changed the entire trajectory of my conversation with Jordyn, I'm not exactly thrilled to have him show up at my car again. I can't shake the conversation. Am I lying to myself? Did this boy hypnotize me into being more concerned about my feelings for him than my friend's feelings?

I don't know why the universe thought it was okay to point me in his direction by making everyone else in the entire world too busy to give me a little time and advice, but the universe was out of order.

"Aren't you excited? We have five requests." He bounces along next to me. Part of me wants to tell him to calm himself. The other part of me wants to be completely covered by his excitement. "Do you have any ideas? Once you do one, I think that'll get us even more requests."

We approach the door, and he reaches in front of me to open it. I move quick, getting to the handle first, like allowing him to open the door would be evidence of me lying to myself.

We get caught in a bottleneck and wade our way through in silence I maintain out of fear. If I share my idea, he'll get even more excited and there will be no turning back. Then again, maybe that's not a bad thing.

"I have an idea," I say decidedly.

I wouldn't have thought it could happen, but his smile shines brighter. I might be more than just completely covered by his excitement. I might be a part of it. I smile too.

"Who's it for?"

The question makes me think about the request and the couple I'm rooting for like they're hometown heroes. And that makes me happy, but also a little more protective.

"We're not supposed to be talking about this. Remember the confidentiality statement?"

He slows our pace and slouches down so his mouth is near my ear. "Whisper it."

I jerk my head back and trip over my feet trying to get away. I don't know if it's the sudden movement that jostles something free in my brain or what, but the memory of how soft his lips are comes over me.

I catch myself in the midst of a lick of my own lips and clamp my mouth shut.

Apparently, I'm the only one impacted by our closeness. He doesn't flinch or anything. He just stays hunched and turns his head a little, making it easy for *me* to whisper in *his* ear.

If anybody, like, say, Maddie, saw that smile and how close we are right now, they would assume more is up between us than PROMposal Queen. Even though *I* know the only reason Mekhi's closeness amplifies the pulse at my neck is because of what Jordyn said last night, I take a step away. Getting between him and a second girl, no matter how unsubstantiated the claim, won't be a recurring theme in my story.

My one step doesn't do much good, though. It's like he's on a string the way he leans in again.

"Do you have some type of personal space issue?"

He blinks at me in confusion.

"You're always leaning in."

"Am I? Sorry."

He creates space between us, but then of course *I* have to lean in to avoid yelling.

"Eliana."

"Oh. I don't know her, but I know Chris," he whispers. "Man, she really likes him. Reading everything she said gave me butterflies."

If we hadn't reached my locker, I would've stopped anyway. Butterflies? Seriously?

He pulls a curl from the crown of his perfectly lined fade and wraps it around his finger as if he's trying to turn a kink into a spiral curl. But since I've had my hands there before I know that kink is going to be a kink.

"What? I can't get butterflies?" he says, confusing my shocked look for disbelief that he has feelings. Which, I mean, is partly true.

The butterflies *are* a surprise. Not necessarily that he got them from reading about someone else, but that he'd *tell me* he got them from reading about someone else. It makes it difficult not to be just as honest.

"Same thing happened to me when I read it." Somehow, that confession alone makes something flutter in my belly.

He nods sharply as if vindicated.

"I have an idea, but I can't get what I need to make it happen." I bite my bottom lip. The thought that Chris and Eliana's promposal might have to wait destroys me.

"What do you need?"

"I want to do a meme. Easy enough"—I tap my finger on my top lip—"but I want it projected big onto the school. I have no idea where to get a projector that powerful."

"That's it?" He raises an eyebrow. "I have a projector."

"You just have a high-powered projector lying around your house? Why?"

"Yes, I do. It's kind of a long story." He gets his phone out of his pocket and hands it to me. "Put your info in there. We need to start setting aside some time. Pool our resources. You busy after school?"

I stare at him a second before I take the phone. Once again Mekhi Winston has made it impossible for me to say that any of this is too hard.

Chapter Twelve

Four days later, in the darkness of the early morning, I pull into the mostly empty school lot. I couldn't eat anything for breakfast, but the pit at the base of my stomach has nothing to do with hunger.

I lace my fingers together in front of my face, look up at the ceiling of my car, and pray that Eliana's promposal is perfect. Mekhi pulls up next to me. I don't care if he catches my moment. It's the first official PROMposal Queen production. If this is a fail, the whole thing is.

Mekhi doesn't have the kind of projector we need. Instead, my dad was able to secure a powerful one from his office. It's built to do the job, except last night I couldn't get my phone to connect to it when I came up here to do a trial run. I spent the rest of the night monitoring the transfer of family videos from our camcorder to an external drive. Now I can use the microdisk without worrying about a Christmas morning video playing instead of the meme I created.

I tap my jacket pocket to make sure the card is still there. It would've been best kept inside the projector, but I'm more relaxed with it on me. I pop the trunk and we both get out of our cars.

He is of course all smiles. He's dressed for the day's high temperature with just a T-shirt and jeans and I'm dressed for the low, wearing a puffy coat and scarf.

I analyze our surroundings. Any sort of light can ruin this whole thing.

For some reason the school's security lights seem brighter than they did last night, and I would swear the sun is making its way up faster than it should be. I didn't account for car headlights either.

With so much out of my control, this promposal is way more adventurous and riskier than the first. And way more visible. Everyone will know if I fail.

"It's going to be too light," I mumble mostly to myself.

"The sun's not supposed to be up for another forty minutes. We're good." He gives me a soft smile and grabs the projector, which I'm grateful for. It wasn't easy lifting it all by myself last night. I wanted to ask him to come along but by the time I had everything all set it was too late to ask.

That leaves me with the stand. I wipe my sweaty palms

on my jeans before I get it out. It's chilly, but everything I'm wearing sticks to me from stress-induced sweat.

When we get to the spot I marked last night, Mekhi carefully takes the projector out of its box and places it on the stand I set up. Even though it's charged to 100 percent, I hook up the backup battery just in case.

Then I slide the card into its slot, and with the cover over the projector's lens, I turn it on. I let out a squeal of happiness and clap when it comes to life.

"Thank you, thank you, thank you," I murmur, ending our working silence.

I'm starting to feel like this could be a success. Mekhi nods as if he's feeling the same energy. But we're quiet again as cars fill the lot, buses pull in, and people spill onto the school lawn.

My phone vibrates with a text from Eliana. "She says his bus is about two miles away."

I hope Chris doesn't get into the building before Eliana's even out of her car. The buses have a designated area, but she could easily get caught up in regular school traffic. He could walk right by me and into the school without ever seeing his promposal. And I don't care what my weather app says, the sun is on the horizon.

It's out of my hands now.

I stare down at my phone, waiting for another update. In the meantime, I invent a whole play-by-play of how this will go wrong.

"This is getting a little intense." Mekhi scratches his forehead as if he didn't expect to feel this way. "My heart is beating fast."

"So is mine." I let out a shaky sigh. "Hopefully this isn't a bust."

Mekhi shakes his head. "When this is over, we have to talk about what I'm supposed to do when you start talking like that. Do you have that little faith in yourself or is your blood sugar low?"

"Ha. Ha."

"I'm dead serious. You doubt yourself a lot."

"I used to have plenty of faith in myself." It's a thought that isn't meant to be shared, but once it's out, I don't take it back.

He's about to ask another question, but I focus on my phone to discourage him. I don't want to explain where that faith went.

Eliana texts again. I hold my breath and look for her.

"She's standing at the end of the walkway that connects the bus loop to the parking lot and he's coming her way, but he might not recognize her."

Mekhi cranes his neck, staring off into the same direction I am.

I spot Eliana, dressed as Chris's favorite character from *Guardians*—a waist-length ponytail, skintight red pants, and a frayed vest. Her cosplay is my favorite part of the entire thing.

I hit Record on my phone and will myself to stand still when what I want to do is bust out in a celebratory dance. This first-ever official PROMposal Queen production is about to come together.

I can't even believe it.

It's all shadows when the girl with the godlike ponytail taps the boy in front of her, but then I take the cover off the projector lens. We're too far away to see the look on Chris's face, but there must be some confusion because Eliana points at the school. The side of the building is lit up with the ladder the characters on *Guardians of Liberty* climb when they reach a goal. Below it, a message reads—*Chris, want to level up and go to prom with me?*

There's a lot of murmuring around me and people stopping and commenting, but I stay focused on the two people lit brightly by the projector now.

"How will we know if he says yes?" Mekhi whispers.

Chris doesn't answer. At least, not verbally. He bends down and kisses the absolute hell out of Eliana. I stop recording. This part should be private. I can't look away, though. I keep my eyes on them. It's as if all these months he's been waiting for her to speak up and she finally did. How can I turn away from that energy?

There's a sharp exhale next to me. It sounds like satisfaction. The only place that exhale could've come from is Mekhi. As much as I don't want to look away from Eliana and Chris, I have to see his face. We did this. Me and him.

Yes, I came up with the promposal, but I might still be working on the form or telling myself to give up on finding a projector if not for him.

His eyes are fixed on them just like mine. "That was cool. We're going to get so many requests now."

As if on cue, my phone vibrates in my hand. It's a notification of a request, which is crazy. How could anyone have completed my questionnaire that fast?

"I told you to stop saying stuff like that." All the adrenaline rolling through me makes my voice crack with the words.

He smiles a little. "It's true, though. You're good at all this. You might as well accept it."

"Thank you" is all I can say to that.

I'm not convinced of myself. For anyone else to be this sure of me is a surprise. His faith in me in *general* is a surprise.

My phone vibrates again, and then again, and another time. I don't even want to look. That could potentially be four more requests in less than five minutes. At this rate, by lunchtime I'll have hundreds of requests and have to drop out of school and disappear. There's no way I can deliver on the promise that Eliana and Chris's promposal has made to the rest of LeBeau High.

Chapter Thirteen

A little after midnight, a text from Mekhi blocks the response to *How did you meet your potential date?* on the forty-second PROMposal Queen request form I've received.

Yes. Forty-two promposal requests have been submitted. As in four tens and two ones. As in forty-two people—two from a school other than LeBeau—want me to help them show somebody how special they are.

I don't need *that* many requests. Especially not in response to what happened two days ago. I love seeing Chris and Eliana walking down the hall holding hands as much as the next person, but I'm pretty confident I can't make that happen forty-two times, forty-two different ways.

It's not just my lack of creativity either. Not even half of the requests have Eliana-and-Chris chemistry.

Even if I were an expert at this—which I'm not—this would be hard. And it's not like I have weeks upon weeks to figure it out. Prom won't wait and neither will Mercer. Coming up with forty-two promposals won't leave much time for business planning.

Why did I think I could start a business the Mercer way? This is why people put four years into the program before they attempt it.

I roll around in bed, molding my sheet and blanket to my body. Maybe being as comfortable as I can will help get some ideas flowing. But when I lie on my back and look up at the ceiling, instead of ideas, I see comments. Comments about how PROMposal Queen isn't worth it or how I ruined promposals.

Seriously, brain, if you don't have anything nice to say, don't say anything at all. I press farther into my pillow and click on the message.

> **Mekhi:** Got a notification about a new PROMposal
> Queen form. All the form says is SOLD OUT and I
> can't log in. I think we got hacked.

I don't respond. I can't handle a conversation with him or anyone else who has expectations for PROMposal Queen with my mind as scattered as it is. This is the part of PROMposal Queen I'm supposed to love and find easy.

> **Mekhi:** I would fix it, but it keeps telling me the
> password is wrong. You have to give it to me again.

I think he could go on with this one-sided conversation for days. But there's no need for both of us to lose sleep over this. Plus, his stress is making me more stressed, and I don't know if I can take it. I need him to stop messaging me.

Autumn: Not hacked.

Mekhi: Form says sold out.

Autumn: It is.

Not even ten seconds later, my phone vibrates with a video chat from Mekhi. My natural reaction is to answer. Without thinking, that's almost what I do. But I snatch my hand back and stare at the phone. Mekhi and I don't video chat. We managed to set up PROMposal Queen without it.

I responded to him to de-escalate. Not to get a call.

I watch as the noise peters into silence, leaving me with nothing but a notification of a missed video call.

Mekhi: Is this about what you told me the other day?

I frown at my phone. What did I tell him the other day?

Mekhi: There's nothing to be scared of. We're going to get more requests.

My mouth drops open. Before I know it, I'm loosening the blankets around me and pressing the callback button. There's a millisecond of ringing on my end before he answers.

"Maybe you don't know this"—I pause for the drama of it—"but when someone tells you something in the bubble, you don't throw it back in their face outside the bubble. It's rude."

He lies there on his belly, one hand under his chin, squinting at me. Shadows and light are falling on odd parts of his face. He looks a little mysterious.

"I do know this," he says simply.

"And you broke protocol because...?"

He jerks his head back as if dodging a swing. "I don't ever break protocol."

"Are we in the car?" I sit up on one elbow, making sure he can see me clearly. Hoping that'll help drive home the importance of exhibit A.

"The bubble is the people, not the location," he says.

"The bubble is the people, and the time, and the place." I tick off the specifications on my fingers. "We're one out of three. Not the time to remember I said I'm scared."

"My fault." He looks away from the camera and bites the skin below the cuticle of his pointer finger. "Does that mean you're not going to tell me what's up? I meant what I said. We'll figure out how to get more requests."

"You've done enough. I have forty-two."

"Forty-two requests? Wow." All his excitement from a few days ago falls back into place.

"This isn't a good thing." Exasperation makes my voice go an octave higher.

He tucks his lips between his teeth to disguise his smile, which makes me laugh a little. For a second, I'm as happy as he looks. But it doesn't last. All I have to do is glance over at my laptop and see the numbers. It snaps me back to reality. I groan and fall facedown onto my pillow.

When he asks what's wrong, he can't hide the smile in his voice.

"I can't give everybody the Eliana and Chris. I can't just make all forty-two of these people's superficial fantasies kiss them when the sun is just below the horizon," I say into my pillow.

"Are people asking for all that?"

"Only two people said it, but it's not a coincidence that I got thirty-eight requests after that promposal," I say. "People want to walk away looking like those two. Anything less than that would be a fail."

I turn and face my phone. Mekhi is all seriousness now. His eyes flit around my face like he's looking for more information. At this point, I don't mind giving it. I need to vent.

"Eliana and Chris inspired me. Even you said they gave you butterflies."

He nods his agreement.

"But most of the requests are just like *I want to take*

somebody hot to prom so my pictures can be cute! and
So-and-So is super hot. OMG his hair! or *his chain* or *his
hoodies.* Like, what?"

He opens his eyes wide. "What are you going to do? Tell
everybody their love story isn't worthy of your talents?"

I sigh. If only he knew how tempting that is.

"No. I can't do that. But I can't take on any more requests
either. I don't want to disappoint people, but right now, I
have no clue how not to."

"Out of forty-two requests, not one is doing anything for
you?"

"A couple, but that still leaves forty."

He's quiet for a beat as if he's stumped. "If you want, you
can tell me about the ones you like. If I understand what
you're looking for, maybe I can help."

That's fine in theory. But while I can say what doesn't
inspire me, I can't pinpoint what does. There's no formula
he can look for in these requests to magically cure my creative block.

On the other hand, anything he's helped with so far has
panned out. So, it's either sit here and read these requests
over and over, looking for something that isn't there, and
fail, or try something I haven't. Getting another point of
view has to increase my chances of figuring this out, at least
by a little.

"One request I like is from Emma, who keeps taking
Jon's Volcanic Coffee order," I say.

He side-eyes me. "You like your requesters to be thieves?"

"Boy, no." I roll my eyes. "The first time, she didn't realize she had the wrong drink until she got to the car. When she went back in to tell him, she thought he was cute, and he was already ordering another drink, and then the next time nobody claimed it."

"That doesn't sound right." He quirks his lips up at one corner. "Please, do not try to get with me after you repeatedly steal from me. How can that girl think that guy wants to go anywhere with her?"

"She was wrong for swiping his drinks. Super wrong. But you have to read how she writes about it. It's sweet. I'm going to do it Saturday. I just need a Cricut. You know anybody who scrapbooks?"

"We have a Cricut, but not for her. She's a thief."

"Yes, thank you. I'd love to use your resources. Can you bring it to school tomorrow or is it heavy?"

He shakes his head vigorously as if this is a battle he has a chance at winning.

"Anyway, if she's a thief, he's a doormat. All he had to do was stop going to that particular location. LeBeau has an unlimited number of coffee choices," I say. "I think he goes to the same place every single day because he wants to buy the girl a coffee. And I'm thinking at this point he's knowingly buying her a coffee. I mean, how many times can you tell the manager your drink never came up without them getting suspicious?"

He stares at me thoughtfully. "Is that how you get ideas? You come up with motives and alibis for everyone and everything?"

"Maybe." I shrug. "I don't know. It seems like there's more to some of these stories than what they put in the text boxes, and when I can fill in the blanks—whether it's completely off base or not—it gets me going."

"This bandit who can't afford to buy her own coffee, but can afford to hire you, inspired you? I can't believe you're letting her get away with that." He clicks his tongue against his teeth. "She's a crook. She doesn't deserve him or you. There has to be something better. I'ma find it."

I chuckle at how deep his beliefs are on this.

"That's why you want the password, isn't it? You just want to read the requests. You don't care about being hacked."

Giggling the way Baby does when she's finally able to get ahold of the thing she's been redirected away from twenty times, he puts a finger up as if to tell me to hold on a second. Then he disappears from my screen. The space he's left reveals the messiest dresser I've ever seen. It's piled with books, papers, trophies, dumbbells, and maybe even a pair of boxer briefs. Not the color-coordinated, perfectly organized space I would expect him to have. It looks a lot like the way I keep my own room.

He comes back with his laptop. When he opens it, the light from the screen takes things from silhouette to full color. Would it have been that hard for him to put on a shirt before he called? Was he just too wound up about the idea of PROMposal Queen being hacked to consider clothes or something?

Not that his being shirtless is a bad thing. It's hard for me to imagine better lighting for his body. It's more about my inability to focus while he has his pecs out here like an advertisement for something called Fit and Chiseled.

I'm not even sure where all of this comes from. He's not an athlete. At least not the competitive kind. Those must be some effective-ass dumbbells.

"What's the password again? I couldn't remember what letters were capitalized."

His words register as an annoying interruption to something I'm enjoying. I unravel myself completely from the blankets, trying to stop the heat rising up the back of my neck from traveling anywhere else.

He repeats his question.

I lace my fingers together and crack my knuckles. I need to get us...me...back on track. I dictate the password.

It's a while before he says, "What about the one from Ryan in the arts academy? He wants to ask his ex. Seems like he's into her."

"She's probably his ex for a reason."

He lets out a short laugh. "We're judgmental, that's why we can't come up with ideas."

"Um, you called Emma a bandit."

"That's not judgment. That's calling it like I see it."

I give a quick one-shoulder shrug. "Same."

He lets his shoulders droop as if I've just stuck a pin in him and let all the excitement out again. "I'm just saying. Try filling in the blanks in his story and see if you can't feel something."

"I tried that. I can't. All I can come up with is she's better off." I wave the idea away with a sweep of my hand. "Other than Regretful Ryan, find another one that gives you butterflies."

"Why are you so mad at this dude?" He leans into the camera and rests his chin in his palm as if he's expecting an answer that's going to open the floodgates of romantic understanding.

I give myself a minute to craft something deep before I decide to go with the first thing that came to mind when I read the request.

"He's using his ex's feelings against her. He says he knows she still likes him, so she'll probably say yes. What is that?"

"He could be using her feelings as courage." He tilts his head in thought. "Maybe he wouldn't ask her if he didn't know for sure she felt something."

"Exactly." I put an emphasis on every syllable of the word. "That's not romantic. Where's the risk?"

"So you're looking for romance and romance is risk to you?"

Honestly, I haven't put a word with what I'm looking for in people's stories. The only thing I'm sure about is not appreciating requests solely based on the physical. I'm looking for something that makes me sigh. But, I guess, romance sums it up.

"Sometimes romance is risk. When you're in the wrong—like Ryan probably is—definitely."

"Okay then. I'll text him and find out more," Mekhi says. "See if he can prove to you he's risky."

I nod my approval. I could've texted Ryan myself, but I saw the least potential in his situation and decided to focus on people with promise. That's why it's good to have another opinion. Somehow, Mekhi sees something I don't.

If he's able to do that with even a couple other requests, that will be fantastic. Surprisingly, the possibility makes the idea that I'm drowning easier to shoot down.

"What if you're not in the wrong? You're just one person who likes another person. What would be romantic then?"

"I feel real strongly about some things, but I'm not an authority," I tell him.

He doesn't look convinced. "Based on all the likes and comments you get, I'm thinking your definition is on point."

I turn over onto my back. For some reason, it's difficult to say these words to his face in this context. The way he's staring at the screen makes me think he's expecting something profound.

Also, before I commit to these points, I want to make sure I really mean them and they're true for me, if he's going to be turning them over in his mind for at least the amount of time it takes to fulfill the requests.

"Anything can be romantic if it's unique to the two people." I perk up, the perfect example coming to me. "Take the bandit and the doormat."

He chuckles and it makes me smile.

"I would never steal somebody's coffee," I say. "And you would never appreciate someone who did even if it was just to get your attention. They could never have the type of experience they have with each other with anyone else."

"True. What else?"

"Pining is nice."

"I can see that."

"Vulnerability. And I don't mean crying together or sharing deep, dark secrets—not that sharing wouldn't be all well and good, just saying. I'm talking about allowing yourself to be who you really are around another person."

I pause for a reply, but nothing comes so I keep going.

"Something more than considerate, but less than selfless." I stare at a spot on the ceiling, contemplating. "I mean, I want to know one person is thinking of the other and what they want, but it's really not cute to be lost in somebody else."

I could go on, but I trail off because I have no idea how to find these things I'm rattling off in the request responses. I peek at him out of the corner of my eye. I hope I've said something that lives up to the intense, thoughtful look on his face.

I yawn. "I'm not saying I expect people to be in love or all these things at once. But there has to be some sort of real connection. All this other stuff doesn't do anything for me."

"Is that how you and Brandon were?"

Based on the way he immediately looks away from the screen, I don't think he meant to say that out loud.

My face goes hot. I don't know if it's the surprise of my relationship coming up in the conversation in general or if it's having to think about my relationship when I've been putting in a ton of effort not to.

"You were together for a while. I thought if y'all had something like what you're talking about, maybe that's why you're looking for it in all these requests. You miss it."

He's staring at his computer screen when he says all this, not me. But there's nothing in his profile—not the hint of a smile or the arch of an eyebrow—to suggest he's joking about me and Brandon having the kind of connection I'm talking about. I mean, I liked Brandon. I liked the way he wanted to be with me and was vulnerable enough to let me know that—but I don't think he let me in on anything more than what he showed everyone else. I'm not sure I let him in on anything more either.

I fill my cheeks with air and let it out slowly. The sudden realization I'm coming to about the depth of my relationship with Brandon feels like my brain is being kind of harsh with my heart. If I had drawn up some idea of what my first real relationship should've looked like, it wouldn't have been me and Brandon. No one could've told me that—not while I was being swept away by the idea of building something perfect. Now, as I'm faced with Mekhi's question, it's kind of obvious.

"Nobody's ever been all those things with me." I yawn again. "Maybe I'm making it harder than it needs to be."

"No. I wasn't saying that. I was...Just give me a chance to look at the requests and find something you can work with." He turns his focus back to his laptop screen. "You have to stop with the yawning, though."

"No more yawning," I say, and burrow my face in my pillow, drifting off to sleep.

I'm still perfectly wrapped in my blankets when I wake to someone saying my name. I can tell by the tone, it isn't the first time.

I open my eyes to find Mekhi staring back at me, barely covered with his pillow bunched under his head. His eyes are only half open.

"Your alarm is going off. Why do you get up so early?"

This is the first I've heard the noise and it's a minute before I can focus enough to tap Snooze.

"If you hadn't woke me up, I was going to sleep right

through that." My admission makes him chuckle. "How is it morning already? Have you been up this whole time?"

"No, and I don't want to be up now."

"Sorry." I drag out the word. "Why didn't you just disconnect?"

He shrugs and stretches. I don't know what to do with my eyes because there's no safe place to look. The glow of the computer in darkness doesn't compare to how the natural light exposes the gold and brown layers of his skin.

There's a hint of hair on his chin like he needs to shave. Since it's something I've never seen on him before it feels like a secret somehow. Something you can only know after having woken up next to him.

"I thought there might be a real reason for the alarm."

"Nope. Just sloth." I snuggle deeper into the warmth of my comforter.

"Wake up," he whisper-yells into the screen. The words jolt me to attention, but only for a second. My eyes flutter shut again. "You're not going to leave me up again while you rest all peacefully."

"Just go back to sleep."

"That's not how I work." He groans loudly. "The sooner you stop being lazy, the sooner you can see my notes on the requests you're failing to see the romance in."

That's all he had to say. I throw my comforter off, letting the cold shock me to alertness.

I pick up my phone, double-take my notifications. Then

Mekhi. I have twenty-seven unanswered texts from him. The latest was sent only a few hours ago.

He leans back, relaxing against his pillow, and grins. "I didn't mean to send that many texts, but I knew if I didn't support all my points you were going to try to battle me."

He's not wrong. I open the first one, anxious to see what he's come up with.

In it, he's breaking down what makes one of the requests special and romantic exactly by my definition. I look at him. I open my mouth, but it takes a few beats before I can come up with something to say.

"You put a lot of thought into this."

He raises an eyebrow. "That's what you wanted, right?"

I just wanted to stop feeling like making PROMposal Queen a thing is impossible. I had no idea what it would take to get there. Now I feel like if someone who needed a definition for romance last night can find it in these requests, so can I.

Only someone who wants to see PROMposal Queen work out would do this. Mekhi can't care as much as I do, or even for the same reasons, but he believes I can do this. Why waste his time otherwise?

"Yeah. It's great. I just didn't expect it. Thank you." I force myself to look him in the eyes, so he knows I'm serious. "If you hadn't called me last night, I think I would've ended up crying."

He breaks the eye contact and nuzzles himself deeper into his pillow. "You're welcome."

I know what he said, but I have every reason to believe that when we get off the phone, he'll fall right back to sleep. He looks comfortable. I'm getting drowsy just watching him.

Just when I'm about to end the call because all I'm doing is lying here looking at him and that's awkward and unproductive, his eyes meet mine. "Sooo..."

It must be getting awkward for him, too, because nothing follows that intro. Hopefully the awkwardness doesn't come from me staring at his body. I'm trying hard not to do that.

Sleep bearing down on me again, I raise my eyebrows to let him know I'm alert enough for whatever he has to say.

"What time should I be ready on Saturday?"

Chapter Fourteen

For the first time since Brandon and I broke up, I eat lunch in the cafeteria. I've been in the library working on the business plan or coming up with promposal ideas, but today, habit led me in a different direction, and I went with it. I'll probably regret it, though. Beginning with Saturday, we have at least one promposal scheduled every day for the next month. Now's not the time for taking breaks.

It's amazing how quickly things can change. Two weeks ago I was out getting lunch with Brandon, and the day before that he was sitting at my table with me and my friends, and the day before that me with him and his.

I try my best not to look in the direction of their table today, but I can't help it. I want to know if someone's sitting in my spot. Have they all scooted down one like it's no big deal? Did he tell them I won't be showing up anymore?

Somebody *is* in my spot. I pick up speed when I walk by. I don't want anyone thinking I'm trying to get back there. I'm not. Even if I do miss it. A little.

I settle in at a table with Reese and one of her teammates, Katie.

Reese looks despondently out at the cafeteria. I follow her eyes. Avoiding Brandon's side of the room, my attention falls on Mekhi. To nobody's surprise, Maddie is draped all over him. To be completely honest, they look cute together.

Rubbing the tension from the back of my neck, I turn back to my friend.

Reese huffs. "When is it going to end?"

"Why are you acting like this? It's the last semester of senior year. You need to be having more fun." Katie twists her box braids into a low bun. She's also a talented basketball player in spite of the fact that she's barely five feet.

Reese glares at me. "I would be having fun, but my best friend is still running around achieving goals. What are you even doing in here?"

I blink at her. "So you don't want me around?"

"I love you, but I'm only entertaining people who can speed up time."

On one hand, I know she's joking, but on the other, I feel like she's overcompensating for her decision to give up on basketball. Hating school is the excuse that gives Reese's decision logic. Eventually I'm going to have to get around to telling her this. She's going to be mad at me, but maybe she'll at least give her decision more thought.

Across from me, Reese clicks her tongue against the roof of her mouth and glances over my shoulder.

"Repeat after me," she says with a roll of her eyes. "I will never get back with Brandon if for no other reason than the way he broke up with me. *He's* the average asshole."

"Girl, I told you I don't—"

"Say it now," she demands.

I repeat after her, mostly verbatim. And I mostly mean it. I don't want to be the type to say a guy is trash because he dumped me, but Brandon definitely isn't for me.

Reese puts on a big smile and rests her chin on her palm. "There. You have your answer. You can go now."

She's not talking to me. She's looking over my shoulder again. So is everyone else on our end of the table. I turn slowly to find Brandon right behind me.

He doesn't seem fazed at all. I definitely am. I turn away from him to take an inconspicuous breath. I'm not prepared to run into him yet. I don't know how to do casual or not say any of the things I normally would. We didn't spend a lot of time being friends before we were more.

"Autumn, I need to talk to you for a second," he says to my back.

"Nope." Reese overemphasizes the *p*, as if to let Brandon know the subject isn't up for discussion.

"Damn. I'll bring her right back," he says to Reese like I'm some type of toy. Then to me, "I can't have a second?"

Can he? I mean, yeah, I want to know what would send him into hostile territory, but that doesn't mean I want to go off and have a conversation with him.

Reluctantly, I get up and follow him to a quiet corner.

"How you been?" he asks once we're out of earshot.

I'm not interested in small talk, but I go along with it. "Good. Same old, same old."

The last thing I want is to be labeled as a crazy ex or a girl who can't get over the boy who dumped her. I used to shake my head about how some girls act with exes, but now I'm sure at least half the time, the dumped girl wants to be left alone.

And if I'm not mistaken, that's why he broke up with me, so he could be left alone. What could we possibly have to talk about at this point?

He looks into my eyes, not like he's trying to connect with me on anything romantic, but something serious.

"I'm only telling you this because I care about you, but you should stay away from Mekhi."

I tilt my head and blink at him. I had no expectation for this little meeting of the minds, but if I had made a list of ten things Brandon might say to me, *Stay away from Mekhi* wouldn't be on it.

"He's been hanging around a lot. Meeting you at your

car, walking you to class." He slaps the back of one hand into the palm of the other as he makes his points, like he's caught me in something.

This feels like an accusation.

We've never talked about Mekhi. Brandon was around freshman year, so it's possible he knows Mekhi and I share some sort of past, but they don't run in the same circle. Why does he care?

"It's not your business, but we're working on a project together."

He chuckles. "Yeah. The promposals. I heard. Why him?"

I cross my arms. So that's the kind of conversation he's trying to have. "Why not him?"

"He's not your type."

"And what's my type, Brandon? Somebody who breaks up with me because a girlfriend is a loose end?"

"Somebody you can trust." He takes a step closer as if we're conspiring. "Maybe you didn't want to break up, but you know I never lied to you."

I press my lips together and look down at my feet. As much as I hate admitting it, that's true. Brandon has zero emotional IQ, but as far as I know, he has never lied to me. He called when he said he would and there were never rumors about him and other girls.

"I'm just telling you. He's not loyal."

I hate to give him the satisfaction, but I am curious. "What makes you say that?"

"I got ears and don't tell me you don't see how he has Maddie S. following him around." He quirks up one side of his mouth. "He's a hit-and-run type of dude. You want somebody like that?"

Her name catches me off guard. Reflexively, my eyes dart to Mekhi's table. The draping is ongoing. But I mean, good for them if that's what they want. Either way, I don't want to talk about Mekhi's love life.

"What he does with his girlfriends has nothing to do with PROMposal Queen."

I start to head back to the table.

"What—what about him stealing other people's work?"

That catches my attention. I turn back. The Mercer wannabe part of me that consumes 99.9 percent of my body has to hear Brandon out. I'm starting to believe in PROMposal Queen. I can't have anybody messing that up.

"We used to be best friends. This is before you guys had your little...thing."

He hesitates before he says the word *thing*, like he can't spit it out or decide what to call it. I'm no help. I can't decide what to call it either. Just like I have no idea where he's going with this.

"You remember the freshman midyear paper?" he says.

I nod. It was tons of research. People notoriously hate that assignment, but I loved it and got an A-plus as proof.

"A few days after it was due, I get called in to the acad

dean and they ask for proof of all my research. They said I turned in the exact same paper as someone else word for word." He smirks. "I find out that somebody else is Mekhi. I guess he thought since we had different teachers he wouldn't get caught, but they run every paper through a plagiarism app.

"No matter what I did, whatever proof I gave, they wouldn't believe I wrote the paper," he says. "The only way for me to get out of trouble was for him to admit he stole my paper, but he wouldn't. We both got zeros and had to retake the class."

I take a step back, studying him. "Why haven't you ever told me about this before?"

The look on his face says this situation was—*is* a big deal to him. I thought we told each other all those kinds of things. More proof that Brandon and I weren't who I thought we were.

"No reason to. I haven't had anything to do with him since." He shifts his weight from foot to foot as his eyes flit around my face. "As long as he stays away from people I care about I'm good, but it looks like he forgot how to do that. I figured it wouldn't be right if I didn't let you know what I know. He will steal your ideas and try to make himself look good while you look stupid."

"Okaaaay," I say slowly, processing everything he's said and lining it up with the way Mekhi acts about PROMposal

Queen. He obviously knows more than I do about business in general. He's always moving ahead to the next step because he's already thought it through. Worming himself into every aspect of the business, even the part I love the most.

All the time he's spending, staying up all night. There has to be something big in it for him. Since he hasn't told me what it is, maybe that means there's nothing good in it for me.

Could he be trying to take over PROMposal Queen? Maybe he thinks it belongs to him since it was his idea. And can I make it any easier for him to swipe it right from under me?

"You're going to let him go his way, right?" Brandon nods as if that'll sway me. "You're going to listen to me?"

I don't know what I'm going to do. Mekhi is part of PROMposal Queen at this point. Mercer has left me no choice.

"I appreciate the heads-up, but what I decide to do with the information isn't your business anymore." I take a step back, then add, "Is it?"

He drops his shoulders and sullenly shakes his head.

"Right." I look him in the eye. "Remember you said it's better for both of us if we break up, to tie up loose ends before we graduate. You can hang out with your boys these last couple months, and I can do me? That's what I'm doing, Brandon. Let me."

I'm not going to lie. It may be petty, but I'm happy to throw his words back in his face.

I don't want to think about Brandon's motives for telling me what happened between him and Mekhi. But I definitely can't let Mekhi take over. PROMposal Queen is mine whether I've let him think otherwise or not.

Chapter Fifteen

On the dreariest Saturday ever, I pull up to Mekhi's house, walk up a long path, and knock on the door. I've never been deep into the Century Park neighborhood, but I remember my dad once saying that when he and Mom first moved to LeBeau, everybody wanted an address here. It was all about the huge yards, big family rooms, and extra-large front doors.

Newer, pricier neighborhoods outshine it now. But Century Park has all the big old trees like my neighborhood that make it feel more like home.

After what Brandon told me, I'd planned to conveniently forget to pick up Mekhi. I need to make sure it's obvious PROMposal Queen couldn't exist without me. The only way to do that is to handle all the promposal planning and execution. But I found out a few hours ago that Jon is actually Jonah, and I need to use the Cricut again.

Yes, I had Mekhi's help on the first official promposal. He helped me see good where I couldn't in some of the requests, but I have most of them sketched out now. This means I'll have more time to dedicate to the business plan. If I don't sleep for the next four weeks, I should be able to make it all happen without anyone in the position to say they did more than me or even came close.

But I can't cut him out completely if I want to meet Mercer's capstone specifications. As I stand there waiting for him to answer the door, big pellets of cold rain begin to dot the ground around me, a precursor to storms we're supposed to get today.

He answers the door in a T-shirt yet to be covered by his hoodie, and furry teddy bear slippers.

"You're early."

"I know. I texted you. His name is Jonah, not Jon. I need to remake the cup holder."

"Sorry. I don't know where my phone is right now." He pats his back pockets, searching for it.

I cross my arms over my chest. "You know we have business. Seems like the first thing to do would be to make sure the lines of communication are open."

He frowns at me. It's the look he's given me at least

once every conversation since my talk with Brandon. Without a word, he opens the door wider and disappears down the hall. I deep-sigh and go in, shutting the door behind me.

I hang my jacket on a rack and take off my boots. There's one picture on the wall. It's of Mekhi and who I have to guess are his mother and sister. They're all about the same deep caramel complexion, but other than that he doesn't share much with the other two. The freckles must come from his dad.

His house is bigger than mine, and the kind of clean it used to be before Baby came along. No dust over the picture frame or random tiny handprints on the wall.

The kitchen is just as spotless. Everything—from the dish towel hanging over the oven handle to the chairs lined up perfectly—is in its place. It's also quiet, like we're the only ones here. I sit on a barstool at the kitchen counter, waiting for Mekhi to come back. I'm careful not to disturb anything. It feels like someone would notice.

The only thing out of place is the ciabatta bread, cheese, and turkey sandwich sitting next to the stove. My mouth waters. I couldn't eat this morning.

When Mekhi reappears, he sets the Cricut down in front of me and plugs it into an outlet on the side of the island. I take everything I need out of my bag to get started.

"I usually use habanero cheese for my sandwiches, you good with that?"

My eyes immediately go to that sandwich. It looks good.

Under normal circumstances, I would love to be the beneficiary of him dropping that thing in a pan of hot butter. But this isn't a normal circumstance. I don't hang out at Mekhi Winston's house and eat his food. I don't want him to think we're that kind of comfortable. That kind of comfortable gets you looking in one hand while he plays his trick from the other.

"No, thank you," I say.

"You don't like things spicy?"

"I love spicy stuff." I focus my attention back on my project. "I'm just going to get this done and go."

"But I have to eat."

"I'm not stopping you. Stay here and eat. I have a prompposal to do." My voice is thick with irritation.

He hums a little. It tells me he's either assessing the situation or counting to ten. I don't care which.

He then proceeds to make too much noise rummaging through pots and pans. I look up to find him pulling a red bag of chips out of a roaster. Witchery Chips. I love them. I could maybe accept one or two of *those*, but it doesn't look like he's planning to offer.

I go back to putting the paper in the temperamental machine just right. He puts a few pats of butter in a pan and lets them sizzle for a second before he drops the two halves of the sandwich in. My mouth waters again. I'm not sure if it's the smell of the sandwich or knowing how good those chips taste.

We work in silence for a while. I feel his eyes on me

sometimes, but I don't look up. I don't want to encourage conversation. When I'm finished, I slide off the barstool.

"You need something?"

His words don't stop my movement. I slide the new cup holder safely into my bag and zip it. "Nope. I have everything together. I'm gonna go, but thanks, though."

After that, everything goes silent. So silent I have to peek at him.

Spatula in hand, he looks at me, at the pan with the sandwich, and then toward the door. "You're leaving me?"

I tap my fingers on the counter as if this conversation is the biggest inconvenience. "I don't want to be late."

"We have plenty of time."

I check my phone to find what I already know. He's right. I have time to spare.

"I got this." I give him a head-to-toe-and-back-again glare. "I don't need you to come."

He blinks and does his spot check of me, the sandwich, and the door again, like he can't piece this situation together. "Nobody said anything about you needing me. I thought this was part of my job."

"The promposals are mine," I say, my words pouncing on his.

He whips his head back. "Did I say they weren't?"

I imitate his movement. "I'm just saying they are."

"Why do you have to—" He pushes a rush of air through his teeth. "Never mind. Bye."

His dismissal is unbothered perfection, and I don't appreciate it.

A crisp, pithy note of laughter bursts out of me. "Excuse me?"

"I said go if you're going." He points the spatula toward the door. "And for the record, I don't have a personal space issue. I've asked around. That's you being how you are. Which I should've known. Don't even know why I tried."

I drop everything in my hands back down on the counter. He's right. I have time for a talk.

"A, you absolutely do lean in. B, please explain. How *am* I? What does that mean?"

He focuses his attention back on the sandwich, uses the spatula to get each half out of the pan, and slaps them onto a paper plate. "I don't lean in, Autumn. And you know how you are. I'm not wasting my time explaining."

"Oh." I drag the word out and nod slowly as if what he's said has led me to some type of epiphany. "I'm a waste of time."

"That." He points a flimsy finger at me and lets it drop. "That's how you are."

"*That* is not a description of behavior." I cross my arms over my chest, trying to maintain my calm. "And you can't be mad just because I don't have time to sit and wait on your feast to cook."

"So this is all about the food. It has nothing to do with me personally."

"Right."

"If the food was done I could come with you?"

"Yes," I snap.

He doesn't turn his head, but he slowly shifts his eyes down to the counter where the finished sandwich steams. Mekhi's calling my bluff.

I'm not sure how he turned the tables on me. I'm not the one whose integrity is in question.

After the way he treated me freshman year. After what Brandon said. That's two strikes against *his* character, not mine. And I'm not sure if it's a coincidence the sandwich is done, or if he played me by picking a fight he knows I won't walk away from. Manipulation is a potential third strike.

Damn his feelings and what he thinks about me. I have to look out for myself.

Then again, there is something to be said for keeping your enemies close. If an enemy is what he is.

I pick up everything and start down the hall. "You better not make a mess in my car."

I have my boots and jacket back on by the time he comes waltzing down the hall after me, sweatshirt-clad and ready to go.

When we're in my car and out of the now steadily falling rain, he extends the plate in my direction. "You want to take a bite before you back out?"

I look down at the plate, then back up at Mekhi. I can smell the peppers in the cheese, and the butter. It looks really tempting, especially with an empty stomach. But like I told him, I don't want his freaking sandwich. I shake my head, expressing my disapproval of him as a whole, as opposed to refusing the food.

"Look. Even though Emma is a con, I don't want to mess up this promposal." He looks me directly in the eyes but keeps the plate of food between us. An edible barrier. "If we don't stop beefing, it's going to be harder to make sure everything goes exactly the way you planned it."

So not a barrier, but a completely mature and professional peace offering. If we're not good, this promposal might not be either. I don't like it but it makes sense.

I give in and grab one of the halves. He holds the plate underneath my hand as I bring it to my mouth. And it's a good thing, too, because as I bite into it some steaming-hot turkey falls out.

"I should've cut it into smaller pieces," he says.

"I'm good. This is so good," I say around the mouthful. I take another bite and then another. I don't want to be enjoying this as much as I am. I want to at least pretend to be pacifying him, but I can't pull it off. "I didn't think I was this hungry, but dang."

He watches my mouth as I take another bite, and I'm sure he's about to make a snide comment about how I'm devouring his masterpiece when I denied wanting any, but he doesn't say anything. He just looks...at my mouth.

I turn the rearview mirror toward me to see where I've made a mess. There's nothing. I look back at him, about to start asking questions, but that'll probably just start another fight. Instead, I back out of the driveway.

At the first few streetlights he holds the plate up to me again so I can take more bites until my half of the sandwich is sadly all gone. As Mekhi adjusts the bread on his half, my attention shifts.

"So...I really like Witchery Chips." Luckily we're approaching a red light, giving me the opportunity to take my eyes off the road and convey my level of thirst for the chips through my eyes.

He looks territorially at the bag he's placed between himself and the passenger door, out of my reach. "I haven't opened them yet."

I soften my voice. "Will you? Please."

"I haven't even taken a bite of my sandwich. The chips come after."

"For the sake of the promposal?" I plead.

He gives me one of the longest, most exaggerated eye rolls I've ever had directed at me. For the love of the chips, I stay quiet and smile. Even I have to admit my tactics are low.

He lets out a sigh that could extinguish a candle from a distance. But then he opens the bag and sets it on the console between us. As the light turns, I reach in, hoping to pull out a potato that folded over into a little taco shell while it fried. Those have the best crunch.

"You know what I can't understand, though? Why no chip company can figure out a way to do a good jalapeño chip." I stuff two chips—neither of them a taco—in my mouth. "It's literally the best-tasting pepper in the world. Just squeeze it on a potato and sprinkle some salt. It can't be that hard. People out here inventing flavors that don't exist in life—like blue raspberry—and nobody can figure out how to properly jalapeño a potato?"

"What?" he says around his own mouthful. "If you're ever at Unique Foods in Ann Arbor try Nothing But the Pep—"

Before he can finish the sentence, I pretend-gag over the steering wheel.

"But they taste just like a jalapeño, though."

I side-eye him. "They taste like old cough drops. What type of jalapeños have you been eating?"

"Should've brought those," he says. "You're not going to leave any for me. Just like my sister."

I stuff a chip in my mouth and make a show of crunching. He chuckles.

"Is that why you hide chips in the roaster? Your sister?"

"Yes. She's a vulture. She will eat my last and not tell me. She just buries the bag in the trash or stashes it underneath a couch cushion for somebody to find later."

I laugh. "Damn. That's rude. Also, I like the *catch me if you can* of it."

He nods solemnly. "Now she has to catch *me*."

We laugh all the way to Volcanic Coffee, the sound solidifying our unspoken agreement to let go of this morning's tension.

Chapter Sixteen

This Volcanic Coffee location is out of the way of school. I have no idea how either Emma or Jonah end up here on their commute. Maybe it's one of those meant-to-be things. Maybe the closest Volcanic Coffee rarely has the drink either of them wants, so they drive past three others to get to the one that never lets them down.

I text Emma to tell her we're on-site, and Mekhi and I head in.

We're twenty minutes early, which is great, because even though I've talked to the manager and she knows what's up, I want to go over everything again. What if the barista she originally talked to about this didn't show today? Anything could happen.

She's busy, though, so we get in line. She's already doing

us a favor, I don't want her to change her mind and decide today is not a good day for high school stuff.

Mekhi and I are backed up to the door, so every time someone comes in or passes by, we end up pressed closer together. By the time I realize I'm sinking into his heat, it's too late to back away without an explanation. And there's no way he won't notice.

He's standing perfectly still. I look up at him to make sure he's awake. Either he's thinking the same about me, or he's been watching me this entire time, because when I look up, he's looking down at me.

He blinks and clears his throat. "I'm not leaning in. It's crowded."

I can't believe he's still thinking about my personal space comment, or that he actually checked in with other people about it. Did he tell them *I* said he has a personal space issue or did he pose it as a hypothetical aside?

I kind of feel bad I even said anything.

"It's not a big deal," I say at the same time he says, "You like coffee?"

I answer quickly to signify I'm up for changing the subject. "I like drinks that happen to have coffee in them. You?"

"I don't like hot drinks."

"Hot beverages are a small fraction of what coffee can do. Especially if you like sweet things," I say.

"I love sweet things."

It could be the way his voice goes deeper when he says

those words or just the way our closeness makes his voice vibrate through me, but I don't think he's talking about treats.

"Me too." My voice is breathy and light compared to his. I nod to two girls putting away laptops and unearthing umbrellas. "It looks like they're leaving. Why don't you go claim that table for us?"

He heads over to the girls and makes a little conversation before they nod for him to sit down.

I try to be patient in line, but I can't stop myself from checking my phone over and over again. Luckily, each time I look at it, no more than a minute has passed. I have plenty of time to check in with the manager. When I finally do, a little of the anxiety leaves my body. She's still on board, happy to have something "so cute" taking place at her location. I have a good plan, and I've executed it well so far. This is going to be good.

Since Mekhi shared his sandwich with me even after our argument, I end up ordering frappés for me *and* him. The barista makes them ASAP.

When I plop the drink down in front of him, he looks up at me, both eyebrows raised. "You got me something?"

"Dessert. You don't have to like it. I won't hold it against you."

"I'm going to like it." He smiles. "Thank you. That was nice."

I focus on the drinks, not sure how to accept his gratitude.

I would buy a drink for any coffee skeptic. I didn't buy it because it's him.

Mekhi moves his straw up and down, pushing whipped cream through the drink. I hate the whipped cream mixed in. I let mine float on top until the end, saving the best part for last. It's funny how his first thought was to do something I never would. I'm a hundred percent sure this is about to be a drink fail now.

He takes a long drag, then frowns and shakes his head. I let my shoulders droop.

"No. It's good. I swear." He takes another sip and nods. "See?"

"You don't look like it tastes good. Brain freeze?"

He glances at the line. I follow his eyes.

Maddie's at the register ordering.

She looks fresh from the salon with her hair cornrowed into a bun. Instead of legs, she's giving abs today with a tiny crop top above sweatpants. That's my normal weekend wear too. I just don't look like she does in it.

I shake my head and look toward the sky. There's no way this is a coincidence—this store is way too out of the way; he must have invited her...to his job. I try and push down the annoyance that bubbles up. I can be professional even when he isn't.

"Pull up a chair for her."

He quickly turns himself completely toward me. "She hasn't seen us yet. She might not."

Huh. So, not an invite?

"She's looking right at us." Ignoring his protests, I wave at Maddie.

I'm not about this awkward *We're ignoring you* scenario. Especially since the last time we were all together, I was an unassuming block. I'm not getting in her way today. Girl, come get your man.

But instead of waving back, she gawks.

I suck my teeth and sigh. She does not appreciate me right now. I'm about to be pushed into something I don't want any part of. I need to clear this up.

"Why are you so mean to her?"

Mekhi almost chokes on his drink, and I slap him on the back. We don't just have Maddie's attention now. We have everyone's.

"Have y'all been talking?" he asks once he's collected himself.

"No. I just remember you acting funny at bowling when she obviously wanted to spend time with you."

"I don't know what I'm supposed to do." He puts his palms up in defeat. "I've been nice. Then I went firm, and now I just kind of stopped acknowledging her."

I rest my chin on my palm and arch an eyebrow, finally catching on. I don't like where this is going. "You're trying to tell me that girl likes you, and you don't like her back?"

"*Like* is kind of strong. It's more like she's after me . . . for reasons."

I let out a bark of a laugh and side-eye him. *"After you?"*

He nods and takes another sip of his drink. His turning to it for comfort convinces me he was being honest about liking it. But now I'm regretting my decision to buy it for him. Mekhi Winston and I are sitting around having dessert and a conversation about delusional girls. The exact kind of girl he reduced me to back in ninth grade. This is obviously some type of pattern with him. Brandon was right.

And I keep letting him weasel his way in. He is truly gifted at this.

Even though he's looking real sorry, I can't bring myself to feel sorry for him.

"Can you do me a favor? Make it look like you don't want her to come over here." He dips his head so we're eye level. If I didn't know better, I'd think he was in some type of mortal danger, he's so serious. "If she comes over here it's going to be a whole big thing and I don't want that."

"If that girl wants to come over here, she's coming over here," I hiss. "And did you not just see me wave at her? What am I supposed to do now? Pretend she disappeared?"

He shakes his head. "She already thinks something's up between me and you anyway. You stay next to me, and she'll know it's not the time."

There are so many problems with what he just said that I don't even know where to start. First of all, I'm not his babysitter, and I'm not down for looking like delusional girl number two so he can fend off number one. What he's asking me to do is putting me firmly on the side of never trusting him.

And then there's that other thing, about her thinking something is up between us. "Who told her something's up between me and you?"

"Not me." He draws me in with those serious eyes again and presses his hand to his chest for emphasis. "She thinks I flirted with you when we were playing pool. But I told her me and you would never be together like that."

"Exactly." Reflexively I return his pointed look and nod agreement. But after it sinks in, *never* starts to feel like an insult, even if it is true. Like, *I would never eat a pile of shit or stick my hand in a beehive.* That's what something with me is equivalent to, according to Mekhi Winston.

Not that he hasn't made that clear before.

If he did happen to flirt with me, it was just useful for getting whatever he needed at the time. Just like when he kissed me before. I don't know why he kissed me then or why he's sitting next to me now. What does he want from me?

And he needs to ask himself why would he bother to point out to Maddie that I'm not worthy in his eyes unless she means something to him?

I check my phone to see if Emma has called. I'm irritated enough with him that I don't want to look him in the face right now.

"I think you like her." I keep my eyes on my phone. "She wouldn't be going through all this trouble if you weren't doing anything to make her think so."

He slides down in his chair and covers his face with his hands. "I don't like her. Not like that."

"Well then, stop."

"Stop what?"

"Stop the thing you're doing to make her think she has a chance." I look back up at him. Our eyes meet and I know he can see I'm irritated.

This is experience speaking. Mekhi does things to pull you in, then acts all innocent when it works. And I find it hard to believe he doesn't know what he's doing. There's no way the person who stayed up all night to help me find romance in the requests is clueless about how this works.

He lets out a sharp breath but doesn't take his eyes off mine. "I'm not doing anything."

I click my tongue against my teeth. "She's just delusional. All on her own. That's what you're trying to tell me? She made up feelings in her head?"

"If I'm doing something, I don't know what it is, and I can't stop doing it because she won't leave me alone."

I look back up at the counter. She's waiting for her drink now and trying to be casual about looking in our direction. She's not having much luck. To be honest, I'm sympathetic. If there was a hint I missed with Mekhi before, I wish someone had shown it to me. It would've saved me a lot of hurt and embarrassment.

"I don't believe you," I say.

He sits up suddenly in his seat, like someone has pushed him in my direction, and looks down at me. "What?"

"I think you're lying about not knowing what you're doing." I speak slowly since he's having trouble catching my meaning.

"Why would I lie about that?" He's wearing a genuine look of confusion.

"I don't know. Maybe that's just the kind of person you are."

I might as well have punched him in the face, the way it crumples. A small part of me feels bad. But if he can call me out on whatever he thought he was calling me out on at his house, I can do the same.

"Hey, Mekhi," a sweet voice says from above us. Maddie doesn't have a greeting for me, though.

Well, he's not lying about that part. She thinks I'm a threat. She's coming out swinging.

That's my cue.

Drink in hand, I push out of my seat and leave them alone. I feel both of their eyes on me, but I don't look back.

I am the least of her problems if she wants to be with him. I don't want anything to do with this. I have actual business to take care of. Something bigger and way more important than the Mekhi-and-Maddie saga I almost let myself be pulled into. They can battle it out.

When I get to the door, my phone vibrates with a text. I'm relieved before I even look. Emma is in the parking lot.

Yes. Everything will go as planned.

Chapter Seventeen

Volcanic Coffee is its own island, surrounded by strip mall parking on all sides. I take a step outside to look for Emma and realize that "in the parking lot" is about as good as saying she's west of Detroit. The rain has gone from a soft pelt to a noisy thud. It immediately seeps through my sweater and makes me shiver. I cover my drink with my hand to prevent raindrops from diluting it.

I do a careful scan of the lot along the front of the store. There are parked cars, and people claiming spots with their blinkers. But no Emma.

The rain is picking up. I should go back in and get my coat, but unless Maddie knows somebody who knows somebody and went out the employee entrance, she's still inside talking to Mekhi. I don't want any part of that.

I walk to the corner of the sidewalk that surrounds the store, and still no Emma. I walk to the next, and the next, faster and faster, because the rain is coming down harder and harder.

Emma: He's here. Where are you?

I stare at my phone. There's no way I could've missed her. I've almost been all the way around the whole building. There's only one thing that could be happening right now. And it *better not* be happening.

I walk faster. The rain keeps pace.

No. Nope. This can't be happening.

Autumn: Where are you?

Emma: In line right behind him.

Mekhi is the last person I want to ask, but I have no choice.

Autumn to Mekhi: Do you see Emma? She said she's here.

Mekhi: No. Where are you?

I wipe my phone screen on my jeans. The rain is officially my enemy.

Autumn to Emma: At what Volcanic are you in line?

Emma: The one by the library???

The library?

Shit. Big PROMposal Queen fail in progress. My muscles twitch under my skin, urging my brain to give them something to do. And as much as I know I need to move, every direction I try to send myself in feels like the wrong one. All I can do is stand here. I have no idea how to get out of failure's line of fire.

How can something I've managed to avoid for most of my life meet me at every turn now?

This is exactly what I was afraid of. Someone putting their trust in me and me not being able to come through for them. And me betting on myself but not being able to change my circumstances.

Mekhi: Where did you go?

The message resyncs my brain with my body. What am I doing? I can't let this happen. Instead of responding, I run back to the entrance.

Thankfully, Mekhi is standing alone outside, holding my jacket and his drink.

"Where are we supposed to be?" Mekhi yells over the

pelting rain before I even get to him. He's obviously figured out the issue.

"The library."

Rainwater splashes both of us as I leap off the sidewalk and land in a puddle. It doesn't slow either of us down, though. But when we finally get to the car, I can't find the keys. Mekhi stands across from me at the passenger door hopping from foot to foot as if dodging the rain. I, on the other hand, am just shivering, more from frustration than the cold.

"Do you have my keys? They were in my jacket pocket."

"I haven't seen any keys."

Without explanation, I run back in the other direction.

He gets ahead of me somehow and thrusts the door to the coffee shop open. I run in ahead of him and ask the people now at our table if they've seen keys. They're a little irritated but get up and let me move the chairs and lift their belongings to check around. They're probably feeling a little territorial with the way I came running toward them.

"Got 'em," Mekhi yells from the counter. "Someone turned them in."

After hurried *sorry*s and *thank you*s, we're back outside in the rain, and then finally in the car. The first thing I do after starting it is crank the heat up and turn one of the vents that should be facing the passenger side toward me. Mekhi side-eyes me but doesn't say anything.

He peels off his soaked sweatshirt and tosses it in the

back. I put the car in reverse and don't look either way as I pull out.

Mekhi gets out his phone and calls the correct location. Within seconds, ringing fills the car, competing with the pour of the rain.

I nearly give us both whiplash stopping at a red light that I either don't see coming until we're on it, or forget is normally here. The one good thing about the weather is there's a lot less traffic than usual. Some people have sense enough to stay put during a torrential downpour.

At the next light, instead of waiting three cycles for my chance to turn, I only have to wait two. It doesn't sound like a huge time-saver, but I feel better telling myself it is. Nonchalantly, Mekhi finds the oh-shit handle and grips it. He can be scared if he needs to. Whatever it takes to put this promposal in the win column is what I have to do.

I do slow down a little, though. The rain gets heavier and heavier the farther east we travel. The radio isn't on, but instinctively I reach to turn it down. It's just so noisy; it's like people are throwing buckets of raindrops at my windshield one after another. Even slowed down to ten below the speed limit, I can't see much.

"If they answer, let me talk so you can focus on driving." He clears his throat as if readying himself to be professional even though nothing has happened to make me think anyone will ever pick up.

I groan. "It might not even matter. No one's answering."

No sooner than I get the words out, there's a whooshing sound beneath my feet and we're floating. Hydroplaning. My stomach drops as the car's tires surf the water, pulling us left, then right. I grip the steering wheel hard and press my back firmly against the seat as if that will stop us from moving forward. But I know it won't. I have no control.

I hold my breath, brace myself because I think we've veered into another lane. A car whizzes by on my side, the driver laying on the horn. A tiny squeal escapes me, and I clamp my eyes shut for a millisecond before regaining myself enough to remember to take my foot off the gas.

My heart unleashes what feels like a thousand beats at once before the tires reunite with the road and the car belly flops with a loud splash.

I put on my hazards and slow down, trying to find the lanes so I can pull over. The wipers only provide a quick flash of visibility, but I manage to inch over until the sound of gravel hitting the underside of the car joins in with the rain.

There are no tears, but my breath hitches as if I've been sobbing. That's when I realize Mekhi's hand is resting near my shoulder. Maybe it's been there the whole time. Somehow his firm but gentle touch is like a conduit, allowing me to borrow some of his calm, and I'm thankful for it.

Still, my heart is in my throat until he says my name quietly. It's not a warning or even a question. It's more like a reassurance, something to say we're okay.

I'm irritated with him about the whole thing with Maddie, suspicious he's trying to steal my ideas, and frustrated that his touch reminds me of the day he kissed me, but still, I'm glad he's here.

I sort of resent him for that too. How can someone who makes me feel all those negative things also make me feel okay sometimes too?

He slowly slides his hand down to the crook of my elbow, and then my forearm, before he lets me go. Where he touched me is about the only place on my body where there's heat instead of goose bumps from the cold of my panic. Second by second everything that's going on around us comes back into focus.

Ringing still comes from his phone. Somehow, it's safe in his other hand. I tell him he can hang it up. We're not going to make it. It's only my second promposal, and I can't pull it off. I knew Eliana and Chris were too good to be true. I don't know why I thought arranging something in such a public place with so many variables was a good idea. This was the worst idea. PROMposal Queen itself is probably the worst idea.

I'm not in a big hurry to talk to anyone, but I have to at least apologize to Emma. My phone has slid to the floor. With shaking hands, I feel around for it. I'm prepared to admit my fault, but instead, post after post pops up from her.

I squeal, in a good way this time. "She asked him."

Leaning over our drinks that somehow remain intact, I

show Mekhi the picture Emma posted. Jonah's giving her the eyes.

I smile down at the phone. "I told you he likes her."

"You were right. I still think dude has to have some pride, but, I mean, whatever makes him smile." He shakes his head. "You should comment. Let her know how hard you tried to get to her."

I shake my head. It's not that I don't want to acknowledge Emma's moment. I'm happy she was able to make this whole thing work despite my ineptitude. But this is part of my *additional information*, and I need it to be more spotless than everything else I've sent. I can't give Mercer a reason to not find a spot for me.

I lace my fingers together on my lap and absently flick my thumbnails against each other. "I'll just refund her and figure out how to make everything else balance out. I don't even care about the money."

"What *do* you care about?" The way his eyes search my face tells me he isn't teasing. "When I first mentioned getting paid for promposals you were against it. Then not even a day later you show up at YBE determined as hell. Can I at least know why that is? What did I almost die for?"

What do you care about?

It's another one of his thoughtful, mood-changing questions. I don't want to answer it. Telling Mekhi I got wait-listed at Mercer is embarrassing enough without the fact that he actually got in.

He puts a hand over both of mine to stop my nervous motion. This is different than the way he touched me a few minutes ago. It's still firm, but it's not as sure. *I'm* not as sure about why he would touch me now and why I would feel it everywhere. When he takes his hand away, I instantly miss the warmth.

"I was just curious. You don't have to tell me anything."

His voice is soft and gravelly at the same time. I don't know how to stop myself from being affected when it's both sexy and sweet. This is part of what got me in trouble the first time. There may not be a question I wouldn't answer if he asked in that voice.

"Actually"—he swallows hard—"you *can* tell me how to get that crushed look off your face. What can I do?"

That makes me look at him and notice the worry lines across his forehead. I would like to smooth those out. This isn't the look of an evil person out to steal my work. I don't know how it's happened, but Mekhi Winston looks like someone who doesn't want me to be upset.

I squeeze my eyes shut and blurt, "I got wait-listed at Mercer. Completing the senior capstone project by signing day is me trying to make myself stand out on the list. I didn't apply anywhere else, so it's not as easy to get over as people think it should be."

When I open my eyes, the lines have taken a step down from his forehead to between his eyebrows, and he's nodding slowly as if processing my words involves complex math.

"Are you sure there wasn't some kind of mistake?"

For the first time ever, I laugh at my situation. Hard. It's better than wanting to cry about it, even if it only lasts for a second.

"I'm not even trying to be funny. Aren't you like top twenty in the class? I'm, like, fifty something," he says. "And I have some questionable things on my transcript."

By "questionable things" I assume he means the cheating incident with Brandon. I'm not even sure how plagiarism shows up on your transcript, and how he can get around that when applying to any college, let alone Mercer. How can he get in with something like that on his record and I can get wait-listed with zero blemishes? Then again, do I even want to know? Will it make me feel better or worse? I'm not sure.

"I'm positive it's not a mistake." I raise my eyebrows. "I made them tell me twice."

He chuckles a little. "Whatever you did, I think you were justified."

I'm not going to lie, having someone other than my best friend whose literal job is to love and support me be just as scandalized by my situation as I am, feels good.

"And you know MBSP, right?"

He nods. "I didn't get to go."

"Well, I did, and I won the scholarship. Now I have a gaggle of people spamming the group chat about how great it's going to be when we all get up there. They all assume I got in."

He grimaces.

"Yeah. So that's how I ended up at YBE. Mrs. Tanner made some calls." I look out at the road because I can't face him when I make this next admission. "To be honest, I didn't have any ideas other than the promposals, which was *your* idea."

"I shouldn't have said that."

I face him. "It's true. I should've thanked you."

"It might've been my idea, but it's not like I could've done anything with it." He leans back against the headrest. "You're the one with the vision. The only one who could make it happen."

I don't even try and hide my smile. "I like how sure you are about that."

"I don't understand how you're not sure."

"Even after today?" My voice goes high-pitched and my eyes wide. "I messed this one up."

He nods sympathetically, but then a quiver of laughter escapes his lips. He slaps his hand over his mouth.

"It's not funny."

I reach out to swat his shoulder, but he catches my hand. We struggle until, laughing, he overpowers me, forcing it flat on the console between us. I try again and again, but every time I reach for him, he forces my hand back down.

On my third try, when he catches my hand again, he says, "You are super soft. You feel like...I don't even know."

My hand goes limp in his and I pull it away.

"Stop trying to distract me from the fact that you're

laughing at me again." I try to push as much annoyance into those words as I can, but it comes out all breathy. And that's a feat because I don't think I'm breathing. Him noticing my softness should feel like a violation, but it doesn't. "Why do you always laugh at me?"

"I'm not laughing at you." He clears his throat and looks at me seriously. "You just get so convicted and everything is so much with you. Most people aren't like that. You surprise me, I guess."

We eye each other, and I realize how quiet it's become. At some point during our conversation the rain stopped and the sun came out. Cars whiz by now at normal speeds. I can take him home without sliding off the road, but I'm not necessarily in a hurry.

I have questions too.

"Why are you helping me? Because it was your idea or were you really that offended I didn't ask you and you needed to prove something?"

He straightens up in the seat and looks out the window. I guess it's my turn for thoughtful, mood-changing questions. He's not laughing anymore, and my softness is a long-ago memory.

"You know how specific some scholarships can be?" he says after a while.

"Yeah, like blue-eyed Black male with one pinky toe longer than all the others planning to major in banana tree leaf exploration."

"Exactly." He laughs a little and drums his fingers on his thighs. "There's one that requires being a Black male with experience developing niche businesses in the service industry. I didn't think I'd be able to apply for it. Most YBE business ideas are product and technology related, but niche services…"

He shakes his head.

"Then you walked in with PROMposal Queen. I didn't even see it for what it could be when I mentioned it in the media center. But once everyone started talking about it, I knew I had to get you to let me work on it. Like I said, you're the one with the vision. I couldn't do it by myself."

I stare at his profile, hoping he'll face me. He already got into Mercer, and getting scholarships isn't something to be secretive about. There has to be more to us working together than that. He could've just told me that back at Lane by Lane.

"Will you be able to go to Mercer if you don't get this scholarship?"

"I could, but I won't. It's complicated."

Mekhi not maintaining any eye contact with me probably means I shouldn't go any further, but it could have something to do with the plagiarism thing and if it does, I want to know. Whether it makes me feel worse or not, I need to know why he might have been chosen over me and if there are any special circumstances.

"What's complicated? It's Mercer." I adjust myself in my seat and scratch my head, trying to figure out how to be gentle but knowing it may be impossible. "There's nothing I wouldn't do to go to Mercer if I got in, especially if I knew somewhere along the way I caught a break."

Finally he turns to me. "Caught a break?"

"Well, you said you had questionable things on your transcript. I was just saying." I backtrack a little. The look on his face is telling me not to go there and I don't feel like another argument.

"You're *just saying*. What makes you 'just say'?"

"Nothing. You asked me a question, I asked you one."

He nods slowly. "Nothing? Not even your boyfriend whispering in your ear?"

"Ex-boyfriend. And what makes you think—"

He raises his palm between us to shut me up. The gesture stuns me into silence. Who is he supposed to be?

"Whatever he is to you, he's been eyeing me like we're about to have a problem since we published that request form. And you..." He scoffs and tilts his head vigorously from side to side as if working out the kinks. "You've been acting funny since he made a big show of pulling you to the side in the cafeteria. It's not that hard to figure out. I thought we could work it out without him coming up, because he's irrelevant to me. But obviously he's relevant to you, so..."

As with every conflict we have, Mekhi keeps his voice low and controlled. I'm learning this means that whatever he's feeling, he's really feeling it. In this moment, I'd say he's pissed.

I try to downplay everything. This isn't the conversation I want to have. "It's not like that. He wants me to be careful."

He steeples his fingers together and taps them against his lips, like he's trying his best to keep it together, not to care. "What *exactly* did he say?"

"Just that you used to be friends and you used his essay and never admitted to it."

He laughs incredulously. "And that's why you felt the need to remind me the promposal ideas are yours? I'm dangerous?"

"I don't think you're dangerous." The words come out so fast and earnestly it even surprises me.

"But you did a few hours ago. And a few hours from now you might again." He relaxes in the seat and frowns. "Maybe your first idea was the right idea. Maybe we shouldn't be doing this together."

I sit up straight. "You're going to quit now? Because I asked you a question? I wasn't even trying to bring up that other stuff or be mean. And maybe I shouldn't have said it the way I did, but I just wanted to know about Mercer. I'm just trying to figure out why not me. You're the one who started getting all defensive."

"Shouldn't I be?" he shoots back, veins bulging in his neck.

I take a page from his book and rein myself in. "I don't know, but don't take it out on PROMposal Queen."

"I don't like having to prove myself to people over and

over again. It never works." He tips his head back on the headrest. "And if you don't trust me, how is this going to work?"

I lace my fingers tightly together on my lap and sigh. "You've proven to me that PROMposal Queen's success is important to you. That's all I need to trust for us to keep working together."

He picks up his frappé but doesn't drink it. He just slushes through the mostly melted sweetness with his straw and looks out the window.

"If I bring up the essay thing again, you can quit," I offer.

After a moment, he sighs. "We should probably go pull up the business plan outline and decide who's going to do what. If you're trying to cover that whole capstone in a month, we have a lot of work to do."

Before he can change his mind, I look both ways, shift into drive, and ease my way into traffic.

Chapter Eighteen

MBSP Group Chat

Devin: We haven't hung out since last summer. We should plan something and take a group shot with our acceptance letters.

"Seriously. There has to be a statute of limitations on how long and how many times you can gloat about college acceptance." Reese smacks my phone to the floor, readjusts my comforter over her shoulders, and turns her attention back to an autobiography about some famous female athlete. "She's the poster child for the auntie you don't want to show up as at Thanksgiving dinner twenty years from now."

I roll off the bed and pick up the phone. Then I pace, tormenting myself with the chat in peace.

What am I going to do?

Should I continue to not respond? Say I'm coming and then cancel at the last minute? Disagree with every proposed time and be the *go ahead without me* martyr? It's not like it's going to be easy coordinating people in five different states.

How long can I stay in this chat without confirming I've been accepted? And when am I going to have this business plan done and enough promposals under my belt to make a difference in my application? Thirteen isn't quite enough to prove my point.

"But you see what I'm dealing with, though? Everyone is all like *Yeah. When? It'll be fun.* Meanwhile I'm praying they pick a date weeks from now so maybe there's a chance I can have something to share."

"You see how that's a choice?"

This is a rare Saturday evening where we both have nothing to do at the same time and we're supposed to be relaxing. Reese is super good at it. I can't be, not when everything reminds me that relaxing isn't what gets me where I'm trying to be. At the same time, I have noticed I need to take breaks here and there or else I end up staring at my computer screen accomplishing nothing anyway.

I stop midpace. "Do I say that when out of nowhere you start talking about post moves and setting screens?"

"You can if you want."

She doesn't even bother to look up at me. I smack her book to the floor the way she did my phone and nod once at my job well done.

"It's not that good anyway." She shrugs and sits up, crossing her long legs in front of her. "When did we turn into bitter bitches? I thought you had to be like forty for this to happen."

I plop down next to her and rest my elbows on my knees. "We're not bitter, just unwritten."

"You don't self-evaluate very well, do you?" She points her finger back and forth between us. "We're bitter."

We both fall back onto my bed, stare up at the ceiling, and sigh. Reese and I have always known we'd be at different schools. A good women's basketball program like State's and an elite business school like Mercer don't have a lot in common.

But this is not how I envisioned we'd end up in different places. And before now, I hadn't been able to imagine how weird it'll be not having her around to call life out the way she does.

I'm going to miss her so much, I feel it in my chest.

There's a knock at my door. Before I answer, Mom comes in with Baby trailing behind her. I get off the bed and scoop Baby up as soon as I can to make sure she doesn't go after my laptop. She has a toy computer that looks and sounds exactly like the real thing, but somehow, she knows it's not.

Reading my mind, Reese puts it out of reach.

This is one of Mom's days off, and she's fresh from getting her roots twisted so her locs are hanging loose past her shoulders. Whatever she has to talk to me about, it must be real important if she got to my room without finding a ponytail holder first.

"Hey, Ms. Angela," Reese says.

Mom looks around the room. "Y'all in a mood. What's going on?"

I shrug. I can't tell her what I'm actually doing. A conversation about college is one I've been avoiding. Mentioning MBSP will get her started.

She holds up a large envelope. There's a blue block *S* in the return area. It's addressed to me.

"Have you heard anything from State yet? They keep sending you all this recruitment stuff."

Her words almost make me drop Baby; then I squeeze her tight as if her little hands are enough to comfort me.

Midbend to pick up her book, Reese goes completely still. I avoid eye contact, even though her energy is pulling me. She must think my ignorance and arrogance are about to be uncovered.

I'm surprised it's taken one of my parents this long to ask about a specific school. I never applied, obviously. My parents just assumed I would, and I never corrected them. They also never picked up on the lack of application fee withdrawals posted to their account.

Baby whines and I loosen my grip so she can slink back

down to the ground. She runs right to the full-length mirror hanging on my door and sloppily kisses her reflection. I keep my eyes on her, not wanting my mom to sense anything off in my eyes. She's done it before.

"A lot of people haven't heard anything yet."

This isn't a lie. There's nothing for her to uncover. Especially when I never said I *should* be hearing back.

She blinks as if she doesn't have all the pieces to the puzzle. I keep quiet. If I say anything more, she'll root it out.

"In the meantime, there's a prospective student day in a couple weeks. It's for juniors but I called and they're happy to have you."

I shake my head. "What if I have a promposal that day?"

"Then you're rescheduling it. You're going. I'll call the other places you applied to as well and see if they have any events. When you get positives back, you need to be ready to decide." She eyes me. "That is if you haven't already heard something and are just keeping quiet. It doesn't make sense that you're the only one everyone's keeping waiting."

I don't say a word. I don't move. I might pass out from limited oxygen intake.

Mom turns to Reese, who finally picks up her book. "Why don't you go too? You've spent a lot of time there for basketball camps and stuff, right? You can show—"

"Mom," I cut in, "Reese doesn't want to go up to State and sightsee."

"I'll pay for dinner wherever you want," Mom says, with

a nod in Reese's direction. As if dinner will entice Reese to visit a dream school that is out of her reach but—in theory at least—still within mine.

"Mom." I take a step closer to her. I don't think she's picking up on what I'm trying to tell her with my eyes. She's being a little insensitive.

"I'll go. There's an Italian place right off campus that I try to go to every time I'm there, if I have the funds," Reese says.

"Perfect. I'll forward the email and let you two work out the details." Mom scoops Baby up, signaling the end of the conversation.

I roll my eyes at her back as she walks out the door. "Thank you for being nice to my mom, but girl, you don't have to go. We don't both have to be subjected to this whole thing."

She narrows her eyes at me. "What *whole thing*? I want to go."

"You do?"

She shrugs and assumes her earlier position on my bed. "It's beautiful up there and it's not like there's anything going on here. Why wouldn't I?"

"I—I don't know. Why would *you* want to show State off to *me*? I mean, I don't want to be anybody's Mercer tour guide."

She picks up the book and studies the cover like it's new to her. "That sounds like jealousy and that's not me. I'm not jealous of my best friend."

I put both of my hands up as if to stop her words from reaching me. "I know. I'm not saying that. At all."

She glares at me. "Well, can you backtrack a little faster, because processing what you said is making me mad."

I sit down on the end of the bed, trying to get my words right. Reese gets irritated with me sometimes, mostly because she thinks anything I'm trying to do or say can be accomplished in fewer words or less time than it takes me, but her being mad at me isn't a thing. Whether she wants to admit it or not, I'm touching on something. Something we need to talk about.

"I didn't mean it that way. You can be happy for your friend and disappointed for yourself without being jealous. I wasn't trying to put that on you." I look around the room, searching for the right words. "I guess—and I know this is my problem, not yours—but I feel bad that you have to give up."

She huffs. "I didn't give up, Autumn. They gave up on me."

I wave a hand in her direction. "See? That right there. That crack in your voice. I don't want you to have to have that, especially when I know if you took a chance, if there was another way, you'd crush it."

"You know what would be even better?" She gives a swift nod with every word. "If I was so good I didn't need a second chance. But I'm not, Autumn. You're the only one that can't accept it. I can."

She says it all with such conviction I almost believe her.

But when she opens the book and starts to read, it's on a page way ahead of where she left off.

I wish I knew how to convince her to believe different.

"Seriously. What are you going to tell your mom?" Reese says, forcing a subject change. "I don't know about anywhere else she thinks you applied, but State doesn't do rolling admissions. You'll have to apply with next year's class. How are you going to explain that?"

I clench a fist and gently tap it against my mouth as I think. "Girl, I have no idea. Let's hope I don't have to."

Chapter Nineteen

I have no idea why Mekhi is video chatting me shirtless again.

We've already talked PROMposal Queen business today and made a trip to the dollar store. I'm supposed to be using this time to be creative, while he adds onto my draft of the marketing portion of the business plan.

I've been doing pretty good. People are still vain, but Mekhi's notes have helped me be a little more forgiving. I'm glad I stopped accepting requests, though; the pressure of seeing the numbers go up on that first day was too much. Now that I know where the end is, it all feels doable. Plus, a sold-out-in-one-day business can't be a bad thing to share with Mercer.

"Are you wrapped up like a burrito again?" he blurts out

before we even exchange a greeting. "Every time we talk you're like that."

I raise my eyebrows. "I'm swaddling. Or I was, until you made me take my arm out."

He's quiet for a second, eyes focused somewhere other than his phone's camera. "Dictionary says swaddling mimics the conditions of the womb. Why are you doing that? Are you fussy?"

"Sometimes. You wouldn't be making fun of me if you knew how many problems I've solved in exactly this position." I lift my chin, proud. "Do you think these promposal ideas come out of nowhere? Next time you need to do some deep thinking, try it."

Without a word, he disappears from the screen.

There's a lot of rustling around until eventually the phone falls and I lose my view.

I giggle. "I didn't mean you had to try it right now."

When his face fills the screen again, he's up to his neck in blankets. He's matched my swaddle with his own. "I got it really tight, my feet are in here good, but how do you get both hands inside without pulling something out of socket?"

I have to work hard not to laugh. I keep my tone even. "I'm not going to lie, it's a skill." I prop my phone up between pillows so he can see my full process. "There's some very careful wiggling and some contorting, and sometimes I have to start over because it loosens too much. But when I get it right, it's so good."

I sigh because I've gotten it right and have been a perfect example of how he, too, can achieve this sort of happiness.

"Your turn," I say.

"I'm good. I don't want to mess it up. It's the perfect tightness." He tilts his head in surprise. "It *is* kind of relaxing."

"Even better if you do it all the way. You have to at least try after you made me take my arm out to talk to you."

He pants. "But I like it this way."

"Whatever. Keep your little off-the-shoulder wannabe swaddle."

He shakes his head but, again, accepts the challenge. He rocks back and forth and side to side. Nothing like my perfect example. The blanket turns into a big mess around him.

"You're going to fall off the bed and hurt yourself. You can stop now."

He looks down at his bare chest, which hasn't made its way back into his swaddle. "Just leave it like this?"

I look down at him, too, and pull my eyes quickly back up to his face when I realize I'm staring at his abs. "That's an option."

My mouth goes dry. I can't believe I said that out loud. I can't believe I thought it. I can't believe I'm *still* thinking it.

He *has* to start wearing a shirt.

"You knew I was going to end up tangled up like this, didn't you, didn't you?" he says with a laugh, thankfully not picking up on my willingness to stare at a shirtless him for however long this chat lasts.

"I had no idea, but seriously. What's up? You don't talk to me unless it's about PROMposal Queen or trying to dispute my feelings about jalapeño-flavored potato chips. Did we get hacked for real this time or something?"

I don't even mean to say anything about the way he steers our conversations back to business every time they veer even slightly off. And I especially didn't mean to sound salty about it. But I'm irritated because I know this particular tension is because of the whole thing with him and Brandon. He doesn't think I trust him, and he doesn't trust me not to bring up the essay again.

I don't know what was going through his head when he stole Brandon's essay, but I don't believe he wants to take all the credit for PROMposal Queen. I think that's obvious in the way I've let him become a very important part of the business. So far, it doesn't seem like he's picked up on that.

He looks away from the screen before frowning sheepishly. "We haven't been hacked and you can't taste-test over video, but I really was curious about you being wrapped up all the time."

"And?" I nod quickly, urging him on. If he's not even going to deny stunting our conversations, then he's probably good with the way things are. And it's not like we *have* to talk about anything other than PROMposal Queen. That's not what we shook on.

"How serious were you about this *PROMposal Queen is sold out* thing?"

I side-eye him. Did he not witness my near meltdown? If nobody else, he should know exactly how serious I am about being sold out. I open my mouth to reiterate my feelings. He doesn't give me a chance.

"This is a good one. It has all the stuff you like. The pining is A-plus-plus."

Every promposal since the coffee incident has turned out right, but I'm not risking my fragile confidence on anybody. I'm well on my way to being able to make a convincing case to Mercer if I stay focused. I don't need anything extra to think about.

And what is this turning into? We have one conversation about romance and this boy thinks he knows where to find it.

"No," I say firmly. "As you know, I haven't even planned out all the promposals I'm already committed to, and you want me to take on another one? Why and how does that make sense?"

He presses his hands together and points them toward the camera as if pleading with me. "Don't decide yet. You know Tyler Ackerman, right?"

I do, but don't get a chance to say so before he presses on.

"After first period, he was talking about this girl, and how they talk but he can't tell what she's thinking, and he's running out of time. He sounded so...clueless. I had to see if we could help. I told him we'd get in touch with him tonight."

"Go ahead and get in touch with him." I nod incredulously. "Tell him you were mistaken in thinking you could make those sorts of decisions for PROMposal Queen."

My voice has an edge to it now. He can't be promising people stuff. It'll block my creativity.

"Come on, Autumn," he says softly, "you said you needed this kind of romance to do your best work. I'm hand-delivering this one to you. It's already been vetted."

His excitement reminds me of the way he was when we first talked about Chris and Eliana. It's the kind of excitement I never imagined him capable of. He always used to seem so chill to me, which is why I thought he and Jordyn would be good together in the first place. But apparently, he just needs the right stimuli.

His excitement is contagious, but I don't want him to know that. He can't be calling me every night with new clients like the rules don't apply to him.

"Who's the girl?"

"I didn't ask. I didn't want to get too attached in case you said no."

I snicker. He's already attached.

I don't need any more requests, but I'm curious. What could someone say to win Mekhi over like this? And it's not like I have to say yes. I just have to hear the whole story.

"If I hear him out and say no, you have to accept it, *and* you can't try and override my Sold Out sign again."

He rubs his hands together, as if everything is going exactly as planned. "Promise I will. Promise I won't."

As he adds Tyler to the chat, I sit up in bed, readying myself to give Tyler a shot. I've had him in a couple classes. Nothing about him ever stood out to me except he's super polite.

When Tyler appears on the screen, red blotches are scattered across his cheeks, and he has to clear his throat three separate times before he responds to my hello.

Not going to lie, his nervousness is kind of endearing. Mekhi smiles and nods as if he's already proven his point. I keep my face blank, not giving away anything.

"I can usually ask girls out on my own," Tyler starts, "but not her. I'm not interesting enough. You get what I'm saying?"

I nod slowly. I've never had that exact experience with someone I've liked, but I can relate to not feeling good enough for something.

"I have her in three classes this year and she talks to me all the time, but I just sit there, looking at her, thinking it's the last time she's ever going to talk to me, but it never is." He pauses and looks quizzically into the phone as if Mekhi or I might know why the girl hasn't given up on him. "These last couple weeks, she's been talking about prom. Mostly about her dress and how she's going to look in it. She asked me if I thought it sounded nice. If I thought she would look pretty."

I lean toward the screen, clamoring for the details. "And what did you say?"

He rubs both hands down his face and blows out a gust of air. "I said 'Sure.'"

"Tyler," I chastise.

"I honestly thought she was looking for a guy's opinion, not *my* opinion," he says. "I couldn't say what I was thinking without sounding creepy."

"What were you thinking?"

"That she's always pretty." He says that part with a ton of conviction.

Probably because he knows my stance on superficial requests, Mekhi stops looking so proud of himself. But it's not like I don't expect people to be physically attracted to each other. That just can't be the only thing.

I don't know if this is vanity or something more, since Tyler won't communicate with this mystery goddess, but the way she has him all speechless is definitely sigh-worthy. She practically asked him to prom already anyway. This *could* be a win.

"Who is she?" I say.

"Jordyn," he says, and the red in his face deepens.

"Black Jordyn?" I say, and turn my ear toward the screen to make sure I'm hearing him right.

His eyes shift a little as if he's looking for Mekhi's reassurance. Mekhi gives him a nod. "Uh, yeah."

I hope he doesn't think I'm going to give him problems about the interracial thing. Jordyn and Tyler wouldn't be the first interracial couple LeBeau High has seen by far. It doesn't faze me one way or the other.

My surprise is all about it being *Jordyn*. Not because I can't see any guy in school falling for her, but because that guy seeking out my help feels like some type of joke. Or maybe it's an opportunity.

I blink at the screen and frown. Jordyn and I didn't leave things in the best way when we saw each other at Kamia's. But she specifically asked me not to allow anyone to PROMposal Queen her. I'm supposed to tell her if someone wants to.

But does that only apply when we're speaking to each other?

I *would* like to talk to her. And she did make it seem like she has a guy in mind. If I had been given a million guesses on who that guy is, one of them wouldn't have been Tyler. But she is definitely putting it all out there for him.

Since when did she become such a flirt? Could've saved us a lot of trouble if she'd discovered she could do this before.

"What did she say her dress is going to be like?" I ask to buy myself some time while I take out my laptop. If it turns out Jordyn has changed her mind about public displays or Tyler and I are both misreading the signals and she's not into him like that, I don't want him to know I've run this all by her.

"Her dress?" Tyler repeats.

Mekhi raises an eyebrow at me. I nod. How does he know this isn't part of my process?

As Tyler does his best to describe the dress and I pretend to understand nothing of what he says, I clandestinely message Jordyn. The most important key to success, in this situation, is making sure Mekhi has nothing to do with it.

I try not to think about it too hard. This is what she asked me for. It's a completely different situation, but I'm happy to show her I know how to follow through.

I'm not messing this one up.

> **Autumn:** You told me to tell you if someone
> wants to PQ you. You've been telling him
> about your dress?

I watch those bubbles on my screen like they hold the key to my life.

> **Jordyn:** He's been listening to me?

I smile, then press my lips together quick to cover it. I have no clue what the other two are talking about and I don't need questions asked.

> **Autumn:** He's describing it right now.

> **Jordyn:** ????

Autumn: I needed time to talk to you before I told him if I could do it or not. He's scared to ask you. You make him speechless. It's very cute. What do you want me to tell him?

There's a long wait, one that makes me wonder if I'm going to get a response.

Jordyn: Tell him to answer me.

Right after I finish reading the text, I look over to see that Tyler's eyes are focused somewhere else on his screen other than the camera.

"That's her," I say. "If you're too scared to ask her to prom or out in general, just act like you already did."

"What?" Tyler and Mekhi say in unison.

"It will work. This once." I put strong emphasis on that last part. There are probably very few situations where he can claim something he hasn't asked for and not get hung up on. "Just ask her what kind of pink her dress is so you can make sure you get the right color tie or corsage or something."

Tyler pokes his lips out. This is the most animated I've seen him. "I don't think she's going to like that."

"Answer her before it hangs up and do what I say. You will win."

He looks at his phone skeptically again. I get those same

feelings I did when I thought Chris might get to school before Eliana. If he doesn't answer, will she call back? Will he ever follow the bread crumbs she's leaving out for him?

"Okay," Tyler says hastily. "See you tomorrow."

And finally, we get the tone that tells us he's disconnected. If I'd been thinking straight, I would've hung Mekhi up and offered to call Jordyn for Tyler. I would love to see this all play out the way Jordyn wants it to.

Hopefully she'll let me know if it does.

I return my attention to Mekhi. "Can I get back to work now?"

"Not until you tell me why you set him up like that." He frowns at me. "You really think she's going for that?"

I can't lie. It's kind of cute that he's worried.

"Well, I know she's not going for a promposal. She told me that weeks ago. Just in case."

He sits up suddenly. "Maybe you should tell me what *you* want. Just in case. If he'd been talking about you the way he talked about Jordyn, I would've tried my best to hook him up. Should I have? You definitely want a promposal, right?"

It's a completely random, harmless question, but coming from Mekhi, it feels weird.

I blink at the screen. Since Brandon broke up with me, I've only thought about going stag or with Reese if she decides not to take anybody. There's no one I want to ask and no one I could imagine asking me.

"If the right person's asking, sure."

He scrunches his nose. "What's the right person? Do they have to fit all those criteria you need to come with promposals?"

"No, but there are some very important requirements that have to be met." I pull my blankets around me again and lie back on my pillows. "I don't want to spend a night that's supposed to be the party ending to my childhood with a cute and fun rando. Not that cute and fun aren't important, because I'm not trying to be bored."

"That makes sense."

"I don't want to spend that kind of time and energy on a person I'm never going to talk to again once we graduate," I say. "I would like it if at least there was some sort of spark. A chance it could be the start of something instead of the end. I don't want to look at my pictures a year from now and not be able to remember the person's name. And I want to go with someone I'm going to want to kiss at some point during the night, or maybe even all night."

When I say the word *kiss* my eyes go straight to Mekhi's mouth. I'm not sure what makes that happen, but I'd like for it to never happen again.

"Potentiality and kissability. The missing links." He rests back into his pillows too. "How will I know if somebody meets your criteria? I don't want to hook you up with a dud."

"If this person exists, I don't know them yet."

He nods slowly. "That makes it easy."

"Anything else?"

"Yes. Should we be sending Tyler a bill?" His eyes go wide. "We need the money."

"Good night, Mekhi." I'm not letting anyone ruin my happy ending.

Chapter Twenty

Mekhi and I have a pattern. If we don't have a promposal after school, we meet at my locker. There we make a to-do list for what's next on the schedule and get to work. But rarely when I get to my hall is he there grinning from ear to ear. It's a smile that would melt most, but I'm cautious. There's no reason he should be smiling at me like that.

It makes me walk a little faster. I want to find out what brought this on, but when his eyes flick over my shoulder and Maddie comes strutting past me on her way to him, the mystery is solved.

Mekhi isn't smiling at me.

Mekhi and I don't talk about Maddie ever. Not since our run-in at Volcanic Coffee. David has assigned her a project, so during the last two YBE meetings we haven't interacted.

But the before-and-after performances to get Mekhi's attention and remind the whole world that he belongs to her are nauseating.

She's at the very end of a rendition of throwing her arms around him like they're long-lost lovers when I join them at my locker. She turns so they're both facing me, greeting me like a happy couple. Her hip and elbow are pressed against him. I can't say whether he's enjoying this or not. He's pressed his other side against the lockers. There's nowhere for him to go.

I acknowledge them with a grunt. They both give me a "Hey." Hers is obviously fake-friendly. His is more of a question. I open my locker. The silence is worse than awkward, it's expectant. It's like they're waiting for me to do or say something. It isn't hard to figure out what.

Mekhi and I speak at the same time, but I'm inherently louder than he is.

"If you guys have something to do, I can get what we need for tomorrow's promposals." I look at the time on my phone as if they're holding me up, and then glance at Mekhi. "I don't need you. You can go."

My attempt at a nonchalant, go-with-the-flow pardon lands like the splat of a tomato right between Mekhi's eyes. He jerks his head back.

Seizing the opportunity, Maddie puts her arm through his and pulls. "See, Autumn has it all covered. *I'm* the one that needs you."

Ugh. Her performance should be labeled FOR MEKHI'S EYES

ONLY. I don't want to see this. And I don't know why she feels the need to show me. He's told her he and I would "never" be together in any way she has to be worried about. He's told me he'll happily fulfill a promposal request for anyone that'll have me. I'm not a threat.

Not that I care what he does or who he does it with, this just isn't professional. I don't try to hide my eye roll before closing my locker.

I attempt to blend into the crowd and go on my merry way, but there's a tug on my sleeve. It's not enough to pull me back, but enough to get my attention. I stop. My eyes meet Mekhi's. His knit-together eyebrows say he's confused. I don't know what about.

"I haven't had a chance to tell you, I've found a way to make myself useful." He lets my shirt go and rubs the back of his hand against his chin. "I'm coming with you."

"But I told you last night I might need help with a shoot today." Maddie says this the way girls do when they know they have undue influence over a guy. It's a true channeling of fairy-tale heroines. Even I resorted to it with Brandon once or twice. Somehow, it works.

I try again to make my exit. This time Mekhi grabs more of my sleeve. I stare down at where he's got me. He lets me go and smooths my shirt as if he thinks his touch is what I'm irritated about. But really, I just don't have time to be caught in a lovers' quarrel.

"And I told you, I can't help you." His eyes dart back and

forth between me and Maddie as if he can't decide which of us is more in need of his message. "Autumn and I have things we need to get done. It's not optional."

Maddie clicks her tongue against her teeth, says a venom-filled "Whatever," and leaves us standing there.

Mekhi leans a shoulder against my locker and tilts his head. "What was up with all that?"

"Obviously she wants you."

Not sure why I can't maintain eye contact when I say that. Maddie's feelings for him are a universally accepted truth.

"I'm talking about you. You're mad. You don't trust me even *that* much?" He bends his knees a little, making our eyes meet. I think he's trying to see into me, but it's working the opposite way. I could swear there's hurt in the way one of his eyes narrows on the word *trust*. "You think I would leave us hanging like that? We have promposals tomorrow and we need to figure out how to be profitable while not accepting any more requests. It's not looking too good, by the way."

The image of Maddie hugging him all tight flashes in my mind. "What else am I supposed to think? PROMposal Queen versus Maddie isn't a fair competition."

He surprises me with that same smile from a few minutes ago and leads me away from my locker. "No competition at all. Especially with what we're about to go do."

Now *I'm* confused. PROMposal Queen is the front-runner in this scenario? On a regular day? But especially today?

I eye him skeptically. "What are we about to do?"

"Well, I'm about to be right," he says.

"Which means I'm about to be wrong?"

"I didn't plan it that way. That's just how it happened." He wiggles his eyebrows. "You remember Ryan, the supposed wrongdoer?"

I stare up at him. "He finally got back to you? Let me hear the reason they broke up because I know you're probably not seeing it right."

"I don't know why they broke up yet," he says. "He wants to meet and talk in person but not at school because Skyla—the ex—will know something's up if she sees him talking to us."

"Wait a minute. You're claiming victory and you have no clue why they broke up?"

He shrugs. "I don't know. Call it my intuition."

I roll my eyes exaggeratedly. Here he goes again. Suddenly a romance expert. I can't tell him anything.

"Where's this clandestine meeting?"

"Everyway Burger. He's covering it."

I sigh. "You have to drive. I only have enough gas to drop my car off at home," I say. "On the way there I'll give you all the scenarios in which Ryan will not make the cut."

He smirks. "Challenge accepted."

At the restaurant, we're directed to a booth, where I slide in. Mekhi gets in next to me and Ryan sits across from us. Everyway Burger is a LeBeau staple. It's on the end of a strip mall and is mostly slightly tinted windows. The rest of the space, from the floor up to the exposed ceiling, is brick. Everything else is a love letter to the burger. Even our table is shaped like a lettuce leaf.

None of us have to look at the menu. We all order shakes and variations on the double burger. Mekhi and I agree on the jalapeño poppers.

"Why did it take you so long to answer Mekhi's text?" I ask Ryan.

In my peripheral, Mekhi glares at me, like he thinks I'm being harsh. Maybe he's right. I can't come at Ryan all accusatory when I don't have proof of anything either way.

Every guy isn't using some girl's care and concern against her or ignoring her altogether. I'm not that jaded. I wouldn't be here if I didn't hope he could prove me wrong.

I jump back in and change my approach.

"This is all me, not Mekhi, and maybe I'm just more sensitive to other people's pain, but in your request you said you know Skyla still likes you." I cross my arms over my chest and lean forward. "That makes me think that if she still likes you, and you're not together, then it's something *you* did."

"I can see how you would think that, but that's kind of my point." Ryan rakes his brown hair back. "I didn't do anything. She broke up with me because it's going to happen anyway when we go to college."

I wince. If there were magic words Ryan could say to get me on his side, these would be them.

I've heard this story before. It's not what I expected. I expected a lot more *what had happened was*. Instead, this is a story I bet I could finish myself. The only exception being I don't want to get back with my ex.

I try to make eye contact with Mekhi, but he's studying Ryan skeptically. Definitely not what I was expecting from him either. Instead, I focus on Ryan again, giving him a proper audience for his complaint.

"I told her we have the rest of our senior year and all summer; why would we give all that time up before we have to?" Ryan says. "Her parents and her friends are all telling her stuff and she's listening to them instead of me. She's trying to be *practical*."

"How long were you together?"

"Since last year."

"Wow. So you guys have spent all this time together, and finally, when it's about to get good, she gets practical?"

I roll my eyes at the idea of breaking up with someone like it's on some getting-ready-for-college checklist.

"I filled out the request after what you did for Eliana." Ryan takes a straw from the dispenser at the table and flicks the end of its wrapper. "It was the day after Skyla broke up with me, and when I got to school a bunch of her friends were talking about how happy they would be if someone did it for them.

"That made me want to do it for Skyla, but by the time Mekhi texted I was mad about the whole thing. My friends were giving their opinions. I started questioning how she could break up with me when I'm a good boyfriend." He sighs and rests farther back in the booth. "Then I got sad again, and I've been waiting for it to go away, and it hasn't. I don't think we should break up at all, but if we have to, we should at least have a better ending than what she gave us."

"Aw," I say, completely relating to Ryan's initial shock and confusion at Skyla's logic. Brandon and I were only together for six months. The fact that Ryan has been feeling this way for so long, and the amount of time they were together, tells me something is different about him and Skyla.

It also helps to cement what I've had to reiterate to Reese every so often over the last few weeks. I don't want Brandon back. It's not just the embarrassment of the way he broke up with me. It's because I don't want *him*. I'm over it. I can say his name, remember us, without feeling the way Ryan looks right now.

No, Ryan's feelings aren't anything I can relate to, but I like having him as proof that they can exist and even linger. Like it's possible to have something so special you'll do whatever you can to make sure it isn't gone for good. I have to help him.

"I'm sorry I doubted you. We—"

Mekhi elbows me. I'm pretty sure it's accidental so I scoot over to give him more room.

"We—"

"We need to chat for a minute." Mekhi looks around the restaurant and then nods at an open table. "We'll be over there."

I blink at him. "But you're about to be right."

He inches out of the booth. "No, I'm not."

I'm confused as hell but follow him across the room anyway. Without missing a beat, the waitress sets our shakes and poppers down in front of us at our new table and delivers Ryan's shake to him.

He looks lonely over there, and I hate that I've made him come here and plead his case. I test a popper on my lips for temperature before I stuff it in my mouth.

Mekhi rests his hands flat on the table and leans in. "We cannot help this kid."

"Yes, we can. You know how many inside jokes and stuff they probably have." I swipe another popper, letting it survive for two bites instead of one. "Let me ask a few questions and we can get this thing going. This is like a Shakespearean tragedy."

"Exactly, but the tragedy is Skyla's not feeling him."

I look at Ryan and his worry brow, and then back at Mekhi. "Of course she is. She's scared."

Mekhi tilts his head and narrows his eyes at me. I eat another popper.

"When he talked about asking her why they would cut the time they had left together short, you made it seem like you wouldn't do that if you were Skyla," he says.

"I wouldn't. If I can be with the guy I like, I want to be with him."

Mekhi nods and opens his eyes wide. "That's what I'm saying. She doesn't like him. He's about to embarrass himself. I mean, look at him." We both do. Ryan's chin rests in both of his palms and he's staring off into space. "That's what he looks like when she lets him down easy. Imagine if she hadn't."

I eat another popper.

"You could be right. But what if you're wrong?" I put my hand in front of my mouth so I don't show him everything that's in it as I talk. "What if it's more like a fifty-fifty kind of a chance and all she needs is for him to show her some solid reasoning for why they should stay together?"

I fill my mouth with another whole popper.

Mekhi rubs a hand across his chin, eyes meeting mine thoughtfully. "You think the chance of public heartbreak is worth the risk?"

"Yes. Definitely." I nod as if it's the purest thought I've ever had. And for me right now, it feels like it is. I get Ryan. "But we don't have to make it public. If he gets a yes, we'll show how even a private ask can be special, probably even more. If it doesn't work, we don't post it."

He taps his fingers on the table a few times before he nods and says, "I can get with that."

"Good. Can I have the last one?" I point at the lone pop-per. "They're so freaking good. We killed those things."

"Yeah." He chuckles. "Go 'head."

We get up and right on cue, the waitress swings by and cleans up the empty popper basket. I don't miss the look she and Mekhi exchange. It could be all in my head, but I think they're making fun of me.

"Sorry about that," I tell Ryan as we reseat ourselves. "We can help you. We're thinking something private, more intimate than we've done before."

"Good." He looks at his phone. "Let's go set up or whatever."

Clearly having taken my hint about the elbow, Mekhi knocks his foot against mine. I step on his. This is a minor issue. Ryan will see reason and give us a few days at least.

"We can't do it right this minute," I say. "Give us a cou-ple days at least."

He shakes his head. "It has to be special, and it has to be today. I think somebody else is going to ask her tomorrow."

That's when I get that pointy-ass elbow right in the side again.

Chapter Twenty-One

"Is it wrong that number two on my list of issues with this promposal is that there's somebody out here getting ready to ask Skyla to prom and thinking they can do it without my help?" I say to Mekhi as we turn into his neighborhood.

Ryan's going home to put on the costume he was wearing the night he and Skyla first talked. It was at a haunted house where he worked. Keeping with the theme, Mekhi and I are on our way to pick up a fog machine.

Mekhi side-eyes me and chuckles. "That person might be thinking how they'd love to have your help but the link to the request form has a Sold Out stamp on it."

I cross my arms over my chest and return the look. "Is that supposed to make me feel bad? Because I feel wanted, you know, and appreciated."

"You would." He shakes his head.

I give him a self-satisfied shrug. I'm not going to be embarrassed about enjoying being in demand for my promposals. It's exciting. It makes me hopeful that if my peers can see what I bring to the table, maybe Mercer can too.

Mekhi parks just outside the garage. It's empty, like the other times I've been here since the Volcanic Coffee fail. His mom and sister are rarely home. That's why we usually get stuff done here. It's easier to focus.

He leads me through a door at the back of the garage to a narrow storage area packed floor to ceiling with stuff. Most of it boxed.

I look around, taking in this party-planning gold mine. "Can you explain why you have all these things? First the Cricut, then the helium machine for the balloon promposal, and now a fog machine."

"All of this stuff came with the house."

"What do you mean, 'came with the house'?"

He struggles with a box that's in the way of the one we're after. I grab the opposite end and move backward toward a table, where we set it down.

"My mom was kind of in a hurry to leave my dad."

Keeping his eyes on the box, he scratches his head. I look away too. I wish I'd asked any question but that one. I can't back out of it now, though, that'll just make this moment more awkward.

"This was a foreclosure she bought 'as is,' I guess you

could say. There wasn't a lot she could afford by herself in the school district otherwise." He looks around the space. "We had a lot of cleaning and fixing up to do and never got around to getting rid of all this."

"I'm glad you didn't," I say, opening a path to a change in subject. "How does it work?"

He turns his attention back to the area we've cleared. "I've never used it before, but I looked it up while you and Ryan were talking and it only takes two ingredients, which we have here."

He squats over a box and opens it. Dust floats up and I shield my eyes.

"Are there spiders in here?"

He gives me a small smile. "I hope so. That'll be good for the aesthetic tonight."

"If you catch a spider and transport it, you're on your own."

"You're for real? You'd miss a promposal because of a spider?"

"I will run out of this room and all the way home and not care if you laugh because of a spider."

He smiles mischievously. It's contagious, but I cross my arms, fighting to remain stoic. "Even if I promised you something good when it's all over?"

He takes the fog machine out of the box, and I follow him through another door to the deck.

"I'm pretty sure there's nothing you could do to get me

to stick around if you're making friends with spiders, but what type of something are we talking about?" I can't help but ask.

He looks at me seriously. All traces of that smile gone. "Doesn't matter. You're going to need to earn it since not only did you hog the poppers, you fixed your face to ask my permission to eat the last one like you were suddenly concerned about my hunger. And you know how hungry I get."

I stand behind him, openmouthed, as he enters a code on a keypad. We go inside the house from the back and head to the basement, where he gets out a gallon-sized jug of distilled water. Then we go to a bathroom on the second level and get a bottle of glycerin. Finally, we get a measuring cup from the kitchen. I trail him around, trying to remember how the poppers got taken down.

He thanked the waitress for bringing them...and then he...he sat there and watched me eat them.

"First of all, that was not an ample serving of poppers," I argue. "Secondly, that was a setup. You could've said something, or reached in. It's not like I held them to my chest or boxed you out."

"I could tell how much you liked them," he says. "There was a lot of aggression whenever you went in for one. I didn't want to get in your way."

"That's on you." I point a finger at him. "You can't hold it against me because you liked watching me eat them so much you didn't want to interrupt."

He does one of his judgmental harrumphs, and I realize I've accused him of liking to watch me eat, which is an odd observation. But what else can I call what he's described?

"It's my opinion—"

He cuts me off with a laugh. "Oh. We're making statements now. This is official."

"You can't say you have something for me, refuse to give it to me unless I earn it, and not expect me to have something very official to say."

"I never said I had something for you. I said, *Even if I promised you something good when it's all over?*" He shrugs. "There's no spider anyway. What are we even talking about?"

"So this is all hypothetical? There's no spider and no something good?"

He does the mischievous smile again and looks away from me. I don't know why, or how it's even possible, but I feel the blood pumping through my veins.

I give that mischievous smile right back. "Mm-hmm. I know what it is."

"No, you don't."

"So there *is* something." My voice is as shrill as a TV lawyer who's just caught a witness for the opposition in a lie.

He jumps, so I know he heard me, but he pretends not to.

"Chips? You found some new chips to taste-test." I'm practically dancing. What else would he think I'd even attempt to try and earn? That has to be it.

"Maybe," he says.

"I've earned them by simply putting up with all the other nasty ones you've put before me," I say. "I shouldn't have to put up with any imaginary spiders. Let me try them."

"I'll think about it." He turns his expression into a pensive one, drawing his forever perfectly moisturized lips into an even more obscene pout.

I scoff. He pretends not to notice.

Out on the deck he opens the fog machine's reservoir, and there are directions inside. It doesn't look like the machine has ever been used.

"Can you look up the fog juice ratio for me while I read the instructions real quick?" he says.

I do need to stay focused, but he's the one who brought up chips, fully aware of my obsession. No, our obsession. I'm not alone in this. With an exaggerated sigh, I look up the fog juice recipe. The more glycerin, the denser the fog. I say the denser, the creepier. Creepy is what I'm going for if I'm reinventing Halloween.

Based on the size of the reservoir, I make some of the one-to-one solution.

"This is elementary," Mekhi says. "As long as it's not defective we should be good to go."

He pours in my solution, plugs in the machine, and turns it on. We wait with bated breath for the thing to heat up. The heat is what causes the vapor reaction.

It takes a minute and even then, the vapor starts slowly.

Once a steady stream emits from the machine, I realize *more-dense fog* is code for *zero-percent-visibility fog.*

"I'm going to the other side of the deck, to see how long it takes to spread," he says.

"Good idea."

We'll need to know when to plug the machine in for the right effect by the time Skyla gets to Ryan's house.

"Can you see me?" he says.

"Nope." I'm surprised. This stuff is amazing. "Can you see me?"

"Uh-uh."

I wave through the fog. "You sure?"

"Positive. This is so cool." He sounds like a six-year-old. "This is going to be good. Too bad we might not be able to record through it."

I don't quite match his excitement. My wheels are turning in a completely different direction.

I wave my hand to see if it catches his attention. When it doesn't, I take one step back, and then another, until I'm walking backward into the door he used a code to get into earlier. He must've disabled the alarm completely because it slides open for me without a peep. Once I'm in the house, I slide the door back in place and tiptoe toward the pantry.

My mom would cuss me out for going in another person's house like this. But for some reason, I'm feeling a little empowered and a lot like messing with Mekhi, especially after that mischievous look he gave me earlier. He can't be holding stuff over my head. That's not going to work.

Plus, it's not like anybody else is home. My apparent lack of home training won't make my parents look bad, or his mom judge me.

Inside the pantry I search for the roaster he pulled the chips out of the first time I came over. I look up. There it is. It's too high for me to reach so I grab the stepladder from the back of the door and climb up.

"Bingo," I whisper as I stare at a brand of chips I've never seen before. Wonder where he found these.

"Put 'em down."

I let out a tiny shriek. Mekhi is behind me.

I have no idea how he got in here without me hearing. He steps forward and reaches for the bag of chips, but I hold it over my head. Since I'm standing on the ladder, he has no chance of snatching them. Without warning, he grabs me around my waist with one hand, lifting me off the ladder. At the same time, he grasps for the chips with the other. I shriek again and clutch them to my chest.

"Stop it, you're going to crush them. Crumbs are inferior!" I yell, but I'm also laughing.

My shirt is riding up a little and his hand is on my one bare side, tickling me. I don't think it's intentional, but it's not helping my resolve. I want to drop the chips and protect myself from his touch.

He pulls me tighter to him, making it impossible for me to touch my feet to the ground.

"Give me the chips."

I laugh harder, but I'm not letting the chips go. They're mine.

"Let me go and I'll give them to you."

My eyes meet his. We're so close, I feel his breath on my chest. My laughter starts to fade as I stare into the uninterrupted night of his eyes.

"You won't."

"I will. I promise."

I struggle, trying to get him to let me go, but his grip stays tight around me. His strength turns into a disadvantage as he loses his balance. By the time he regains it, I have him pressed against the wall and he still hasn't let me go.

"Stop fighting me."

His voice is breathy and deep and vibrating right through all my soft spots. I try to wrestle myself out of his arms again, but he pulls me even tighter to him, to the chest I've resentfully memorized over the last few weeks.

"*You* stop it." I try with everything I have to put some authority behind my words. But I sound a little weak, even to myself.

"*You* started it." There's a warning in his unwavering focus. I know that look. My heart nearly pounded its way out of my chest the last time I fell for it.

He's close enough to notice I'm holding my breath. Waiting for his next move.

Am I really wishing for something to happen when a few hours ago I thought he wanted to forget every responsibility he has and go spend time with some other girl? Is he really about to let something happen when he's made it clear he doesn't want me that way? But why would either of us let anyone this close if something wasn't in the plan?

A kiss?

It would be so easy, a fault of gravity even, to touch my lips to his. One little kiss is all I want. But this is exactly what happened before. He pulled. I fell in. Do I want that again?

"What are y'all doing? And why is it so freaking foggy in here?" A woman's voice brings me back into my right mind.

My mouth goes dry as I slide down Mekhi's body and his hands travel all the way up mine... just to make sure I don't fall. As soon as my feet hit the ground, I step away.

Thank God it's only his sister, Taj. And her smile says she's more entertained than scandalized. Today, instead of the faux locs she's worn the other times I've met her, she has a teeny-weeny afro. The hair must be the reason I didn't notice the resemblance to Mekhi before. Because right now, it's impossible to miss.

Mekhi uses the distraction to go for the chips. I dance out of his reach and hide behind his sister. The movement helps to shake off a little of whatever it was he tried to put on me through his eyes. That's a lot of power to use for one bag of chips.

"He hides chips in the roaster," I blurt.

"Really? You're going to play me like that? Tell my secrets?"

Whatever he was trying to do a second ago is apparently still in play. The gravelly tone of his voice, and eyes that will not find anything else to look at other than me, haven't gone anywhere.

"I'm sorry," I say to Taj. "We're testing a fog machine for a promposal."

She looks between us, lips turned up. "You tested the machine in the house?"

"No." Mekhi closes the pantry door behind him. "We let fog inside when we opened the door. But I turned the machine off. Hopefully it goes away before Mom gets home."

"If you tell her it's for your business empire, I'm sure she'll be proud," Taj says.

For some reason, he doesn't look convinced. He has a worry brow.

Now I feel bad. The fog wouldn't be in here if not for me.

"Are you going to be in trouble?"

"No. He won't. He's ridiculous," Taj answers for him, and rolls her eyes.

That makes me feel better, except why would Mekhi think there'd be an issue? Why would he be ridiculous?

That's not a word I would associate with him in any other circumstance.

"Anyway"—Taj eyes the bag—"those chips smell so good."

I check Mekhi's position before I hold the bag away from me and notice the hole.

"Look what you did." I laugh. "We have to eat them now. Otherwise, they're going to get stale."

"Where did they come from?" Taj asks. "I've never seen these before."

Mekhi shakes his head. "I'm not saying where they came from. Just taste them."

Taj looks from him to me, confused.

"I love jalapeños and spicy chips and personally believe there is no jalapeño chip that properly honors the true taste of the pepper," I explain.

"And you're trying to prove her wrong?" Taj says to Mekhi.

"It can be done," he says.

I shrug. "I actually want him to win."

Because I don't trust him in this situation, I take out two chips for myself before offering the bag to them.

When we all have a sample, Taj says, "Same time."

We all three nod and then put a chip in our mouths.

It is so nasty.

Mekhi's shoulders droop. "You don't like them."

"I haven't even said anything. Let me at least chew it."

"I just watched you eat six jalapeño poppers in a five-minute span," he says. "I know when you like something."

I stop pretending, hold my mouth still in the hopes that my tongue will lose its sense of taste, and as best I can without letting the chip flavor touch any other part of my mouth, ask for a napkin to spit this travesty into. Taj grants my wish.

"I'm sorry." My voice is small. "I wanted to like them."

He shrugs like it's no big deal, but disappointment comes through in the way he ducks his head a little.

"A chip is a chip," Taj announces. "Can I have them?"

"Yeah." He waves the bag away. "We have to go before we're late anyway."

I stand up straight, his words reminding me I'm not here to chill with Mekhi and Taj, but for business. I tell Taj it was nice to see her again and motion for Mekhi to follow me out of his house. But as he comes near me, all I'm thinking about is not letting him get too close.

Again.

Chapter Twenty-Two

"Twenty-three and one," I say.

I ruined our perfect record. How was I supposed to know Skyla would bring her new bae to the promposal and make out with her before she even got out of the car? Ryan deserves better.

The sun is long gone now, and except for the light from the dashboard, it's all shadows in Mekhi's car. Not that I'd know what he was thinking even if I could see every angle of his face. When Mekhi looks at me, even in the brightest light, it's hard to tell what's on his mind.

I have no idea if I was the only one thinking what I was thinking in his pantry. Yes, he was in a little bit of suspended animation, too, but maybe it was awkward for him instead of tempting. If I'm being honest, I'm still tempted two hours later. He seems unfazed.

"It's still an elite-level winning percentage."

"True."

"But, man." He puts a fist to his chest as if he's being gutted. "Ryan's face. I was embarrassed for him, and Skyla... that girl."

I rest my head against the window. "I wish we could refund his money."

He gives me a narrow-eyed glance. "After all that stress? Is that the precedent we want to set? We don't guarantee yeses. And, um, we're on the verge of not even being ramen profitable."

"I'm not saying we're going to, but that was more than a no." I exhale a sad laugh. "And he bought us dinner."

"That was a snack. And I didn't even get my share. I'm still hungry."

"Your tapeworm is not his fault or mine. He shouldn't have to be heartbroken *and* broke."

A refund isn't going to fix things for Ryan, but it's the principle. He put in all this effort, has been suffering since Skyla broke up with him, only to get his heart completely shattered tonight.

Mekhi turns into my neighborhood and glances at me. "You right. He doesn't deserve what happened. But—"

"I know. I know. Capitalism and compassion are mortal enemies."

We go around corners and past several variations of my house before he pulls into the one with the forward-facing garage. For some reason the house is completely dark except for a soft glow of light coming from the family room. It's only eight. I can't imagine that anyone other than Baby is already asleep.

Mekhi shifts into park. "After all that, I gotta ask you..."

He pauses, and I sit up even straighter than before. Mekhi is forever asking me questions—usually debatable ones—and I'm rarely prepared.

"Ryan took a risk and he got his heart broken. Is that still romantic to you?"

"Yes." I don't even have to think about it. "The ending was tragic, but yeah."

"I know, man." He covers his eyes and shakes his head as if blocking a bad memory. "I could tell he wanted to reach out and touch her the whole time."

I turn my whole body toward him. "I didn't pick up on that."

"It was kinda obvious, like he didn't know what to do with his hands," he says. "And, you know, when you like somebody that much you want to touch them. You make up reasons to do it."

I can't say I've experienced wanting to touch someone all the time. That's not the first thing that comes to my mind.

"When I like somebody that much, I want to kiss them. It's all I can think about."

I don't realize I've said that out loud, and what I've

admitted to with those two sentences, until they're met by silence. He even stops tapping his fingers on the steering wheel.

Heat flares up my neck. I mean, I don't think it's a secret I wanted to kiss Mekhi way back when. That was the energy I gave. But I don't want him to know it meant so much to me. Especially not with the way I looked at him back at his house. If he realizes how close I was to trying to kiss him, he'll think I like him, which I don't. He's just cute and we're spending a lot of time together.

At least I think that's all it is.

And wasn't I trying to throw him at another girl a few hours ago? A girl I think he likes? What am I doing having any type of reaction to him, lustful or otherwise?

I'm looking everywhere but at him. I can't think of any way to cover all these thoughts other than putting more words between us.

"You should probably come say hi," I finally say. "You're a random person dropping me off. My parents get touchy about that kind of stuff."

He clears his throat, seemingly an effort to forget my comment. "You sure? It's late."

I want, more than anything, to agree and let him disappear, and get away from this incredibly awkward moment. But I'm not lying about my parents. Also, with the exception of me talking out of turn, I'm having a good time. I don't want it to end.

"It's not that late yet," I assure him. "And you can eat too. One of my parents always cooks and it's usually something good."

"I don't want to be coming up in your parents' house all late begging for food."

"And I don't want to be answering a hundred questions about what's wrong with you that you can't speak."

I take out my phone and text my mom to make sure everyone is properly dressed because we're having hungry company. She sends back a thumbs-up and lets me know what Dad made.

"Do you like chicken enchiladas?"

Mekhi shuts the car off and is out of it before me. I let the garage door up and head for the door that leads to the kitchen, but he stays a few steps behind. I have to wave him inside.

"Are you coming or not? My mom's going to be yelling about letting the cold air in."

He doesn't say anything but shuffles along. Once we're in the back hall, he takes off his shoes, and taps his hands on his pockets as I hang up my jacket.

As many times as he's seen me tense and unsure, seeing him in the same spot should feel like a leveling of the playing field. It doesn't. I want him to feel comfortable in my house the same way I do in his...preferably without the going-in-the-pantry part. My mom would not respond well to that.

I smile encouragingly. "I wouldn't have invited you in if my parents weren't cool."

He nods but keeps tapping his fingers on his jeans. I stare pointedly there. He stuffs his hands in his pockets then.

We step into the kitchen, where, across from us in the family room, my parents are sitting together on the reclining love seat watching something with the closed captioning on.

"Oh. I see," Mekhi mumbles from behind me, as if he's just solved the world's greatest mystery.

I hope that "I see" is an agreement that my parents are cool people. I can't think of anything else worth seeing in my house. It's way more cluttered than his, but that's not the kind of thing you note out loud the first time you visit somebody.

Especially not Mekhi. He has manners that make a good first impression. I'll have to ask him about it later, though. I don't want to put him on the spot after telling him everything would be good.

"This is Mekhi from school. The one I'm doing the promposals with. Mekhi, those are my parents." I make my way farther into the kitchen and to the fridge.

"Nice to meet you," Mekhi says. "Autumn said it was okay if I come in. Is it okay?"

Mom smiles warmly. "Sure. Wash your hands and help yourself."

Dad doesn't say a word. I turn around slowly and look

across the room again, and it's as if he's been waiting for eye contact with me this entire time.

"This is your business partner?" He puts vocal quotes around the words *business partner* as if the term is in question. "The one you've been spending all the time with."

"Yeah, we ended up meeting with this guy Ryan and doing what I guess you'd call an emergency promposal, which put us behind on getting ready for the ones we have tomorrow. We've been pretty busy."

During my explanation of our day, my father is looking at Mekhi, who has not moved an inch since I introduced him. I wave him over to the sink. I can see what Dad is thinking. Something more is up between me and Mekhi than what I'm saying, but I don't justify the idea with a reaction. Just because the only other boy I spent this much time with was my boyfriend doesn't mean every boy I spend a lot of time with is.

Even though I don't know what would've happened if I'd had about five more seconds in that pantry alone with Mekhi.

I blink at the TV and then my parents. "Can someone explain why the TV's on mute?"

"Baby only wakes up when we turn the volume on." Mom puts her palms up to signify her cluelessness. "We can talk as loud as we want, though."

"Why is she so weird?"

Mom tuts. "You're both weird."

A chuckle comes from the direction of the sink, but when I look at Mekhi he's wearing a straight face. When he's finished washing and drying his hands, I give him everything he needs to plate, warm, and eat the enchiladas I take out of the fridge.

"How much can I have?" He whispers, but with the house being so quiet, his voice still carries.

I laugh. "How much do you need?"

"Take as much as you want," Mom chimes in.

"What's your last name, Mekhi?" Dad asks.

Mekhi goes completely still. "Winston."

"And you're a senior?" Dad eyes Mekhi as if there's a wrong answer to this question.

"Yes."

Mekhi stays frozen a few beats. Then suddenly, his eyebrows shoot up as if he's realized my dad has initiated a staring contest and intends to win. He offers a polite nod and smile before turning back to me.

"Where's your plate?" He whispers so low this time I'm pretty much reading his lips.

"I'm not hungry. I had an entire popper appetizer all to myself, remember?"

He swallows hard. "You're just going to watch me eat? All three of you?"

I roll my eyes, get a plate, and put half of an enchilada

on it. After his food is warm and I put mine in the microwave, I don't bother telling him he can go to the table. I can see he's not going without me. When we get there, he waits until I pick a seat before he chooses the one right next to me.

"Spicy," he says with a mouthful.

"Why didn't you warn him?" Mom says.

"He likes spicy." I give an impressed nod in Mekhi's direction. "It's a good surprise."

Mekhi nods his approval and eats and eats until there's no doubt. I mostly watch him, just like he was afraid of. When his plate is clean, I slide my untouched food over to him. He inhales that too.

When he's finished, he takes a long breath as if he'd suspended all other bodily functions while he ate. "Thank you, Mrs. Reeves. That was so good."

Dad wastes no time calling Mekhi out on his error. "You mean *Thank you, Mr. Reeves*. That's my recipe."

"Sorry. I didn't know." Mekhi ducks his head. "Thank you, Mr. Reeves, and Mrs. Reeves and Autumn Reeves."

Dad grunts, and Mom and I tell Mekhi he's welcome. He rinses our plates, announces he's going to go, and is back in the hall putting on his shoes before anyone can accept or reject.

"Make sure you reiterate to your dad how much I enjoyed his food."

My dad was out of order, but witnessing Mekhi being so shook makes me have to hold back a smile. "I will."

"Thank you again too."

"You're welcome."

He moves toward the door, but before he can get out, I remember something.

"What was the 'I see' when you walked in?"

He smiles. "Nothing."

I frown at him. It definitely sounded like something, and since he doesn't want to tell me what that something is, I have to know.

He sighs. "Your parents."

"What about them?"

"They were all snuggled up on the couch," he says.

"And?"

"And"—he scratches the back of his head—"they're cute. That's all."

I wave my hand toward the family room dismissively.

"That's how they always are. My mom works four twelve-hour days in a row where they barely see each other, so when she's off they're usually in each other's faces."

He nods. "Now I see how you got to be the way you are about certain things."

"How am I about certain things?"

"You know"—his eyes gleam with an emotion I can't quite identify—"romantic."

I don't think about my parents' relationship, and definitely not about how it relates to me and what I think about anything. At the same time, for some reason, I'm happy he no longer thinks my need for inspiration deeper than surface level has anything to do with me missing Brandon. And I think I'd be into romance as much as I am regardless of how my parents are. Otherwise, what would be Mekhi's excuse?

"You need to look in the mirror," I tease. "You're the one noticing people wanting to touch each other, not me. You're the romantic."

"Don't get all defensive." He swallows hard and laces his fingers together. "I think it's sweet."

Wait.

I side-eye him. Am I sweet or are my parents sweet? Do I even want to know the answer to that? I'm not sure if I'd be disappointed or relieved if he said he was talking about my parents.

"I—" He stops himself. His forehead crinkles. "I meant you."

I feel my forehead mirror his. First of all, he's reading my mind. Secondly, what? "Me? I'm not sweet."

He scratches his head again as if even he's confused by his comment. "Must've been some excellent enchiladas, then."

I laugh out loud. Too loud. I don't care how weird Baby is, that's going to wake her up.

"I need to go before I end up having to thank your dad for something again."

My laugh disintegrates into a giggle and eventually a sound more somber than I expect. "Yeah. You better."

I don't let the garage door down until he's backed out of the driveway and the glow of his headlights has disappeared.

Chapter Twenty-Three

I've never been so interested in a conversation, yet unable to stay focused on it, in my whole life. Sydney is explaining to the group how she was finally able to get an investor for her hair care product line. Lack of an investor, and her age, have been the things holding her back.

An investor would've made PROMposal Queen unstoppable. An investor could make PROMposal Queen a thing again next year, and even the year after.

But it's hard to stay focused on Sydney when she's sitting next to Mekhi and all I've been thinking about the last few days is kissing him. I keep reminding myself what happened after the first and only time we did. But that thought also reminds me of what kissing him felt like. It's a vicious cycle. A cycle I think he can read on my face.

And it's not like one kiss is going to cure me. I'll just want another and another and another because I like him. It's not about spending too much time together or working on something that could help us both get where we want to be. It's about him.

I mean, every boy in this room is smart and driven, but the way Mekhi goes about being those things draws my attention. And once he has my attention, I notice everything. How he licks his lips right before he inserts himself into the conversation. The way he nods anytime someone asks Sydney a question, like he's affirming, *Yes, your question is valid.*

The reason I have no clue what to do about my feelings is also *about him.* Not just the way he's treated me in the past, but the person sitting on his other side. I really don't know if he likes Maddie or not. Yes, he chose his commitment to PROMposal Queen over her, but knowing what I know about him, I wouldn't expect anything different. It was only a big deal because she made it one.

Every time we make eye contact, Maddie smirks at me like she's won something because she's sitting next to him and I'm all the way across the room. Clearly something is happening to make her think she has a chance.

And he told her we'd never be together. Never is like... never.

David saying something about PROMposal Queen pulls my attention away from Mekhi.

I look up to find David chuckling. It could be my own insecurity, but that chuckle feels a little knowing. I sit up in my seat, refocusing myself on business.

"I'm sorry. What?"

"I was just saying how we'd love to have a PROMposal Queen report, since you had to miss the last meeting to prepare for a promposal."

I let myself slump in my chair. Mekhi nods at me, signaling I should be the one to talk.

David looks from him to me. "It can't be that bad. I keep up with your social media. You're busy. Plenty of happy clients out there."

"We're broke, David." I drop the news as a matter of fact, no emotion attached to it at all.

The reaction around the room is half surprise and half knowing harrumphs. As if some people thought PROMposal Queen would beat the small-business survival statistics and others had their doubts. I personally can't believe I ever wasted time worrying about getting requests and generating ideas. Even with those two things checked off, the outcome is the same. It's embarrassing, and extremely unworthy of Mercer. I'm supposed to be showing them a success, not a fail.

David's smile remains, but it's betrayed by the way his eyes dart around the room. He's thinking hard.

"We didn't have time to do a cost analysis or anything like that," Mekhi chimes in. "So we're not charging enough.

And if we had charged what I think we should've, we might not have as many requests."

"You'd have to weigh that. It's possible that one client for the cost of two might be more lucrative. That's certainly a lesson to apply in the future." He puts a finger up. "But before we go too far down that road, let's figure out if we can turn things around for you all right now. Can you meet your customers' needs and keep your promises in the short term?"

My eyes shoot to Mekhi's. I don't know how to answer that.

"We can"—he nods slowly—"but the queen has really high standards and—"

"Hey. There's nothing wrong with standards," I whine.

"You're responding to queen references now?" Mekhi teases, and everyone laughs.

I let my head fall back and groan deeply, pretending to be irritated. The reality is, I like it when he teases me. Especially now that I know he does it to lighten my mood most of the time.

His voice is laced with laughter when he says, "You didn't let me finish. I'm not saying there's anything wrong with high standards. That's one of the reasons you're so good at this. I'm just saying you're sacrificing some of your own goals for those standards. That's all."

"What was one of your goals?" David asks.

My phone vibrates in my pocket. I ignore it. There's no

phone rule, but most people here are respectful. Phones stay quiet and out of sight during this group time. I don't want to be the one to break the unwritten understanding, especially when people are trying to help me.

"Profitability, but that's not going to happen." I make eye contact with David again. "It would've been nice if I'd had time to get an investor from the start."

David shakes his head. "Investors usually require repayment."

I groan again and shut my eyes.

"That wasn't meant to discourage you," David says. "Consider an inventory of your resources and tailor your promposals to those resources instead of the other way around."

I open my eyes. "That's actually a good idea."

"Your surprise confounds me," David says, and the group laughs again just as my phone vibrates and vibrates and vibrates.

I pull it out of my pocket and sneak a look.

It's my mom. The first notification is for a call. The very last text is just Autumn? I scroll to the very first one—Come home now. Then I don't care what you're doing.

Chapter Twenty-Four

I know nothing's wrong with Baby or Dad. My mom wouldn't send a cryptic text if it were something like that. She also wouldn't sound like my own life was in danger if I didn't come home immediately. Honestly, her messages had me tripping over myself to get out of the meeting.

As soon as I get in the kitchen, Mom holds her hand out. I stare at it, then back up at her. Her hair is already tied up for the night and she's wearing a sky-blue long-sleeved pajama set with cotton clouds printed all over. She's supposed to be asleep so she can be well rested for the first day of the four twelve-hour shifts she'll work this week. Dad sits at the table sipping something caramel-colored and fragrant out of a short, intricately decorated glass.

I realize at that moment that whatever I've done, I didn't

just do it, I *did* that. Every hair on my skin's surface transforms into a needle with the finest tip.

They know.

Dad peers at me from the rim of his glass. "Well, don't just stand there. Say something."

Mom is normally the one to deal with any issues around the house. Most people assume it's because she's the intimidating one. But no. She handles things because when Dad is angry, every word, every look, every shift of his body is a threat. I've only ever witnessed this directed at other people two or three times and feared what would be next. I've never experienced it for myself.

Our relationship is my first example of loving someone too much to be angry at them. But that's not a thing anymore. He's pissed. His words make me drop my car keys on the hardwood floor three times before I can get them in my mom's outstretched hands. Neither of them even has to say that's what she wants from me. I just know. Without a word, she joins Dad at the table. He slides the drink to her. She sips it and sets the glass back in front of him.

I don't have time to try and piece together how they found out. And it doesn't even matter.

"We're waiting," he says.

I take a step into the kitchen. They simultaneously sit up straight in their seats, as if I've made an aggressive move and they're on the defensive.

"I realize how stupid it was now, but I thought I'd get into

Mercer. It wasn't calculated or anything. I didn't expect it to be an issue."

My voice shakes, not because I'm going to cry but because of how open the floor is. It's like they're waiting for me to say something nonsensical and walk myself further into the doghouse. I don't want to go, so I stop talking.

"That was an extremely arrogant and immature choice. One you knew better than to make, but you know that's not why we're here."

Dad calling me arrogant and immature—things he's never said to me before—without even the slightest twinge of emotion in his voice stuns me. If I could gather myself enough to be able to figure out what the bigger problem is, I wouldn't be able to give voice to it.

Mom finally speaks up. "You lied to us, Autumn. Straight to both of our faces. About something that impacts your future. You had the chance to tell us that first day exactly what kind of situation you were in, but you lied, and you kept lying."

She stops to take a breath. I can't cut in and try to explain myself because just like Dad's tone surprised me, so does Mom's. She's hurt.

"It is literally our job to help you navigate bad choices. Why wouldn't you trust us enough to give us a chance to do that?"

That's why Dad led the conversation? He was covering Mom...because she's up against a rare thing that would make her question herself? Me?

"At the time it felt like a situation that I got myself into so I needed to get myself out of it." I take a step closer to them as if proximity will help me get my point across better. "I trust you guys. I was just so embarrassed."

Mom narrows her eyes. "In front of us? You thought we'd judge you?"

"In front of everyone, especially myself. Why do you think I'm trying so hard to turn this around?" I let out a shuddering breath. "Yeah, I want to go to Mercer, but even more than that, when I sit for even a second, all I do is think of all the reasons I fall short. That's hard, Mom."

Dad slides the drink in Mom's direction for her turn, and she puts up a hand to refuse it.

"It is hard. I'm right there with you." Her eyes bore into me, revealing glimpses of sympathy. "But I don't get why you would lie to the two people who are always going to hold you down. It's self-destructive to you and disrespectful to us."

My tongue feels thick, and a lump grows in the back of my throat. I don't try to find a defense for what she's pointed out. There isn't one.

"What worries me is what you'll think you need to lie about in the future." Dad grips the glass as if he's imagining bad choices future Autumn can make. "There are going to be consequences for this. As far as your mom and I go, no car until we feel like giving it back. Don't even ask.

"But the life consequences are going to hurt you more.

You may end up staying around here a semester or two. Even though that's fine with us and ten years from now it may not even matter—"

I scoff at that idea. There will be so many people deep into their dreams by then, and I may not be one of them.

Dad nods as if I've proved the point he's about to make. "We know it's not what you want and you'll be miserable, but you'll make it work. But there will be other choices, bigger ones that have way more impact than you can ever imagine. That's why we want to make sure you get this lesson now. We don't want you to repeat it when there's more at stake."

I literally cannot imagine anything being bigger than the opportunity to attend Mercer. I just can't. But I get what they're trying to say. And I do wish I could have just been honest with them. I have enough stress worrying about Mercer. I didn't need covering my tracks added on to it.

"I'm sorry," I say.

Chapter Twenty-Five

The next day, Reese comes at me all super aggressively *telling* me I'm going to support the girls' soccer team in their first-ever semifinals appearance today, promposal planning be damned. Apparently, we need to wallow in other people's happiness. Especially after everything exploded with my parents.

I'm lucky to be going out, but my parents stuck to their word. I have to live out the impact of my decisions and park the car. Still, they both had little to say to me at our normal breakfast run-in.

Reese drives. Three of her teammates are packed in with us. We look like a clown car when we finally spill out in our opponents' jammed parking lot an hour and a half later.

Reese looks around and shakes her head. "Man, if we

got this kind of support just one of my four seasons playing basketball at LeBeau, I know we would've done big things."

"The masses love women's soccer because the US men's team sucks," Katie says. "Men's basketball does not."

I spray my face with the sprinkler fan I've brought and offer it to Reese, who waves me off.

"If I start with that now there will be no relief for me later."

It's a random summer-like day in spring. We're all wearing some form of shorts and tank tops. Tomorrow we'll be wearing thick jackets again. Reese hangs back with me. The full parking lot means a long walk for us to the stadium entry. We stick out here in a way we wouldn't at our own school. Diversity isn't a thing this far northwest of metro Detroit.

There's a wolf whistle. We both turn around to find Mekhi and AJ a few steps behind. I know the whistle had to come from AJ because A, Mekhi would never wolf-whistle at me, and B, AJ is pointing blame at him and aggressively denying responsibility.

Mekhi waves. That's when I realize I'm staring. I whip back around. Reese got to him before I could this morning and explained that whatever we had planned was canceled. So other than passing him in the hall once, we haven't talked today. He doesn't know he's the official PROMposal Queen chauffeur yet. To be honest, I kind of hate telling him there's another thing I need him to do.

Reese leans down and whispers, "Girl, he wants to grind on you. He looks like he's imagining it right now."

I sigh deeply. I don't feel like repeating all the reasons I know she's wrong, including having the opportunity to grind on me and not taking advantage. He has repeatedly declared himself not interested.

"What I need is to finish up these last few requests so I don't have any more excuses to talk to him. It's getting uncomfortable."

"I believe that's called sexual tension. If you want to get past it, you have to go through it."

There's a tug on a curl below my left ear. It tickles. I don't know how, but I know it's Mekhi. But when I turn to my left, he isn't there. I turn to my right and there he is grinning down at me. He's wearing basketball shorts and a black T-shirt. On one hand, black is a bad choice on a day like today. On the other hand, it makes his eyes stand out.

I spray him with my fan. He flinches but not even a second later says, "Do it again. That felt good."

I spray his face and neck. Then he lifts his shirt for me to spray his belly. As many times as he's phoned me shirtless, I've never been privy to muscles as low as what he's showing me now. There's a three-second delay on anything other than looking. When I do pull the trigger, I try not to notice the way his muscles tighten when the cold droplets land.

"No reentry," Katie yells from up ahead. "Y'all better use the bathroom now before you go in. Don't let them stamp you with something they've been pressing against everybody else."

"Ain't nobody stupid," AJ says, and pulls out his ticket, which causes a ripple effect among all of us.

District finals are different than other games. To make sure they don't oversell, tickets are sold only at the two participating schools beforehand.

"Did you see what I did with my ticket?" Mekhi asks AJ, his easy smile gone.

"Is this a setup for a magic trick?" AJ says.

Mekhi huffs and keeps checking his pockets and patting himself. Somehow the first thing my brain goes back to is his hands on me in his pantry.

"It's a seven-dollar ticket," Mario, one of their other friends, says. "I'm sure they'll let you in if you explain you lost it."

Katie points to a huge sandwich board.

NO ENTRY WITHOUT PREPURCHASED TICKET. ABSOLUTELY NO EXCEPTIONS!!!

Mario pokes his lips out comically. "I'm thinking he's going to need a ticket."

Mekhi turns to AJ. "Can I get your keys? It probably fell out of my pocket."

"What if you can't find it? You going to sit out here for two hours?" Mario says.

Everyone knows what Mario's thinking. A Black kid loitering in a parking lot in this part of Michigan is liable to be suspected of something and/or have someone called on him.

"I'll go with him," I offer.

I'm not protection from anything by any means, but I can be a buffer—or a videographer. Or maybe just company. Everyone nods their agreement as if they have a community say in what Mekhi and I choose to do with ourselves. AJ hands Mekhi his keys.

The entire walk to the car he encroaches on me. I know he's trying to be funny because every time I put distance between us, he closes it. Then when I look up at him, he gives innocent doe eyes. Only to do it all over again.

Knowing he's just trying to get a reaction out of me because I said he has a personal space issue doesn't stop heat from spreading to my lower belly and up my chest. I watch him, trying to see what Reese sees. And I don't know.

Maybe? Possibly?

If he wanted something from me, he would try to get it. That's what he's shown me in the past.

And I'm not sure I've done anything to convert a *never* into a *we'll see*.

When we get to the car, he opens the passenger-side back door and I open the one on the driver's side. We leave both open so we don't suffocate, and meet in the backseat. The middle seat separates our spaces. I want to make it one space. Autumn and Mekhi's space. But I focus on the safest thing—looking for the ticket.

But no matter how many crevices we stick our hands down or times we retrace his steps, when the national anthem starts playing, Mekhi is still ticketless.

"I have no idea where that ticket is." He leans against the hood of the car. "You want to do something?"

There's just as much question in his voice as there is in his words. It's as if he's not sure he should even ask. Why he'd be so awkward about it, I have no idea. He knows I wouldn't leave him sitting out here alone.

"We can get ice cream somewhere. I'll buy you the biggest one. AJ won't mind as long as we're back when the game is over."

It's an offer I would never refuse, even without the extra added incentive. He wants to hang out with me, and it doesn't have anything to do with PROMposal Queen. For the record, there's nothing I can do to stop myself from reading into this.

"Answer one question first, soft-serve or hard ice cream?"

Why am I not surprised? This boy thinks soft-serve is real ice cream. And I'm not sure if everyone in this township agrees with him or they just have something against the real thing, because all we find is soft-serve everywhere.

I refuse to accept it and we end up at a grocery store freezer aisle choosing between my favorite brands.

"I'm thinking something with berries and chocolate. What do you like?"

He tuts. "You don't care what I like."

I come very close to telling him I do care and exactly how much. Instead, I grab a fistful of his T-shirt and pull him closer to the freezer. It's a completely unnecessary touch that I ultimately regret because it makes me want to touch him more. Also, his nonresistance makes me wonder if I could've grabbed his hand. Would he have gone along with that too? I want to test that boundary so bad.

I look up at his picture-perfect profile. "Choose."

He reaches in and comes out with a gallon of a raspberry-and-chocolate-chunk concoction.

I salivate. He smirks.

"You are such a martyr," I say.

He strides past me, stopping in front of the sprinkles.

"You can't put those on my ice cream."

He looks down at the gallon he's holding like a baby. "You can't eat this whole thing by yourself."

I raise an eyebrow.

He raises one in return. "Before it melts?"

I concede with a shrug. He's got me there.

The sun is low when we get back outside, transforming the sky from a bright blue with wispy clouds to an opaque orange. We end up on a bench outside the store. Mekhi spreads star-shaped sprinkles liberally over his half of the container. Meanwhile, I dig in with one of the spoons we snagged from the hot soup counter.

"You happy?"

"Yes. Thank you," I say around a mouthful.

Without looking at me, he nods a little. It's almost like he's happy to have made me happy. I don't know what to do with that. The entire last hour has been very, very curious.

Though I believe the sprinkles ruin the integrity of the ice cream, it looks like he's enjoying it, too, at least a little. I still outpace him two spoonfuls to one.

He's the first to call it quits, citing his need for real food. He wipes the corner of his mouth with the back of his hand. "I called you last night."

He's resting on the bench contentedly, staring out at the busy parking lot. Everything about him says this is a casual comment, but it doesn't feel casual. When you call someone and they don't call you back and you mention it, it suggests you feel some type of way. Snubbed? Ignored?

I mean, why bother mentioning it when the person is sitting right next to you now, ready to hear whatever you have to say?

"I kind of checked out last night. I didn't see you called until this morning. I figured I'd talk to you at school, but then Reese rearranged my day and I didn't really see you."

I swirl my spoon around, making a path in the softened ice cream. "Was it important?"

He lifts one shoulder and shakes his head. "I don't know. You jetted out of the meeting like something was wrong. Reese said you need happiness in your life. You good?"

Hold up. Wait. Mekhi was...*is* worried about me? Like, he's been thinking about my well-being for the last almost twenty-four hours? And this ice cream is supposed to bring me some happiness?

Somewhere out there is an AP English Language and Composition metaphor about me and this melting ice cream, but I'm too shook to come up with it.

I bet these are the kinds of things that have Maddie twisted, why she won't leave him alone. Concern from any other person is simply kindness. Concern from a boy you like is sweet, endearing, and something to read into.

My stomach tightens. I won't read into this. My self-destruction has boundaries.

"I'm good. Just the usual Autumn drama."

"You don't want to tell me about it?"

"It's not that. I mean...y-you already know most of it anyway," I sputter. I do want to talk to him about it. I just don't want to have feelings about him while I do it. "My parents found out I was lying to them about applying to other schools. They're not happy."

He frowns exaggeratedly.

"They've nominated you the official PROMposal Queen

chauffeur by taking my car." Needing to use both of my hands when I talk, I toss the melted ice cream in the trash a few steps away. When I sit back down, we're a lot closer than we were before. It's where I've wanted to be this whole time. "This is going to sound cliché as hell, but the worst part is they're disappointed in me and worried. My mom thinks I don't trust them. Like, if I could slap myself in the face with any real force, I would."

"Well, you *can*."

I shake my head. "I'd just duck."

He chuckles softly, which makes me do the same until one thought leads to another and the reality of my situation settles in again.

I massage the back of my neck with both hands. "They're going to question everything I say now."

He releases a deep sigh. "And that's going to feel like shit."

"You sound like you have experience with that."

"I live that," he grumbles.

The first thing that comes to mind is the essay. That would definitely make parents question their kid's word.

But this feels bigger than that. He's wearing the same look from when he mentioned he could go to Mercer without the scholarship but wouldn't. His eyes are vacant, like all of his feelings are stacked up in front of him and he's trying hard not to see them.

"How's that?" I say.

He starts to say something, then presses his lips together as if thinking better of it. "We don't have the same kinds of secrets, Autumn."

"They sound pretty similar to me." I swallow hard. "To be honest, I feel like you're always helping me out and I don't do anything in return."

"I'm just doing what we agreed to."

"It's more than that." I look down at my hands. Sitting here with him is like an honesty spell. I'm about to say a whole lot and I can't look him in the face when I do. "Since we've been working on PROMposal Queen you've made me feel like I can do things I didn't think I could. You make me feel like I can't fail. I want to do the same thing for you. You never give me the chance to."

"There's nothing for you to help me with. Your situation just reminded me of certain things." There's an attempt to bring some lightness to his voice, but we've spent too much time together for me to believe it's real.

I blink up at him. "If there was something I could help with, would you tell me?"

"Yes." He pushes a long, heavy breath out of his mouth. "I don't know. It depends."

He picks at the skin at the edge of his thumbnail as he looks at me. I'm not sure I want to know what he's thinking. It doesn't look like happy thoughts.

He slouches down and rests his head against the top of the bench.

"My parents are divorced. You know that." His voice is gravelly. When he looks at me for an answer it's the shortest of glances.

I nod and sit up straight. He's actually going to tell me.

"I found out my father was cheating on my mom, and I didn't tell her."

The way his voice goes up at the end of the sentence tells me there's more, but it's quiet for so long I think he's waiting for me to say something.

I open my mouth to answer but nothing comes out.

"She found some condoms. She asked Taj about it, and that was strange because she'd bought them for her before so it wouldn't be a thing." His forehead crinkles as if he's confused all over again about what happened. "When Taj said they weren't hers, she took this breath, and I knew what she was thinking. The same thing I had been for a while. The same thing I knew."

He glances quickly at me again and presses his hands against his thighs, almost as if he's embarrassed. "And I knew she wasn't going to ask me. She didn't have a reason to."

I don't know when this all happened or why he's embarrassed about this particular part of the story. But Mekhi's the sort of person it wouldn't surprise me if he is a virgin, and it wouldn't surprise me if he isn't. The way he kissed me, I'm sure he wouldn't pass up something he wanted.

"I said they were mine. I knew she didn't believe me when she didn't ask any follow-up questions." He closes his eyes and sighs. "So not only did she have a cheating husband, she had a son she couldn't trust, who protected him."

I reach out and put my hand over his where it rests on his thigh and wrap my fingers under his palm. I don't let the electricity we make force me to pull my hand back. Neither does he, and it's impossible for him not to have the exact same force traveling through his body. I scoot closer. And everything—his hand in mine, him telling me all this—is making my heart beat so fast I'm a little bit light-headed.

"I'd always tried to make sure she didn't notice the things I did about my dad, but this was the first time I ever volunteered a lie." He shakes his head. "Everything was different after that."

Things start to come together in my head. "Is this why you need a scholarship?"

He nods. "I can't take my dad's money. I don't want it to look like I want to have anything to do with him."

Mekhi shouldn't have lied, but there's more than one way to look at this. "Have you ever talked to your mom about it?"

He side-eyes me and lets a short, incredulous snort escape.

"I'm just asking because to me it seems like you were trying to protect your mom, not your dad. And yeah, you lied to her"—I raise my eyebrows and nod—"but she has to understand why."

He shakes his head slowly, definitively. His chest is heaving like he's challenging me or even angry. At least he wants me to think so. But I've seen what those things look like in his eyes. This isn't it. Mekhi is sad.

"I don't think that's how it works, Autumn. People get an idea in their head about you, and that's it."

I squeeze his hand. "Maybe this time will be different."

He doesn't say anything. He doesn't look at me. He doesn't move. The only way I know he's at least heard me is his breathing slows.

I don't know what he's thinking or feeling right now, but he's beautiful. Not in a way I would tell Reese about, but in a way that makes me want to make things better for him somehow.

"Are you going to at least try to talk to them?"

He takes a deep breath that comes across more like a surrender than frustration, and nods.

"And you won't be all secretive and embarrassed or whatever. You'll tell me what happens."

He smiles a little and looks me in the eye. Mekhi's eyes on me register in my body like a soft touch. "I promise. You'll be the first person I tell."

Keeping his hand in mine, I slouch down on the bench like him and rest my head against his shoulder. Not just because I think he needs me to, but because *I* need to. I want to be close to him.

More importantly, I have this feeling nothing like this will ever happen between us again. It'll never be this quiet.

The sky will never be this beautiful. I will never have this kind of courage again.

With his free hand, he taps a rhythm on mine, and I feel it like my own heartbeat. He's officially touched me enough today that I can't keep ignoring what it does to me and that I want him to keep going. I want to keep going.

I turn to him. He stops the drumming, but it takes a minute before he looks back at me. If I weren't so afraid of the answer, I'd ask him what he sees. Why is he letting me be this close to him? Why did he before?

Is it different this time? Can it ever be different?

He gives me a small, lopsided smile. It feels like permission.

So I kiss him. There's no warm-up. No brushing my lips against his to test the idea or pressing mine to his to see if he wants something deeper. I take everything all at once. Partly because I want it. Bad. Partly because right before our lips touch, I see something other than want in his eyes, and I don't want him to tell me what it is.

I've done it. I'm kissing Mekhi Winston on a bench in front of a grocery store after we shared secrets and a gallon of ice cream. And that ice cream tastes better on his lips than it did coming out of the carton.

Is it possible for a kiss to feel this good if I'm the only one who wants it? And would his hand be on my hip if he didn't want this?

Right when I'm about to believe this is happening, he pulls himself away and says my name the way moms do when they catch you doing something they know you know better than to do.

The energy making its way through me transforms from something that feels good to something that makes me want to disappear. With a thud, he presses his head back onto the bench again and rubs his hands over his face.

"This is supposed to be a PROMposal Queen—only thing, Autumn."

Suddenly, the heat of the day is on me. I'm sweating. I can't even imagine what I look like to him. What he must've been thinking when he realized what was about to happen. I can't find my voice to agree or disagree or tell him I under-stand. I just sit there staring at some plastic bottle that looks like it's been run over a hundred times but can't manage to get out of the way.

I guess senior year is not just a year for my failure, but also a year for repeating mistakes.

He stands. "We should get back. The game'll be over soon."

There could be a million reasons why he doesn't wait for my response before heading back to the car—and yes, I want him to turn back to me and say he made a mistake today and before—but the only reason I can build a case for is that Mekhi wants to forget any of this ever happened.

Chapter Twenty-Six

Just like Mercer, State is around an hour and a half away, but in the opposite direction. There's not much to see on the ride up. Reese talks about things she wants to show me when we get there, but none of it is enough to keep my mind off Mekhi for the entire time.

Since I kissed him two days ago, there have been zero bedroom video chats, let alone casual conversation. And we've managed to take care of the prompossals we had on the schedule without looking at each other.

Well, I looked at him.

A lot.

He didn't look at *me*. Mekhi says only what needs to be said. I go back and forth between being hurt about being rejected by him for a second time and feeling like an asshole because I took a moment of friendship and tried to turn it into something else.

When we arrive on campus, the scene is picture-perfect. Or maybe I should say even better than the pictures. The stone and ivy are gorgeous in person. Mercer is old, too, but the buildings are more spread out and there's more cement than trees. I'd be lying if I said it had anything on State in that way.

If I applied to go here and got accepted…next year, it'd be hard not to imagine finding time to sit underneath one of the many huge, hundred-year-old trees that beautify the campus. I kind of want to sit under one as we drive up.

If only a beautiful campus were all I needed.

We park in the visitor spots designated for the program. For the first time in weeks, the weather feels like spring as opposed to winter or summer. I try not to let that influence me either. Pretty much everything reaches full beauty on a day like today.

As soon as we walk in, I'm glad Reese decided to come along. I don't know anyone. This is pretty much how it would be for me as a student. Plenty of people from LeBeau end up here. I just don't know any of them that well. And with a population of thirty-five thousand, it's easy to lose track of someone you didn't make an effort to see for four years in a way-smaller space.

I get the feeling this meeting is supposed to feel cozy, because of all the large buildings and auditoriums this program could be in, we're stuffed into a small space in the library. I check in and get a name tag, and we find a seat in the middle of a row slightly toward the back. At first, the seats on both sides of us are left empty, but someone from the admissions office asks us all to scoot in as much as we can.

We're between a dad and a girl who I would mistake for a middle schooler instead of a high school junior.

As expected, a general overview of the university is given, followed by a presentation by the actual business school students. I already know the differences between State and Mercer. State is a good school, but the prestige of Mercer, along with the never-ending list of alumni that work for themselves, as well as at all different levels of business, is a thing State can't match.

But I have to be open to it and how it can work for me. This could be where I end up at some point. I may have to make State my Mercer. I'm sure Reese knows all of State's strong points, but her eyes are glued on the presentation. It makes me wonder what she's thinking.

After all the formalities, students around the room identify themselves as campus tour guides. We join the group closest to us, which consists of two families and two friends.

At the very last second, one more person joins.

A person I know.

At least I think I do. They say everyone has a doppelgänger, and that maybe makes more sense than what I think I'm seeing.

"Is this one of those *what happens at State, stays at State* types of situations?" Reese whispers, mistaking my staring for something other than what it is.

"Ugh. No. I think that's Julian from MBSP," I whisper back.

"The one who's always hating on you?"

I nod. "But it doesn't make sense that he would be here. I can't believe he didn't get in either."

Julian isn't my favorite person. Mostly because he isn't too fond of me. But he's brilliant and driven and one hundred percent Mercer. I have to get to the bottom of this.

As soon as we make eye contact, I say hello.

"Hey, Fall." He laughs. He thinks it's the funniest and most original joke ever.

I roll my eyes. He runs a hand through his slightly wavy hair. Julian is one of those people who gets the awful *what are you* question. In the three weeks of MBSP I never heard him give the same answer twice, and I believe every one of them.

"What are you doing here?" he says.

I'm not going to try and be all coy about this when we're in the same situation, but it's hard to admit I didn't get into Mercer to the person who openly wished for my downfall. I imagine the only difference between me and Julian is when I got wait-listed and accepted it, I wondered what was wrong with me. I'm sure Julian wonders what's wrong with Mercer. I wonder if he got full-on rejected or if there's a chance for him too.

I clear my throat. "The same thing you are."

He smiles knowingly at that. Reese introduces herself.

The tour guide gives us the plan for the next hour and tells us that if at any point we need to leave, let him know so he doesn't think he's lost someone.

The three of us keep ourselves a little separate from the group. I wonder if Julian's reasoning is the same as mine. The visual part of State is the part that doesn't need a sell. Some of the little facts we're given are interesting, though, like when and under what circumstances some buildings were constructed and by whom.

Presumably to keep us all interested, our guide asks what each of us plans to major in.

Julian says finance. I say general business administration because unlike Mercer, State doesn't have an entrepreneurial studies program. As stealthily as she can, Reese tucks herself behind us to avoid answering. She's been okay so far. I hope she's not feeling out of place now.

"Didn't you want to do something with event planning or something like that?" The words *event planning* come out of Julian's mouth with extra emphasis as if they're disgusting on his tongue.

I nod and look down at the water flowing under the bridge we're crossing. "I started a promposal service. I like doing it."

"I heard about that."

I jerk my head back in surprise. "You did?"

Up until this point our voices have been low enough to not be disrespectful to our guide, but my words get everyone's attention. I apologize in a whisper.

"Yeah, people have been talking about it in the chat."

"I haven't seen it." Not that my missing something in the chat is a surprise since I mute it more and more now.

He offers me a smug smile. "Private group."

I try not to let it bother me that there's a group chat where I'm being talked about. I *am* part of a group chat that's named in honor of Julian and his downfall. And it's not like I didn't know someone would question my silence.

"Guess you don't need Mercer after all. Rejection motivates you." He raises an eyebrow as if he's just made a point that should totally change my way of thinking.

I stop walking, not caring if I lose track of the guide. Apparently, Julian doesn't care much either—he stops too. Reese's eyes ping-pong between us.

"I didn't get rejected. I got wait-listed."

"Wait-listed." He chuckles. "You know how hard it is to get off a wait list? It's not like there are a lot of people turning Mercer down."

I cross my arms over my chest. "Just because you're all out of chances doesn't mean you have to downplay mine."

"Out of chances with who? I got in." He turns his nose up as if something stinks and takes in everything around us. "I'm here with my brother. This is where he wants to go for some reason."

My stomach drops, and not in that happy roller-coaster way. In that I'm-about-to-die-of-embarrassment way. Am I so in need of someone who feels my pain that I would fall into this trap?

"Wonder what they're doing with that scholarship money. I hope it's not too presumptuous to ask because I'm about to."

"Is that what this is about? That scholarship?"

He nods brusquely as if it's so obvious. "Why you? I can use that money."

"You know what? I have no idea. But if everybody at Mercer is going to be like you, then I don't want to be there."

"I'm exactly what you want to be like, that's why you haven't told anyone from MBSP about your situation," he says. "You're still hoping to get in."

I look for the group, like we're going to find them and rejoin the tour.

I pin him with the sharpest eye I can without making way for the tears I feel building behind my eyes. "Promposals might not win me another innovation award, but I've done more with PROMposal Queen in six weeks than people do with businesses in an entire year. I'm going to get in."

My voice wavers on that last line. I'm saying it because it's a reflex to defend myself, but I'm not sure I believe it. Am I going to get in? Should I stop dreaming, apply to every school with rolling admissions, and go wherever I get accepted?

He shakes his head as if he's been hit with some flying object he had no idea was coming.

"Wait. That's what the promposals are all about? The fact that you think something as cheesy as promposals will impress Mercer proves you don't belong there." He sucks his teeth. "If I were you, I'd distance myself as far away from PROMposal Queen as I could. Nobody at Mercer's going to respect that. They'll probably love you here, though, standards being what they are."

"PROMposal Queen is just for now. When I get in, I'll show Mercer I have more to offer."

He nods incredulously. "Yeah, I'll be waiting for that announcement. Hopefully they let you know soon, put you out of your misery."

Somehow, before I can come up with another word in my own defense, I let him be the first one to walk away.

I may have to accept that what he's saying is true. Maybe PROMposal Queen isn't good enough. Maybe the idea didn't send off any signals in my head the first time Mekhi mentioned it because it isn't enough to push me over the hump, whether it's profitable or not.

The group is long gone. I'm not even going to pretend to try and find them.

"We'll have to do our own tour." I unclench my hands and stretch my fingers, trying to relax. "You know where the business school is?"

Reese blinks as if she's trying to hold herself together. To be honest, I'm surprised at how quiet she stayed during the whole interaction with Julian. My best friend fighting my battles would've made me look even more ridiculous, but that's a lot of restraint for her.

"You know what would be nice?"

I shake my head slowly because the pause she leaves makes me feel as if she expects an answer. But the way her lips are twisted and her eyebrows knitted says she's daring me to speak.

"If the person who called me a quitter wasn't a quitter herself." She stomps her foot. It's like a release of the energy she'd been holding in the entire time. "Why did you let him talk to you like that?"

I hop back and gawk at her as if her stomp landed on my foot.

"Are you talking about me? When did I call you a quitter?"

"You said I gave up."

"That's not a quitter."

"It is. Giver-upper isn't a thing," she snips. "And I'm not even mad at that. You were kind of right. I'm mad at you because you talked about your own business like it was nothing. After all this time and all the work, you fold the minute somebody like Julian comes around?"

I sigh and squeeze my eyes shut. "Just because PROMposal Queen is something to me, doesn't mean it will be to everyone else. How do I even know?"

She clucks her tongue against her teeth and releases a sigh just like mine. "I have no idea, but you at least have to pretend until you and everybody else catch on."

"I do that most of the time, but the MBSP chat and even YBE meetings make me feel like everybody else is better at everything."

She shrugs and looks me dead in the eye. "Maybe they are better. Now. But that's not a permanent thing. You're literally the person who showed me that. I thought you believed it. I'm going to keep playing basketball because of it."

I grab her arm. "Excuse me? You what?"

"When you said I had to give up, all I kept hearing was I *had* given up and maybe it was too soon," she says. "A year or two at a good junior college and maybe I will be as good as or better than everybody else. Maybe I'll have something that makes me special. I have to see. And I don't plan on talking about myself like how you talk about PROMposal Queen."

"That's me." I shake my head at myself. "Pitching my business like even I don't like it."

She blinks at me in question.

"You kind of had to be there."

I'm thankful she's here right now to remind me that I started PROMposal Queen because I believe in myself. I have to keep doing that.

We wander around campus doing our own tour—finding

the biggest dorms and the business school. I try to see myself here. It's not what I've wanted, but maybe I can do it.

By the time we decide to go home, Julian has spilled my news in the chat, with the funny story of how and where he ran into Autumn Reeves.

Chapter Twenty-Seven

Julian's announcement literally made the MBSP chat glitch. Since then, making PROMposal Queen even bigger and better, and perfecting the business plan that shows how I got there, are all I've been thinking about. The only thing Mekhi and I haven't worked out is the profitability piece. It succeeded in theory, but in practice we're barely breaking even. If not for Mekhi's gadget-filled garage, PROMposal Queen would be bankrupt.

It's been hard for me, but for the last few days we've kept it PROMposal Queen only. I can't deny that keeping it that way is also part of the reason all we have left to do is fine-tuning and proofreading the business plan. We're more focused than we've ever been. Mekhi's good to go. The scholarship requirements are way less intricate than what's required for the capstone.

All of this means Mekhi and I don't have much reason to talk as often as before. But when Skyla, of Ryan fame, tracks me down, there's no one I want to tell but him. He's the only one who'll get it. And since I'm serious about the whole confidentiality thing, there's no one else I *can* tell.

I'm great with the self–pep talk and convince myself it's okay to seek out Mekhi for an impromptu meeting. Still, by the time I get to his usual table in the cafeteria, I've counted to ten twice and cracked my neck and all my fingers, but the air still feels cold in my lungs as if there's something in it other than oxygen.

There's an empty seat between him and AJ. Taking it as a sign, I sit on the stool with my back to the table.

Mekhi whips his head up from his lunch and blinks. That's a sign too. Not a good one.

" 'Sup," AJ says on my other side.

Thank God he's here to break the ice. I smile at him. Surprisingly, it's unforced.

As he drinks the juice from a cup of peaches, his eyes flick over my head to Mekhi and then back to me.

"You guys have PQ stuff?"

I can't help but glance from AJ to Mekhi. "Not planned. I just wanted to tell him something."

That sounds a lot like Mekhi isn't sitting right here, and I almost wish he weren't. My voice wouldn't sound so hoarse.

I wouldn't be sitting here rethinking every decision I've ever made.

"Um, excuse me," someone says indignantly from above me. Maddie.

Immediately, I flash back to the last YBE meeting. Her death glare gets better and better. It's not so much the look that intimidates me as her sophistication. It's the way she keeps her shoulders back and faces forward, yet still manages to look down at me.

She motions exasperatedly in my general direction.

"Oh." I look from her to Mekhi to AJ. "Were you sitting here? Nobody said anything."

"The tray was your first clue," she says, glancing from me to the table and back.

I turn around. And yep. Right there in front of me is a tray with nothing but buttered pasta and rolls on it. Sitting in the seat this girl has claimed next to the boy she's claimed— whether he likes it or not—is an honest mistake. But for some reason, I feel like excusing myself under the table. Mekhi knows how to discard unwanted girls. He's good at it. If he didn't want her around, she wouldn't be. I'm a hundred percent sure if not for the promposals, we'd be done.

Maybe I do deserve a little of her disdain.

AJ looks down at the opposite end of the table. "Can you guys scoot down?"

I put my hand on AJ's shoulder to get his attention. "It's not that serious. I'll handle it myself."

It's not like I need Mekhi's help anyway. I wanted to share a promposal-couple scandal with him because I knew he would get it, that's all. Maddie probably has way better secrets to tell.

I try to swivel out of her way, but before I can, AJ's moving one seat over.

"Nobody wants to sit next to me? I see how it is," he says.

Maddie doesn't make a move to take the empty seat. I scoot into it. It's less of a declaration of competition than remaining where I am or leaving.

AJ hunches down and whispers, "Go 'head. Talk to him."

I peek at Mekhi. He's super focused on his tray. I face my own empty spot at the table.

"You needed to talk to Mekhi, right?" AJ's voice is loud enough to get everyone's attention at the table. Even Mekhi looks in our direction. Not at me, but close enough.

"Our first no came looking for me," I say.

His eyebrows shoot up. Normally, if something I said got his attention that way, it'd make me smile, but all I can do is nod. He still hasn't spoken to me.

Maddie leans forward to take a bite of her pasta, obstructing our view of each other. We both lean back and so does she. We lean forward again. His attempt to actually see me is promising at least.

"One guess what she wanted." I try to bring lightness to my voice. If nothing else, I want PROMposal Queen to be normal. That's something we got right.

He shoves fries into his mouth and shrugs. I tilt my head and nod, urging him to make a guess. He doesn't give me anything. He just stares at me, waiting.

I let out a long breath and mumble, "She wants a promposal. For him."

He turns back to his food. "Interesting."

His voice is low and undirected. He could be talking to anyone. That's all I get. He's not disgusted. He's not scandalized. He's not surprised. And "interesting" feels like a lie.

If not for the eyebrow action a few seconds ago and his attempts to see around Maddie, I'd think he didn't care. I'd wonder if this was the same person who was completely invested in Ryan and Skyla just a few weeks ago.

Or was he? That whole day—when he sat next to me rooting for Ryan and then feeling sorry for him, when he said I was sweet—was he just caught up in a moment that's passed?

"Which one was this?" AJ says. "I don't see any nos on here, and I don't think I'd forget something like that."

When I turn back to him, he's scrolling through PROMposal Queen posts. When AJ first eased me into conversation, it felt like a save. Now his words weigh on me like a punishment. I want to leave, but I have some pride. I'd like my exit to be graceful.

"Oh"—I swallow hard, trying to regroup and make sure the sinking feeling in my stomach doesn't come through my voice—"we don't post the nos."

"You don't post the nos," Maddie says, a hint of disbelief

in her tone. "Do you know how many more followers you would have if you did?"

I want to ask her if she knows how much this is none of her business, but I don't. My attitude isn't all about PROMposal Queen. Some of it is jealousy. I can't help feeling it, but I don't want to act on it. I don't want to embarrass myself any more than I already have. I came to speak to someone who looks like it pains him to give me the time of day.

"Way more," AJ cosigns. "I bet the nos would get the most shares and comments."

I nod. "But we—"

Reflexively I look to Mekhi. He understands where I'm coming from on this issue. From a business and personal aspect. I expect him to jump in. There's no doubt in my mind, before I kissed him, he would've. But he just sits there, looking off into nothing with his chin resting in one hand while he dips fries in ketchup.

He's bored. Not just with me, but with PROMposal Queen. The thing that's most important to me, that I've been sharing with him. All because I kissed him? You'd think it was the worst thing that's ever happened.

For the first time in weeks, *we* feels wrong. There's no *we* if only one of us cares.

"*I'm* in it for the happiness. I want to see people get who they want, not abused in the comments."

Maddie clucks her tongue. "Basically, you guys are lying. You have everybody thinking you always get yeses."

I scoff and roll my eyes at her. "I never said that. It's not good business to showcase people's hurt feelings."

AJ smiles, obviously trying to take the conversation in a different direction. "The one you did with the meme on the school. That one is my favorite."

I appreciate his effort, but the heaviness in my chest tells me any chance at polite discourse is lost. Nobody gave Maddie permission to critique my business.

"That one was nice, but I liked the one at the end of the softball game where you guys had all those tiny softball balloons with the girl's name mixed in with bubbles." Maddie looks dreamily in Mekhi's direction. "That was really sweet."

He glances at me. "Her idea."

He says this with the enthusiasm of someone that's been told they need their nose hairs plucked one by one.

"That one was okay." AJ shrugs. "Probably third on my list."

"What was second, then?" Maddie asks.

"Hold on." I put my hands up between both of them. "Y'all are not about to rank my promposals."

I put my heart into every single one. And yeah, some shine more than others, but all of them mean something to the giver and the recipient. They mean something to me. They *are* something. I don't need them critiqued.

"Why not?" Maddie does this thing where she looks around at all of us and lets her mouth settle into a frown.

I guess it's supposed to be a look of innocence. "Everybody else is."

I do the same, glance around the group the way she did. They all look like they know something I don't.

She lifts up one corner of her mouth and pulls out her phone. PROMposal Queen is already up on her screen. My cheeks burn before she even opens her mouth. A girl like Maddie doesn't make statements like that unless she has evidence.

"Maybe not ranking them, but definitely having opinions." She slides her finger along the screen. "I'm trying to find where somebody said the last one was 'lame and not that creative.'"

I try my best not to read the comments anymore, but I know she'll find what she's looking for. At this point, I'm resigned to everyone discovering my faults and reveling in my downfall. May as well let her have this one.

AJ reaches across me and grabs her phone. She laughs but doesn't fight back.

I can't help thinking the save came from the wrong person. Mekhi Winston is going to sit here and let Maddie dog not just me, but PROMposal Queen? That's what we're doing?

I wait a second for him to prove me wrong, but there's nothing. Or maybe I'm waiting for my own perfect words and a way to say them without sounding as hurt as I am. Without much thought, something bubbles up.

"Anyway"—I lick my lips and breathe deep—"I just came over here to say me and Mekhi don't need to meet anymore, and he doesn't need to come to the promposals. The ones I have left are pretty much set."

He looks at me. Not in my general direction, but at me. He tilts his head and opens his mouth. He's finally going to say something. But do I want to hear it? There's a good chance he's going to call my bluff and brush PROMposal Queen off like it's nothing. Right here in front of his best friend and his...situation.

And I'm going to look like an asshole when I'm scrambling to take back everything I've said. Because I don't want anything I've said. Even though I keep getting hurt, I just want him to talk to me, to explain it. I want to understand how I keep misunderstanding his feelings. I want to see PROMposal Queen to the end with him.

But that's not what I'm about to get. I see it in his face.

I shoot out of my seat, sure not to make eye contact with any of them. "Cool, then. I have stuff to do."

I don't wait for a response. I head for the quickest route through the tables and out of the cafeteria. I'm so focused on being away from them, I don't recognize that Mekhi is following me until I get to the door and pause to avoid a collision with some juniors. Mekhi's tennis shoes squeak and I turn to see him just barely keeping himself from running into me.

I push my way past the juniors. My need to get out is

stronger than my need to be accommodating. Mekhi keeps pace but stays out of my line of sight.

"Can I talk to you for a minute?"

I let my nonresponse be my answer and keep walking, to where I'm not sure. He had a chance to talk, but he wanted to stay quiet and let his *girlfriend* say whatever she wanted about PROMposal Queen as if it's a joke. If I say one more word, he's going to know exactly how much he's hurting me. If he doesn't already.

How could he not know? Why doesn't he care even a little?

"Autumn? One minute. That's it. I promise."

I stay quiet and head toward the doors that lead to the athletic fields. I don't know why. I just don't want to be inside anymore. When I make it outside and Mekhi's still on my heels, I realize he's not going to stop following me until we talk. But I don't want to hear anything he has to say. I don't want it to be *his* conversation.

I whirl around. "You should just be with her."

He's caught on his tiptoes again, about to run into me. He sways backward, catching himself. Both of his eyebrows are lifted as if asking a question all on their own.

"Maddie."

His shoulders slump and he rolls his neck, like he's exhausted or something.

"You know how to show people what you feel or don't

feel. You know how to get your point across." I put the fist of one hand into the palm of the other and crack my knuckles. Anything not to look back up at him. "If you didn't have feelings for her, she would know and you wouldn't have sat there saying nothing while she tried to turn PROMposal Queen into a joke."

He nearly cuts me off. "You're right. I should've said something. But the whole thing caught me off guard." He stuffs his hands in his pockets and rocks back on his heels. "I didn't want to be an asshole and say everything I need to say to her in front of you. I don't want you to think it means something...about you and me."

He's right. If he had gone off on Maddie in front of me, I wouldn't have seen it as just a defense of PROMposal Queen, I would have seen it as a defense of me. I would've turned it into something it wasn't. But still.

"You act like PROMposal Queen doesn't mean anything to you. You don't care about Skyla and Ryan. You weren't going to tell me what people were saying."

"It means something to—"

"No." I shake my head and keep my eyes focused on my hands, which are now pressed against my thighs. "The scholarship means something to you."

"PROMposal Queen means something to me. You can't say it doesn't just because you don't want me to be a part of it anymore."

His voice is stern when he says this, but I don't believe him. And it's not just about the kiss. It's him. I don't get him, and I don't like that feeling.

"We're in a great place with the business plan and you can write about the outcome and projections for the scholarship without helping with the last few promposals."

I don't say this with quite as much strength as I did at the table. No one's here for me to be spiteful or strong in front of. I'm protecting my feelings at this point. Yes, I want to spend as much time as I can with a boy I like, but only if he feels the same.

I glance up at him, catching his eye just long enough to know he's been watching me this entire time. And also, he might be holding his bottom lip between his teeth to keep from saying something. It can only be about one thing.

I press my hands harder against my thighs and grip the bit of slack I find in my jeans.

"You didn't want to kiss me. I couldn't see that until right before, but I did see it and I kissed you anyway and made everything weird. I know this is my fault, but I want to end PROMposal Queen on a good note. Not with you feeling obligated and me feeling…"

I point and flex my foot, trying to come up with the right word to complete my thought, but can't. I look up at him, hoping he won't insist that I do.

Now *he's* not looking at *me*, but back toward the door we

came out of. He's massaging the back of his neck with one hand and tapping his pocket with the other.

" 'Kay," he says barely loud enough to hear.

After a minute of nothing but the normal sounds of LeBeau High junior/senior lunch period on a spring day, he turns away from me and goes back into school.

Chapter Twenty-Eight

I thought I needed romance to get my creative juices flowing, but apparently *lame and not that creative* is muse enough. My last three promposals are for the least-romantic, most vanity-based requests I've received. They aren't last because I was saving the best. They're last because I couldn't come up with anything until I realized that if people aren't asking for a romantic promposal, then they don't necessarily have to have one. Despite the lack of romance, it can still be unforgettable. Besides, after everything with Mekhi, I'm not feeling very romantic.

Another lesson I've learned is that if I ever do this again, the cost will be based on the promposal idea. You want an elite promposal, you're going to have to give me elite-level money. I'm not being greedy. My elaborate ideas and people's elaborate wants can get expensive.

I can't be counting on my dad's office, Mekhi, or the art teacher who loves what I'm doing to help my promposals come together. I have to be self-sufficient.

The aforementioned art teacher is the only reason I'm able to turn today's promposal into what I want it to be. She knows where to get the best reflective paper for the cheapest price. During third period, all ten rolls of it come tumbling out of my locker. Based on the assistant principal's "recommendation," lunch is the best time for me to pull this one off. I know this because after I asked to be excused from a small portion of class to make it work, it went further and further up the chain of command. Even janitorial services weighed in on cleaning up afterward and what I'm using to affix paper to lockers and walls.

The other thing that comes wafting out of my locker is one bright yellow origami sun. I look around, expecting to see someone, but the hall is empty.

Written on the sun is *1 of 10*. I guess I should be expecting nine more of these. Or maybe nothing at all. Last year someone slid ketchup packets into my locker vents and exploded them all over everything. I was pissed. I cleaned it up and that was it. It never happened again. I'm pretty sure it was one hundred percent random. As this probably is.

Either way, I don't have time to worry about it. I don't

have a lot of time to make this work, or someone to assist me in case something goes wrong or I need an extra set of hands. Since the cafeteria incident, I haven't heard from Mekhi at all. I haven't even seen him around school. I do, however, keep walking myself back from calling him to talk about my ideas. Before I kissed him, I think, he would have been proud of the progress I've made about seeing people's requests for what they are.

I'm beginning to think I'm never going to find that out. The reality is, after graduation, it's not like we're going to run into each other. Even if I end up at Mercer, we could still never cross paths. And I can't see either of us sliding into the other's DMs. Not that he would want to slide into mine.

He's over it. Or more likely, never been into it.

All these thoughts play in my head as I tape reflective paper over lockers and to the walls, wishing I had more than two hands to make things go faster and a little more perfect.

One thing that hasn't changed through all of this is my nerves. I'm hungry but can't eat, and all I can imagine is this idea not shining the way I envision it, or getting a no. Luckily, the other three nos have been in a more private setting. There'd be no hiding this one.

And still, no matter what anyone says, I want to get attention for PROMposal Queen through great prompostals, not broken hearts or jilted clients. Even if it means pushing past my own tastes and standards.

Of all the requests, this one is the most vain. Lauren thinks Sheppard's gorgeous hazel eyes and blond hair complement Lauren's blue eyes and brunette hair, and will *really help bring out my gold dress*. I would've thought someone was trolling me if not for the fact that I've had both Sheppard and Lauren in several classes since elementary school. I don't think Sheppard will mind being reduced to nothing more than gorgeous hazel eyes and blond hair. Not having heard anything about them dating in the past is one of LeBeau High's greatest mysteries.

There's no doubt in my mind that what would make both of them happiest is being able to see themselves, and each other, without interruption. And I'm just as happy to make that happen.

Once I have everything set up, I take pictures. In my excitement with some of my early promposals, I didn't get any before shots. By the time they were over, it was too late to capture what I'd done. My work had either been destroyed as part of the plan or as a cost of being at school with nearly three thousand people who will trample anything.

When I'm finished, it's one minute after Sheppard's teacher is supposed to excuse him from class, and four minutes before the bell. It doesn't surprise me that he hasn't been let out. His teacher was not happy to have his class interrupted for a promposal.

If the promposal didn't involve motion detection, Sheppard's timing wouldn't be that big of a deal. But if he's late, hundreds of people could end up thinking Lauren's asking them to prom.

Lauren pushes up to me in our designated hiding spot. She's also late. "Where is he?"

I shake my head. In a minute, I'm about to go get him myself. The only reason I haven't is that my presence would pretty much give it all away. It's not like I've ever spoken to Sheppard without a specific reason. And in the last few days, I've noticed that people either light up or try to hide when I come around, as if anticipating they're about to be surprised in the best or worst way.

"There he is," I say.

I'm not surprised to see him looking around for someone to blame for his being extracted from class, but I am caught off guard by how long it takes him to notice the reflective paper with a message in large letters especially for him on it. Any longer and there will be a promposal malfunction.

Finally, he sees it and laughs to himself as he reads it.

Mirror, mirror, on the wall, who would be the best prom date of them all?

As I'd hoped, he walks as he reads, and he gets to the end just as the bell rings. Then he looks into the infinity mirror I made with literally millions of reflections of Lauren and sets off the motion sensor. Lauren's voice rings out across the hall through a speaker I attached.

"Well, me, of course. Sheppard, want to go to prom?"

Sheppard doubles over in laughter, and when he pops

back up, the reflection speaks again. Lauren and I laugh too. There's more laughter, some slow claps, and eyebrow raising as she waltzes over to him. He nods exaggeratedly in answer to her question.

Of course, I record it all. Including the part where she demands he take the mirror down so she can put it up in her room.

It's funny how they look just as happy as all the romantic couples I set up, but in a different way. And I'm just as happy to see them happy.

If Mercer ends up saying no, I'll be crushed, but I know that with or without Mercer, I'll find a way to keep this happiness in my life and others'. And I won't be afraid to tell anybody how much I love it.

Chapter Twenty-Nine

Kamia must not mind the energy Jordyn and I leave in her house, because once again, our appointments are one after the other. I'm still riding on my high from the Mirror, Mirror promposal, but I can't promise good vibes. It takes two.

Again, Kamia's running behind schedule. As she waves me toward the couch, she's also saying goodbye to a client with a finished dress in hand and nodding Jordyn toward the makeshift office/dressing room.

"Did you pick up the bras I told you to get?" she says to me.

I nod. I've been to a formal before, but this is the first time a decision about undergarments has ever been so in-depth. A regular bra vs. braless vs. sewn-in pads vs. pasties. This is a whole thing. As usual, Kamia has a measuring tape draped around her neck, and another helping hold her big bun of braids in place.

Jordyn and I pass each other in the tiny hall with just a hello. We haven't spoken since her almost promposal. The only reason I know everything worked out is because Mekhi told me Tyler said so.

I can't even face her anyway. Not after spending the last week accepting that she might be right about me lying to myself about what was important to me when our friendship fell apart. Especially not when I'm right back where I was—completely infatuated with Mekhi Winston. And once again, he's not interested.

I have zero pride.

"Hey. Can you come in with me?" she says when I've already passed her. "I need an outside opinion."

"Outside" bothers me, but only a little. After everything, we still ended up here, giving prom dress approvals just like we would've if nothing had ever separated us.

"I can stay and see yours, too, if you want," she offers.

"That would be cool." I don't try to tamp down my overly enthusiastic answer. I just change direction and follow Jordyn into Kamia's second bedroom, where I sit in a chair in the corner.

There's a beautiful pink dress attached to the mannequin. Not all of the seams are together, but it's already a pink dream. Jordyn will be beautiful. I'm pretty sure she'll see that without me telling her, but I do anyway.

"It's going to be so pretty on you."

"It looks just like what you wanted," Kamia says. "Exactly how we drew it up."

Jordyn doesn't say a word. She just stares at the dress with an unreadable expression on her face. Kamia looks over at her, a question in her eye.

"If you have a problem with anything, we haven't passed the point where I can work it out," Kamia says. "That's what this fitting is for."

"Are you speechless?" I ask. "Like in a good way?"

Jordyn nods. I'm surprised I still know her so well.

Kamia lets out a sigh of relief. "Let's get it on you, then. This is why I love what I do."

Jordyn steps into the closet/changing room to get out of her clothes. Meanwhile, Kamia carefully unpins the back seam of the dress and pulls it away from the mannequin. When Jordyn says she's ready, Kamia heads in and gives strict instructions that she is not to open her eyes until she's told otherwise.

After a while, Jordyn comes out of the closet with her eyes closed and Kamia holding the dress together at her back. Kamia helps her up onto the pedestal. I hold in my reaction. If I make any sudden sound or move, Jordyn will open her eyes and see herself in the mirror before Kamia gives the okay.

As Kamia fusses with the top, Jordyn tells me how nervous she is about going to prom with Tyler. Neither of them has ever dated anyone outside their race. From what I see at school, I don't think Tyler can even say he has a Black friend.

"He's always seemed cool," I assure her. "I don't think you should be worried about it."

"We're good. I'm talking about everyone else." She pulls her braids over one shoulder and plays with the ends. "We're taking pictures at his house with all of his friends, and he said his grandparents are coming. I told him everybody better know I'm Black before I get there. Any shocked faces and I'm out."

"I don't know." Kamia's lips set into a line of skepticism. "You might not want to give them a chance to mobilize."

"Maybe, but, I mean, if he's stepping out like this and not trying to keep you a secret, then he probably has a handle on his people or knows how to *get* a handle on them," I say.

"You right. You right." Kamia steps away from the pedestal. "Okay. Open your eyes."

When Jordyn finally sees herself in the mirror, there's at least a smile so it's easier to tell how she feels.

"Now, I want to talk to you about this hem. I'm a firm believer in only having one sexy element to any outfit or else it becomes trashy," Kamia says. "We're already going there with the plunging back. The hem needs to be at least an inch, maybe two longer than we talked about."

Jordyn blinks in disbelief. "Are you calling my dress, the one you made, trashy?"

"No, I'm saying you can take any garment from classy to trashy with just a few tweaks. I'm perfectly fine if that's what you want to do. I'm not above trashy every now and again myself, but it's a time-and-place thing." Kamia meets Jordyn's gaze so unflinchingly, I would bust out laughing if not for the delicate state of our relationship. "If this is your time and place, be my guest."

As Kamia kneels to show us the original hem they talked about and her new suggestion, Jordyn gives me a look that says *Can you believe this bitch?*

I *can* believe Kamia. It's her reputation on the line. Parents—as in my case—are paying for these dresses; if she has us out here looking scandalous, she could lose customers. All that aside, even without the trashy ideals, I think Kamia's right. The longer hem looks better.

"You don't want to be pulling on the dress all night. Every time you sit down, stand up, or dance, you're going to be adjusting if you keep it short," I say.

Jordyn puts a hand on each hip and looks at me pointedly. "But does it look better?"

I nod. "Yes, it looks beautiful."

"Okay, let me unpin her and you're next," Kamia says as they head back into the closet. "I had so much fun working on your dress, Autumn. At first, I thought maybe it would be too simple, but once I started getting into all the small details you want, I realized how sophisticated it's going to be. It makes you the jewel, you know."

"Cool," I say.

"Why are you acting more excited about Jordyn's dress than you are your own?"

I shrug, and then when I remember neither of them can see me, say, "I'm excited."

And I am. I want to see my ideas turned into something beautiful too. It's just that having this small part of the way I imagined things would be come true makes me want all the parts that aren't going to happen even more.

Kamia emerges from the closet with something behind her back. I figure it's my dress.

"If you want to see this piece of work," she says, "you're going to have to at least sit up in your seat."

I readjust myself and she rolls her eyes as if she's disappointed with my effort.

"Come in the closet," she instructs as Jordyn comes out. "You don't get to see this until it's on your body."

I make my way to the open door with Kamia keeping her back to me so I can't see the dress.

"You can go without a bra, but we don't want your nipples showing either. I tacked in some padding so we can see how that works. I can pull them, and we can go one of the other routes if you don't like it," she says. "Let me know when you're ready."

I slide out of my clothes and keep my back to the door. My dress only has side seams, so I kind of give up on modesty as she slides me carefully in. She ushers me out with the same directions she gave Jordyn, who doesn't hold in her reaction the way I did.

"Girl. That's instant Instagram fame right there," Jordyn says.

"Too true," says Kamia. "And I was thinking of adding a belt, or something that looks like one, using the sparkle she bought for the sleeves and hem. Her waist is small and the more we accentuate that the better everything else looks."

"How do you think she should wear her hair?" Jordyn asks.

Judging by the sound of her voice, she's gotten up out of the chair and come over to the pedestal.

"Like I said, it's all about her, so nothing too much. I'll make something nice to pin in it using the sparkle or the fabric...probably both," Kamia says.

I clear my throat to get their attention. They've obviously forgotten I'm a living, breathing thing. "Can I open my eyes, please?"

"Oh yeah, but you have to be excited because this is too pretty not to get hype about," Kamia says.

I open my eyes. Kamia is right. This dress definitely does accentuate everything. And in a weird way the dress looks a little sexier than Jordyn's, even though hers shows way more skin. But mostly I love the color. "I love it. And I like all your ideas. Thank you."

"That's it?" Jordyn rolls her eyes. "You're not even smiling."

I push every ounce of happiness I can find in my body into my voice. "I love it. Seriously."

Jordyn purses her lips. "Are you worried about Mekhi not liking it or something? Because you can probably show up in a paper bag and he'll be all about it."

"Wait. What? Who's Mekhi? Not the ex?" Kamia's eyes flit between us excitedly as she tugs on the dress, molding it to me.

"No. Not my ex. Not—not my anything," I stutter out. This is not a conversation I expected to have with these two.

"But you're working on locking it down?" Kamia nods as if answering her own question.

I shake my head, but my body rejects my words as warmth works its way from my insides out. If this is what happens just thinking about working on anything with Mekhi, *actually doing it* might take me out completely.

"Why not?" Kamia says. "You don't like him?"

"She doesn't want me to be right." Jordyn's words land like the unexpected punch line of a joke.

I try to turn and face her, to see if she's serious, but Kamia has a very strong hold on me and this dress. As if she knows exactly what I want, Jordyn comes and stands right in front of me.

"I don't get why you can't admit you like him." Her eyes grow wide as if she's exasperated and over it. "If you had before, we'd still be friends. I knew he liked you anyway.

That was obvious. Whenever you went up to him and tried to make something happen between us, he only saw you."

The heat I felt from thinking about Mekhi turns cold on my skin. I try to move. This time just a step toward Jordyn to better plead my case, and still, Kamia holds me in place.

"You were being so shy, and I—"

Jordyn cuts me off with a shake of her head. "I wasn't being shy. I wasn't being seen. If I can admit it bothered me that every time he saw you, I was right there and he never noticed me once, you can at least stop gaslighting me. It's been three years."

"Girl"—Kamia holds the chalk in the same position she has been since Jordyn mentioned Mekhi—"you need to start from the beginning because it's kind of hard to root for you right now."

I cross my arms over my chest. I'm about to tell the events exactly as I saw them and it's not going to make me the hero of this story. Not that I'm trying to be a hero. I just want to be forgiven. I want my apology to at least be taken under consideration.

"I didn't even know who Mekhi was until you pointed him out at the first pep rally. You remember?"

Jordyn nods her agreement with my story so far.

"I thought he was cute, and even though he hung with AJ and all them, he seemed kind of quiet. Like he was cool not being around a bunch of people or into something all the time." Even though the heat from earlier is rising again, I try my best to keep my face neutral. Not only do I not want to prove Jordyn right, I resent my body's reaction to thinking of Mekhi. "I thought he was perfect for you.

"And seriously, every time I talked to him it was for you, I promise. But then he started finding me, and I'm not going to lie, I noticed that. I liked it. I started looking forward to it." Even now, a smile builds inside me just thinking about it, but I push it down. "I never outright admitted that to myself then, so I couldn't admit it to you because I felt like the worst friend. But I seriously thought as soon as I let him know you were interested all that would stop.

"The day he kissed me—"

"Ooh, girl. He didn't," Kamia interrupts. She puts her chalk down and sits on the edge of the pedestal to listen. The side of the dress that hasn't been marked yet gapes open. I try to tuck it all together under my arm.

"Before he did that, I had decided I was literally going to sit him next to you in the cafeteria, force you guys to talk, and walk away." I put my hands up to signify releasing any hold on the situation, and I have to quickly pull the dress closed again. "I had a whole cute thing planned, but *he* found me first."

I hope the way this part of the memory plays in my head doesn't show on my face because it's a sweet memory. I liked the way he looked at me as he caught up to me in the hall and we walked together up the back stairs, close enough that I felt his heat. Closer than two people who are just platonic acquaintances would. That's not from having a ton of experience. That's just from the comfortable, but at the same time electric, feeling I had while it was happening.

He ran his fingers along the sleeve of my I'M GOING TO BE A BIG SISTER T-shirt as he congratulated me on being adjacent to such a great accomplishment. I was so excited for my parents. I was never supposed to be an only child. When I thanked him, I guess that excitement must've come through on my face because he said, "I like it when you smile like that. I wish I could make you smile like that."

Those words knocked the wind out of me somehow. Instead of centering the conversation on my friend, I asked why he wished he could make me smile, knowing there was no answer that would do anything other than make me feel closer to him.

He shrugged and said, "I just want to."

My heart beat faster even as our pace up the steps slowed. With his hand still on the hem of my T-shirt sleeve, he inched even closer. At the time, I told myself the invading-of-my-personal-space part was either all in my head or a coincidence, but afterward I knew it wasn't either one of those things. He wanted to be closer to me. Still, I could've dodged everything and changed the whole mood.

He stopped on the landing between the second and third floor and said, "Can I try? To make you smile like that?"

I gave a barely audible mix of "Yes" and "Mm-hmm." I don't remember anything between my answer and when he kissed me. At first, I thought that while I liked that he kissed me, I wasn't going to like the way he kissed. But that idea faded from my mind fast. I loved the way he kissed me. Since then, I've come to the conclusion that my doubt was either about betraying my best friend, or a fear that I would do something to make Mekhi not want to kiss me again. Then the door to the cafeteria opened and closed. I pulled away but Mekhi was still searching for my lips, trying to reestablish that magnetic connection.

I ducked out of his reach and took a step back the way we came instead of toward the cafeteria. "I gotta go."

I don't give Jordyn all the gory details of how it felt to kiss him because A, it's rude, and B, Kamia's commentary could potentially escalate the situation. I don't deny my fault in any of it, though.

Jordyn's lips twist with skepticism. "Why didn't you come tell me what happened?"

"I didn't know how to bring it up and by the time I did, you weren't talking to me. I tried for days. You already knew somehow. I don't even know how it got out. I don't know who opened the door and what they saw or if it was just him bragging about being in the back hall with somebody like every other guy." I search her eyes for any clue that I'm getting through to her before continuing. "Then when I went to talk to Mekhi, he told me in front of all his friends that he probably shouldn't have kissed me because he didn't like me like that."

"He said that?" Jordyn and Kamia ask in unison.

I adjust the dress around myself. "He did. Now I'm right back in the same situation. I kissed him the other day and he stopped talking to me. He barely even looks at me."

The feeling in my chest changes from anger to disappointment. "I mean, yeah, I had some doubts, but I didn't think he'd be like this. If nothing else, we're friends. He tells me things. We laugh. He has more faith in me than I do sometimes...I don't know. Maybe I shouldn't have risked it."

Jordyn fiddles with her braids, pulling them all over one shoulder and running her fingers through. "What about the promposals?"

"I could tell he didn't want to be involved anymore so I told him he didn't have to be."

Braids still in hand, Jordyn nods over and over like she's processing a lot at once, even more than I've told her.

"Until now, that day in the back hall, that's the only time anything ever happened between y'all? Ever?"

I look at her pointedly. "Yes."

Jordyn stands there, hand on hip, looking at me. I think she's about to call bullshit on some part of the story, but instead she says, "You were late. I was coming to find you. I'm the one who walked in and saw you guys kissing in the stairwell."

I look away from her and back, letting the dress fall open again. This time Kamia grabs it and holds on. It's not hard putting myself in Jordyn's place back then. As much as I hate seeing Mekhi with Maddie, them lip-locked would be the pits.

"When I saw you guys kissing like that I figured it had been going on awhile, like that whole time you guys had a thing behind my back."

"Jordyn," I say sharply, unable to hold in my disbelief that she would even think something like that.

She tilts her head and crosses her arms over her chest. "For real, who has a first kiss like that?"

"It was my first kiss, yeah, but I don't know if it was his."

"That too, but I mean people don't kiss each other like that when it's the first time they've kissed. He had his hands everywhere. He looked real comfortable." Her eyes flit around the room as if the full breadth of the memory is coming back to her and she's trying to unsee it. "Like he'd been there before."

I blink. I never imagined the kiss looking the way it felt to me. I feel oddly vindicated. I'm not the only one the kiss fooled. Jordyn saw us and thought it meant something too.

With her eyes squeezed shut, Jordyn nods several times again as if she's coming to a decision. "I'm the one who told people you guys were spending time in the back hall," she admits.

That makes sense based on what she's already said, but my brain hadn't made it there yet.

"Yes, I knew what people would think, but it's not far

from what I thought," she says. "I was hurt. I didn't care if either of you were."

I can't believe Jordyn is the one who saw us. I would be hurt and mad, too, and could've come to the same conclusion she did and maybe handled it the way she did. What I don't get is why this all sounds like she's leading up to an apology.

"A couple days after I saw you guys, he asked me why you wouldn't talk to him anymore. It was the first time he ever really talked to me, and it was about you. I didn't know you'd stopped talking to him. And I didn't realize you'd never even told him I liked him.

"When he asked me, I said, 'Because she doesn't like you.'" She looks down at the floor as if for the first time she might be feeling remorse for the part she's played in my situation. "He looked at me like he thought I was joking, but when I didn't take it back after a few seconds, he said okay and started doing something on his phone. I'm pretty sure he believed me."

I stand there, letting it sink in. And I imagine the way her words might have hurt Mekhi, knowing I deserved it and he didn't. I realize maybe the reason he told me we didn't mean anything is because he thought we didn't.

This should make me feel better. Instead, I feel like an even bigger idiot than I did when I was under the impression Mekhi wasn't a good dude. If he'd led me on, some of the blame for everything was on him, too, even if just for hurting me. But I'm responsible for all of it. I hurt him after he took a risk for me. None of this would've happened if I'd just said no and not let him kiss me, or told Jordyn the truth the second I started developing any sort of feelings.

Whether he could verbalize the idea or not, he knew what romance was before I gave him my definition.

I can't blame him for not being able to see me that way again. I wouldn't even know how to ask him to try.

Since I'm here with Jordyn and she knows everything, I start with her. "I'm sorry. I should've done things differently. I should've been honest and trusted you to at least try to understand."

"Are you going to try and work things out with Mekhi too?" Kamia chimes in.

I side-eye her, expecting Jordyn to do the same, but she surprises me.

"You have to." Her lips quirk up into a sad smile. "We lost three years of friendship and while I'm sure it didn't all come apart just because of a boy, something more than a few forbidden kisses has to come out of it."

I laugh. "Oh, I learned a lot."

She chuckles a little. "It didn't stop you from still trying to be a matchmaker."

"Oh, whatever. I'm good at that," I say.

"As long as it doesn't involve Mekhi."

I nod. "True."

We both let out a wistful sigh.

"I am going to talk to him, though," I say. "When I got crushed, all I wanted to know was why. If he was crushed, I want him to know there's no reason for him to be."

She smiles. "Good."

This isn't the perfect reunion I've sometimes imagined for me and Jordyn, but it's a start. One that says anything is possible for the future of our friendship.

Chapter Thirty

The next morning, Reese and Jordyn converge on me at my locker as two different-sized sunshine origami fall out. I now have one through six of ten. I toss them in my locker with the others. This origami situation has gone from random to weird real fast. But not weirder than having my old best friend and my current one speaking at me in unison.

"Did you talk to him?" they ask.

I lean back against my locker, pressing it shut, and stare back and forth from Reese to Jordyn as they look quizzically at each other. I'm a hundred percent sure what's happened here is unintentional. Especially since last night, when I told Reese everything, she was not happy with Jordyn. It doesn't make me any more optimistic about the way my answer will go over, though.

I look at them both from underneath my lashes and shake my head.

Reese drums her fingers on the locker next to mine. "Why not?"

I look to Jordyn for a smidge more compassion, but she has the exact same energy as Reese, tapping her foot impatiently.

"Jordyn, you don't know this, but Reese, you do. I had to submit a business plan to Mercer. Everything needed to be perfect before I sent it."

"And of course it was perfect and you sent it in, right?" Reese asks.

I nod, mostly responding to the second half of the question. I didn't submit the business plan because it was perfect, but because I was running out of time to play my last card with Mercer. Now, all I can do is wait.

Reese puts on a wide, placid smile. "Congratulations. Following the submission, did technology fail? Did you not have five spare minutes to talk to him?" She puts her hand up, prominently displaying five fingers.

"Of course she did. Avoiding him doesn't have anything to do with the business plan," Jordyn says.

"Me explaining everything to him isn't going to magically make everything okay." I look back and forth between them again. One of them has to understand where I'm coming from. "He's never said he feels anything for me. It's the opposite, and I don't care how he tries to spin it, there's something up between him and Maddie."

Reese is shaking her head before I get the whole thought out.

"I talked to AJ this morning." She lets out a deep exasperated sigh as if the task took her to her limit. "According to him, Maddie and Mekhi are not a thing."

Jordyn and I lean in at the same time, equally hungry for details.

"He said Ms. Maddie, and that's Madelynn, not Madison, don't get it twisted, and her little friends had some pact about sleeping with a senior." Reese clucks her tongue against the roof of her mouth. "She put the full-court press on Mekhi, whatever, whatever, and he was kind of feeling her. Like for real."

This shouldn't be a surprise to me. I've suspected all along he likes her. But I hate having it confirmed.

"One of her friends told him what was up, and he was like *Why are you pretending to like me when you could've just said what you wanted*, and she was like *That's how it started but that's not how it is now*, and he was like *Bye*. Ever since, I guess she's been on a crusade to prove herself because obviously he liked her or else he wouldn't have gotten so mad."

Even though it crushes me to see any girl think she has to prove herself to get a guy, I can't help but see Maddie's perspective. "She has a point."

"Whatever." Reese waves her hand. "If he wanted her, he would've been forgotten about that pact."

"Reese is right," Jordyn says. "Mekhi doesn't seem like the type to string her along like that if he really cares."

I'm about to concede the point when a familiar voice cuts into the conversation. "Hey?"

Reese, never one to miss an opportunity to dislike Brandon, makes a gagging noise toward the spot where he's inserted himself in our meetup. "Why can't you just go away?"

Never one to be outdone, Brandon steps right in front of Reese and leans a shoulder on the locker next to mine. She would be completely blocked if not for having an inch or so of height on him. She's about to smack him on the back of the head when, to my surprise, Jordyn pulls her away.

Brandon waits until they're out of earshot and whispering animatedly at each other before he says anything. "What's up with you?"

The question isn't casual. It sounds like an accusation, and his eyebrows are drawn together like he's confused about something. I don't know what he could be accusing me of this time.

I shake my head to signify that nothing I'm willing to share with him is going on with me. "What's up with you?"

"About to go to class."

"Same."

He nods slowly, looking down at me from the tip of his

nose each time his head goes back. "I was getting all my plans finalized for prom and everything. The car. The suit. The dinner."

I side-eye him. I have no idea what's going on, but I'm trying to be polite. I don't hate him. "A lot of things are all booked up."

"Yeah, right. Good point. It would be hard to add someone to a reservation. You have to have your counts right."

I'm sure this is true, but none of this is anything I'm worried about. Reese and I are going to Southern Cuisine, where her uncle's a chef. A reservation isn't a problem.

I eye him and start walking to first period. He falls in step with me. That better not be what this is about. Brandon thinking I want to go with him.

He adjusts his backpack and clears his throat. "I haven't heard anything about who you're taking."

Oh. Maybe he's trying to figure out how to tell me he has a date. I haven't had my ear to the ground for this information. I am curious as to who this girl is, but I'm not going to be jealous or hurt. He has nothing to worry about with that.

"There's nothing to hear." I try not to sound disappointed about that. Not having a date isn't a big deal. It's the not-having-Mekhi-as-a-date part that I don't like.

"I'm going stag. Just me and my boys," he announces.

My eyes flit around the hall, searching for meaning in all of this and finding none.

Brandon presses on. "We're not combining with any

other groups or anything. We're focused on what we want to do."

Oookaaay. "As you should be."

"It's cool to have girls around, but then the focus shifts."

"Can't have that."

He smirks. "I know you're trying to be funny."

The contrast to the way I feel in this moment and the way I do when walking next to Mekhi is stunning. It's not that I'm dreading walking with Brandon. But the most I am is mildly curious about what brought this on.

"Uh-uh." I shake my head. "You're funny all on your own."

"But you get what I'm saying."

I shrug. "Sure. It's all about you and your boys."

"But there are a couple parties after. We're probably going to Devin's first."

I'm beyond confused at this point but play along. "Everybody's pretty hype about that one."

"Yeah, so if you're going to be there, we can catch up then."

"Oh." I blink. "I guess. If you want to."

"Of course I want to catch up. You know I still care about you." That comment is followed by a look that I think is supposed to mean *period* or *full stop*.

"Thanks for saying that," I say, genuinely.

Even if I'm over him, it's not a bad thing to hear.

At the same time, I have no clue what we'd catch up on

that would be meaningful. Can you reminisce on something in the recent past? I could try, I guess, if that'll show him I'm not walking around hating him. But aren't I showing him that now? I mean, this is a nice, civil interaction.

He sighs, relieved. About what, I have zero clue. "Okay. I'll see you after prom then."

"Sure," I say.

He nods and walks away. I play the conversation back in my head over and over, wondering where the plot was and how I missed it. He's going stag. I don't want to go with him, but we'll see each other after.

It isn't until I get to the door of my first period that I think I get it. I bust out laughing. There's only one thing I haven't considered. Probably because it's unbelievable. At the same time, it's on trend with the unpredictability of my life right now. I might have just agreed to meet up for a cliché-ass prom night booty call.

Never going to happen. Brandon and I have all the closure we're going to get. No need to start up anything else.

But on the other hand, Mekhi and I don't have anything close. Reese and Jordyn are right. I have to talk to him.

Chapter Thirty-One

As I walk up the steps to Mekhi's house, the night sky is clear and beautiful. If we were any other two people, this would be romantic, the perfect backdrop for saying everything I feel and having him tell me he feels the same.

But as soon as he opens the door, I know that fantasy won't be realized.

Even though he didn't ask questions or refuse me when I messaged him to borrow the Cricut again, it's clear he doesn't plan on this being a conversation. He's holding the tool out to me like a baton I'm supposed to grab blindly and run with.

I have no room to be offended by anything he does, but it still hurts. He's always made me welcome at his house, but now he's telling me something different. He doesn't want me here. If I didn't have so much to say, I'd leave. But I have to get this out.

Plus, Reese is my ride. If I get back to her car without having at least tried to resolve this, she will lose all respect for me.

The silence is so blatant it makes every second I stand there in front of him feel like a minute. I either have to take the Cricut and go or start talking. I wave it away.

"I'm sorry. I don't need to borrow that." My voice cracks. I clear my throat even though I know that won't fix it. My nervousness will just show itself some other way. "I want to talk to you and I felt like I needed a reason."

He licks his lips and tucks them between his teeth. A few more of those minute-seconds tick by before he steps out onto the porch, closing the door behind him.

His message is clear: I can say what I came to say, but I better not get too comfortable.

My heart is beating so fast that standing feels like work. I sit down on the top step of his porch and try not to be discouraged by having to look back at him to get him to join me. With the distance he keeps between us, I can barely call it sitting together.

"Freshman year, I designated myself the wingman for Jordyn. She really liked you."

His eyebrows knit together, and he sits up straight. "Wait. What are we talking about?"

"You know what I'm talking about. Before."

I wait, prepared for anything, but he just rests his elbows on his knees.

"She can be shy unless you know her. She'd been talking about you for a while. She was scared to say anything. I thought I could help her."

I glance over at him. He's not looking at me. He's focused on connecting and disconnecting the steeple he's made between his knees with his fingers.

"Long story short, I could see the things she saw in you and I started to like you too. I figured it would go away if you guys actually talked and were together. I know now that probably was wishful thinking. But the day you kissed me...The day we kissed I was going to sit you next to her in the cafeteria, so you could get to know each other."

I look at him again because I want some sort of reaction. He doesn't give me anything.

"Even though I felt a certain type of way about you, you weren't for me." After a long sigh, I pause because I want to get this part right. "I wanted to kiss you, but I knew I shouldn't want to, and I didn't like the idea that I wasn't loyal. I knew I should be a better friend than that."

Mekhi stops pressing his fingers together and lets them fall between his legs. It's the only clue that he's listening to me. I want him to listen, but physical proof that something I've said has even the smallest effect on him makes it that much harder to keep going.

"Anyway, Jordyn saw us and the first time I talked to

her about anything after that day—you included—is when we started PROMposal Queen." I'm talking fast now, just trying to get it all out. "I never told her I didn't like you. She was just hurt, which I get. She thought we were together behind her back or something and that was basically the end of our friendship. Then you treated me like trash in front of everybody and I felt stupid for thinking you liked me. I despised you."

He looks at me, then back at his hands twice before he says anything.

"You do realize that when you finally decided to talk to me it was a whole week after I kissed you, right?" His voice is hard. "I called you so many times before that. I tried to talk to you at school and you acted like you didn't see me. You started taking different ways to class."

"I wanted to straighten things out with Jordyn first. I knew if she saw us together or heard anything, we'd never be friends again. But she—"

"Confirmed what I was already thinking. I don't know why I even asked her."

"But I'm saying, she didn't tell you the truth."

He shakes his head. "If you really liked me, you wouldn't have put me in the position to have to ask someone else how you felt or make me think I had to say the stuff I said so you could stop feeling sorry for me. You would've explained the situation."

The idea of Mekhi thinking I felt sorry for him makes me

slow to respond. There's so much I want to address, but I don't think his current patience level will let me go to all those places right now. I attack what I think matters most. Why didn't I speak up?

"Explanations didn't feel like an option at the time. I had to make quick choices and every choice had consequences."

"Why explain things now?"

He's looking at me with barely a blink, like he thinks he's going to find an answer written on my face. I hope he sees I want to fix things between us. That I'm not playing a game.

As hard as it is, I return his steady look. "I'm telling you this because I like you."

He nods curtly and the set of his jaw is firm. "And you think I like you?"

"I thought maybe you did, but I honestly don't know now." I hold my breath. "Do you? Like me?"

Instead of answering, he goes back to steepling his fingers.

I wipe my hands on my thighs and let out a shaky breath. It's okay. Like I told Reese and Jordyn, telling Mekhi what actually happened doesn't mean everything's going to turn out okay. It doesn't mean he'll want what I want.

"Remember when you said Ryan was wrong for using Skyla's feelings against her?"

"That's not what I'm doing," I shoot back. But am I? Would I be here if I didn't believe there was hope?

"That's what it looks like to me. You think you can say anything, do anything, not trust me until someone else says

314

it's okay, and I'll shake it off, or wait around like I did before, because of how I feel."

"I do trust you. I have trusted you."

"No, you haven't. The other day you tried to tell me I don't care about PROMposal Queen." One side of his mouth quirks up in disappointment. "That was bullshit, Autumn."

"I shouldn't have said that. I'm sorry." I wrap my hands around my knees and pull them close to my chest. "And I don't expect you to shake it off or wait around. I don't expect anything or think I have the right to expect anything. I just...if there was a chance you...You kissed me back for a second, and then you changed your mind. If what happened before was why..."

"I didn't change my mind." His voice has none of its usual depth. It's like he's not sure if he actually wants me to hear him. "I remembered what it feels like when you decide you're done with me, and I didn't want to have that feeling again."

And that's really what it boils down to. This isn't about if he likes me. It's about if he's willing to take a risk for it.

I gather all the courage and sincerity I have and try to make it come through in my voice, my words, and the way I look at him. "Nothing like that is going to happen again."

"It already happened. It's been happening." He blinks and looks up at the sky. "Like I told you. I don't like having to prove myself all the time. I mean, what's going to happen when there's no Jordyn to plead my case? Only me?"

"Nobody has to plead your case. *You* don't have to plead your case."

He frowns and scratches his head. "Jordyn is the only reason you're here giving me the time of day. It doesn't have anything to do with me and who I've been the entire time."

I start a sentence but don't finish it because he's right. I'm here because of what Jordyn told me. I had planned on giving up.

I wipe my hands on my thighs and let out a shaky breath.

"I'd like to think I would've realized what I'm missing out on eventually," I say. "But I guess I would be too late anyway."

I don't sit and wait for his response. He knows what I want him to say. And we both know he's not going to say it.

Chapter Thirty-Two

I spend most of the next day trying to figure out how I could've handled last night better. The truth was the only card I had to play. I don't see Mekhi in the halls at all. He's the one doing the avoiding this time.

After school, I don't notice the huge origami star stuck to my locker until I'm right up on it. This one looks a bit more like a sunflower than the others. Something's written on the front in black Sharpie. I read it without taking it down.

You haven't been reading the stars so everything's not yet clear.

I can't wait to fill you in. Open this star. It's all in here.

I look around, asking everyone if they saw who put this big-ass star on my locker. Of course, nobody saw anything. But someone around here has to know something. I'm obviously being watched if the star-giver knows I haven't been opening them. And how could I have? Some of them were so tiny I would've torn them up trying to get them open.

Opening this one is easy, though. The print is small, so I have to hold it right up to my face to read it, but before I do, I peek around to see if anyone's watching. No one looks the least bit suspicious.

> I wasn't surprised you were voted most likely to
>   brighten everyone's day.
> That's exactly what happens every time you come
>   my way.
> You're always so cute, and you have the best hair.
> Every time you walk by I can't help but stare.
> I get jealous sometimes when you're hanging with
>   that other dude.
> I wish you could remember how I used to get you in
>   the mood.
> It would be an honor to have you on my arm again.
> I wish you could see me the way you did when you
>   were my girlfriend.
> They call you PROMposal Queen, well, I'm about to
>   be the king.

Meet me outside the caf after school so we can do this thing.

I blink. Read it again to make sure I'm seeing what I think I'm seeing.

Yes, they call me PROMposal Queen, and I was Brandon's girlfriend, but the origami can't be from him. Brandon would never.

Then again, his behavior *has* been bizarre. After that talk in the hallway, he's been going out of his way to make sure we don't see each other. One time, he stepped behind someone and into an alcove when we spotted each other in the hall.

He told me once he liked me for months before he ever got up the courage to say anything. Maybe he went the other way when he saw me in the hall then, too, and I didn't notice. I can attest to wanting to be seen by the person you like, but also feeling naked when it happens.

This is from Brandon?

This is from Brandon.

And it's for me.

But it doesn't make sense. Either this is a joke, he's having some kind of dumper's remorse, or he somehow believes this is a way to guarantee he gets some on prom night. Something is definitely off, and I need to figure out what it is.

I take a deep breath and get ready to handle whatever's about to happen. If I can make it through the awkward aftermath of my conversation with Mekhi last night, I can deal with anything.

I take the long way, making sure I don't run into Reese. On the off chance that this is real, I don't want to subject Brandon to whatever sort of ridicule she's going to come at him with, deserved or not.

As soon as I round the corner to the cafeteria entrance, a deep-voiced "No" rings out. Brandon stalks toward me. I take a step back. This isn't the welcome I'm expecting. Even on the day he broke up with me he wasn't visibly disgusted to see me. But now, every spot on his face that can be pinched and creased, is.

"No. This—Why are you still doing this?" He holds up an origami that's strikingly similar to what I've been getting all week.

He's staring directly at me, but I look around for someone else he could possibly be talking to.

"I asked you about this the other day to try and see where your head is. You said you understood how things are with us. But I kept getting these suns with this wack-ass poetry that could've only been from you." He turns away dramatically and then back. "I don't understand. I broke up with you. I was nice about it. I said we could still be cool. I convinced all my friends to go stag to prom so you didn't get hurt seeing me with somebody else. I don't know what else I could've done."

I don't say anything. I can't. I'm too shocked. I was sitting around minding my own business and he wanted to be with me. Since we broke up, he's the one that's been seeking me out. Not the other way around. But no matter what, I would never humiliate him the way he's humiliating me. I wouldn't do this to a stranger, let alone anyone I claim to care about.

What did I ever see in him?

I hold my dismantled star up to him, poem out, press it to his chest, and let go. I don't wait around to see if he catches the paper before it falls to the floor. All I want is to be out of this school and away from him.

I keep my head down on the way to Reese's car. I try to open the passenger door even though I know it's locked. Since this whole thing started, I have never wished I had my car more than I do right now. I want to be by myself.

My phone dings, and a notification slides onto my screen. A new comment on our last promposal. I tap it.

The hyperlinked words PROMposal Queen Gets a No stare up at me. I lean back against the car and click it. It's me and my sad little face as Brandon says no. From this angle, and in this context, it looks exactly like what the headline describes: I asked Brandon to prom, and he rejected me in the worst way. There's no reason to question whether or not the video is legit and no one in the comments does. They proceed to dragging me instead.

Do for others what you can't for yourself lol.

Fraud

Bruh. He didn't have to play her like that though.

The look on her face at 1:25. Crushed.

Sad to watch.

Can she refund her own money?

Wow. I bet these are the same people who went from loving my promposals to being very unimpressed. I shouldn't care, but I do. I have a professional reputation and somebody's trying to ruin it. I delete the comment with the link, but it just keeps being reposted under different account names. So I turn off the comments, but it doesn't matter. The video already has more than a hundred views and fifty comments. People know where to find it.

What would happen if someone from Mercer's admissions committee saw this? Does this negate my accomplishment of starting a business? That thought makes me physically ill. That video could ruin my chances with Mercer for good. Maybe better planning could've protected me from anything like this happening. Mercer may want someone who can anticipate this kind of problem and prevent it.

The best thing I can do is delete my business plan from my application. A simple search for "PROMposal Queen" will lead to this debacle.

From my phone, I log on to my applicant page, quickly scroll down to <u>Submit Additional Materials,</u> and click. *You may submit documentation only once* stares back at me from a text box. No matter how many times I close the box and click the link, the response stays the same.

Shit.

I pace the side of the car, wondering where Reese could possibly be. There's a pressure behind my eyes. I take a deep breath to push it away. I'm so glad I didn't say anything to Brandon. If I had spoken, tears would've fallen and that would've been a disaster. That video would've been edited so many ways that no matter what I said, no one would believe those tears weren't for him.

There must be a way to fix this. A way to prove to Mercer, and maybe even myself, just how special I am. The thing I can't do is crumble. I've wallowed enough about all of it. I sit on the ground in front of the passenger's side, making myself think this all through, willing myself to figure it out.

Maybe to give myself the best chance to get into Mercer, I need to show them something they've never seen before. The part of myself I hate to show. The part of myself that lost me my best friend. The part of me that no one knew enough to add to a recommendation letter.

To do that, I'm going to need help. As much as I hate to, I message Brandon.

Chapter Thirty-Three

Reese stretches her long legs out across the chaise on our deck, making herself comfortable. When I finally caught up with her at school, she was stalking the halls searching for Brandon. Lucky for him, he'd already left.

"You should give him a script. You can't go live without knowing exactly what he's going to say. He might start feeling himself again and thinking you want him."

Brandon gives her a quick, beady-eyed glance. "Hold up. Why are y'all acting like I did something? We both got played. I'm a victim too."

"You better be telling the truth." Reese eyes him up and down. " 'Cause when I find out who's responsible for making my girl look desperate, there's going to be a price."

"But I didn't do anything," he stresses from his spot on

the other side of the deck. It's about as far as he can get from Reese and still hold a conversation.

"Oh, you did a lot," I snort. "I'm all humiliated and you're running around looking like the guy I can't stand to lose."

And the pile-on isn't dying down either. There are an infinite number of jokes that can be made about a promposal planner who calls herself PROMposal Queen and can't get a date to prom, and we're only on number 306. I don't want to say that there are more comments on my rejection than on any promposal, but that's how it is.

He cocks his head to the side. "Would it be that bad if you still liked me?"

I roll my eyes. He can answer that question for himself, since he's the one who made the idea of still being liked by me seem like his worst nightmare. I'm still mad about that. I'm probably more mad at him for that than I am at the person who set the whole thing up. The scheme couldn't have worked without Brandon reacting the way he did.

But feelings or no feelings, it's the principle of the thing. He shouldn't have gone off on me like that. He can at least see that part of it. When I asked him to come help me set the record straight, he didn't fight me on it. And I'm not giving him a script. This needs to be real.

"Can you brush your hair before we do this?" Reese frowns. "You look like you had a rough day."

"Why you gotta be so mean?" Brandon says.

Reese twists one corner of her lip and rolls her eyes so long and deeply the flutter of her lashes resembles a moth near a bright porch light. "Now you want to defend her? When legitimate points are being made in the form of statements as opposed to 'wack-ass poetry'?"

Brandon groans. "Where we doing this?"

The one thing these two can agree on is finding the best light, and when they do, we tell our side of the story, sitting right next to each other, proving I'm not broken...or hopelessly in love with Brandon.

When we're finished, I post the first comment to the video.

PROMposal Queen Isn't Perfect.

PROMposal Queen's first and only posted rejection is mine, and I'm okay with that.

Brandon and Reese hover over my shoulder, watching my phone, waiting for comments to start popping up. We all jump when a voice I'm not expecting to hear says, "Your mom let me in."

Mekhi is standing right outside the sliding glass door to my house.

I sit up straight. I want to see him. I love seeing him, but at the same time, it creates a drop in my belly that's equal parts excitement and hurt feelings.

He sees it. The way he can't even meet my eyes anymore tells me he might even pity me. How embarrassing is that?

Reese smiles and offers him her spot next to me on the

deck stairs. Brandon doesn't budge from my other side, but his body goes tense, and he takes a deep breath. Mekhi keeps his distance, and his hands in his pockets.

"Um, hey," I say, and stutter through the beginnings of a couple different sentences before I finally settle on "How long have you been standing there?"

"Long enough to see you have everything under control." He glances around as if taking in the whole scene, even though there's nothing to see. "I expected you to be taking this whole thing way differently. You were so upset in the video, and since I know what all of this means to you I—"

"What does it mean to you?" Brandon asks as if this is information he's entitled to know.

Mekhi gives something between a glance and a glare in Brandon's direction. "Can I talk to you alone?"

Reese looks from me to Mekhi to Brandon. "Oh. We were just about to leave."

"Speak for yourself. I don't have anywhere to be." Brandon puffs up a little and eyes Mekhi, who's rubbing a hand across the back of his neck and looking everywhere but at me. I see it in his eyes when he comes to a conclusion. "Oh, hell no."

I think he's reacting to the fact that Reese has him by the shirt, because he gets up and takes two steps away from me. But they're also two steps closer to Mekhi, which multiplies the tension by about a hundred. I stand up, too, even though I have no clue what's going on. This can't be about me. Neither of them is that invested.

"Did you have something to do with this?" Brandon looks at me and lifts his chin. "I told you messing around with him would get you in trouble."

Mekhi laughs incredulously. "That's right. I almost forgot. You're supposed to be a good guy and I'm the one who gets people in trouble? That's funny."

Brandon laughs, too, but neither of them even tries to fake a smile. "Naw, bruh. You funny."

"You're the one with the jokes, telling people I stole your paper. Still." Mekhi pins Brandon with an antagonistic glare. "You know it's on my transcript."

"It's on mine too."

"It should be. You cheated."

"You need to grow up. Get over it." Brandon's voice has none of the passion Mekhi's does. It's one big shrug.

The conversation isn't hard to follow. Processing what I'm hearing, on the other hand, makes Mercer's capstone course look like light work in comparison.

Brandon sought me out for the sole purpose of lying to me. I believed him, adding cheat to the list of reasons I had not to trust Mekhi. I told Mekhi all this to his face. He never corrected me. I never questioned it even though it shouldn't have taken me that long to realize Mekhi would never steal anything from Brandon.

This is why Mekhi doesn't believe I trust him. I took Brandon's word over his and never let the person Mekhi has shown me he is prove it wrong.

"I was over it. Your name never came out of my mouth until you had something to say about me. And even then, I didn't say much." Mekhi takes his hands out of his pockets and flexes his fingers. "You know how many times I wanted to ask Autumn how you got with her, and didn't? But you're warning her about me based on something you did?"

With every word Mekhi inches closer to Brandon, who doesn't back out of the way. Reese must notice it too. She's nearly between them now.

I eye Brandon, taking in all the things about him that I used to appreciate but that do absolutely nothing for me now.

"Why did you lie?" I ask him. "You could've just stayed out of it."

"I didn't plan it, but you weren't listening to me." Brandon actually does shrug this time. "I broke up with you so we could finish senior year without being tied down, not so you could go be with somebody else. Especially not him."

Mekhi takes another step. Reese puts a hand up and gives Brandon the evilest of eyes. "We need to go. For real this time. Stop trying to prove how big of an asshole you can be. We can all see it's infinite."

Brandon gives that eye right back, not budging.

Mekhi steps backward and takes a deep breath. "I'm the one who needs to go."

"No. You don't." I try to make eye contact with him, but he's not letting me. "Can you stay for a few minutes? Give me a chance to apologize or try to explain what was going through my head when Brandon told me about the situation. Why didn't you just tell me what really happened?"

"Would you have believed me? Taken my word over his?"

"You didn't give me a chance."

"But would you have believed me?" He looks me in the eyes then and raises both eyebrows. "That's the question, Autumn."

I just stare at him. I want to say yes, but I don't want to lie. If he'd told me his side of the story when I approached him about everything, no, I wouldn't have believed him.

"I didn't know you then."

"But when you got to know me, did you even...Why did you look so surprised just now?"

"I—"

Mekhi shakes his head. "Never mind. I didn't even want to get into all that. It's pointless. I just came to tell you Maddie planned this whole thing."

"What?" I shriek.

"I knew it. I warned you," Brandon says.

"Maddie?" Reese whips her head back in disgust. "That bitch."

She's typing on her phone, spreading this information before it's even sunk in for me. I can't do more than notice my body shaking with anger. All this because Mekhi doesn't like her. It's not like he's even with me or I stole him. Everything between them happened before me.

"I thought she was good after we talked, that she understood you don't have anything to do with what's going on between me and her. But I guess not. I'm sorry." Mekhi stuffs his hands in his pockets and rocks back on his heels. "I've been trying to get her to take it down. But I guess you don't need that now."

"Don't even worry about it," Reese says. "This is her last time. Trust me on that."

"Okay then, I'ma head out," Mekhi says only to me, and walks away, taking the long way around the house instead of going inside.

I watch until he's out of sight. I want to ask him to come back and talk to me, but why? At this point, we have no other reason to interact again. If he's okay with that, I don't want to try and force anything else out of him.

Chapter Thirty-Four

"Tassel on the right. You haven't graduated yet," Mom says as we walk toward LeBeau for Senior Honors Night.

I check the tassel, which seems to be bouncing around on its own. This is the third time she's told me. She's right; I still have a couple weeks before I can say I've graduated high school, but also, her emotional attachment to this tassel is questionable. I have this feeling she wants time to stop, and me to keep this tassel on the right side forever.

My suspicions are confirmed when Dad takes her hand the way he would Baby's and pulls her back with him. I appreciate the block, but he's not any better. He got out the good video camera as if his phone can't take sufficient video of me anticlimactically receiving a cord for National Honor Society and a certificate for the Seal of Biliteracy.

I pull Baby close. "If you really want to be a miracle baby, find a way not to grow up. I don't think they can take it."

As if she knows exactly what I'm trying to say, she takes the hand that isn't wrapped around my shoulder protectively, puts it on her chest, and says, "Baby."

We both giggle. I let her slide down my hip, pass her off to my dad, and lead my family into the auditorium.

All of the National Honor Society kids are being recognized today, so Mekhi's here. I glance around, looking for him. Just so I can know where he is and so my heart doesn't fall to my stomach when he catches my eye on accident. It's like, I get the message his silence is sending—I need to stop liking him—but my heart doesn't register it.

I spot Jordyn in quiet conversation with a girl next to her. I don't know what's going to happen with our friendship, but I do know I don't want her and Reese to gang up on me ever again.

I take my alphabetically assigned seat. As usual—and thankfully—I'm between two of the most domesticated seniors at LeBeau. One tells me how nice I look and complains about their own attire and hair until I tell them they look great, and the other congratulates both of us. When those formalities are over, we all stare straight ahead and wait. My hair is uncharacteristically in a crown of two braids tonight to make sure my cap stays on, making me more difficult to spot, but still, I slouch down in my seat a little.

I don't know what compels me, but I turn. Almost directly behind me, three rows back, is Mekhi. He looks like he left the barber's chair and came directly here. I've learned the difference between what his hair looks like when his barber has brushed and tamed it the way he wants, and after the fact when Mekhi has washed it and not fought or organized the kinks in any way. He looks good. He always does, but I like his hair better his way.

As much as I love seeing him, it hurts. It hurts to care about him. Pangs of want don't leave space for getting sentimental about this being one of my last times in this room as a student.

He looks up like he can feel eyes on him. Even though I've spotted him first, my heart still drops when he catches me staring.

I face forward and busy myself with my phone until our principal gets up to welcome us. Unlike award shows, the program begins with some of the more prestigious honors, and we work our way down to the ones that include large groups of the student population. Some of the awards are obvious, foregone conclusions. Everyone knows who's been working the hardest and participating the most the last four years. Those are all the people with happy posts to schools even more selective than Mercer.

The principal's remarks aren't long or boring. I'm surprised I've never realized until now that she's kind of funny.

She introduces Mrs. Tanner to present the first award, for citizenship.

Mrs. Tanner starts by reminiscing about the day she first met this student. She can usually pick out the freshmen in the class who'll end up in the office for some reason or other within the first month.

"Normally, it's the ones who look like their shoes are made of fifty-pound weights as they come in from the parking lot and bus loop on the first day," she says, and pauses to soak in the chuckles. "But I worried about this student for a different reason. This one looked completely unfazed. She smiled and bounced in. And I thought, *She is in for a rude awakening. She'll be in the office—maybe crying—before the week is over.* I was prepared to deliver my speech about how change is good and developing a growth mind-set and on and on.

"As expected, she was in my office in the first week." She puts her finger in the air to emphasize the number of weeks it took this student to show up. I prepare myself for this person's bounce-back story. "But she wasn't there to get help for herself. She was there to get help for a junior crying uncontrollably in the hall. Shows what I know."

She pauses again, letting the laughter die down before she continues.

"I remember thinking to myself later when one of our staff came back to the office with this particular student—how many others walked by and didn't think to say anything," Mrs. Tanner says.

"I found myself leaning on this student a lot too. When someone needed extra hands for a project or to show a new student around, she was the student I could count on. Not that she never turned me down. Just this year I asked her to help with outreach for one of our programs—I don't want to embarrass anyone, so I won't name the program—but she looked me in the eye and asked, 'Mrs. Tanner, are you asking me to do this because nobody else wants to?' Following that, she looked at me with such disappointment. Totally shamed me."

She gets more laughter and looks around at everyone. When I said that to Mrs. Tanner, I didn't think it was all that funny. I felt like she was trying to take advantage.

Mrs. Tanner is talking about me.

She goes on with a few other stories about the times when I didn't turn down her asks. She brings up PROMposal Queen and how she isn't surprised that helping people get what they want is a brainchild of mine. My neck gets hot at that point. Mekhi has to be staring daggers into it. The promposals themselves were my brainchildren, but the idea of promposals being a business was his. I hope he knows I've given credit where it's due. I've never told anyone it was all me.

"When the committee got together to make their senior

award recommendations, only one name came to mind, and no one disagreed. This student exemplifies what it means to be a good citizen among her peers and of the world," Mrs. Tanner continues. "All of the intangible things we want and need in a friend, a student, a coworker, or an employee and can't put our finger on but know them when we see them— all those things are Autumn Reeves."

Mrs. Tanner makes eye contact with me as she says this. I've known it was me for the last three minutes, and everyone around me says *Congratulations,* but still I put a hand to my chest to confirm. She nods encouragingly. When I stand there's an ear-piercing whistle that can only be from my father.

Onstage, I shake the hands of the teachers, principals, and counselors I pass before I get to Mrs. Tanner. She hands me a plaque and flowers. I can't do anything but smile. I wasn't expecting this award or for Mrs. Tanner or anyone else to remember anything I've done at LeBeau. I wouldn't have expected it even before Brandon told me I hadn't set myself apart.

To be honest, it seems a little unfair to get an award for actions it cost me nothing to take. These teachers don't know everything either. Would I have been the easy choice if Mrs. Tanner had known about the situation with Jordyn way back then? But maybe that was the growth part, and good citizen or not, I couldn't have skipped that.

I fumble my way back to my seat, careful not to look three rows behind me.

Even though every other recognition I receive is my name preceded and followed by someone else's, I spend the rest of the program unable to curb nervous sweating under my romper, at the backs of my knees, and where my ankles are crossed.

After the last recognition, students are told to file out first for refreshments in the hall. I head right for the water. I don't even walk away from the table before I gulp it down and get another bottle. Waiting for Reese, I slide out of people's way, nod at any congratulations, and offer them back.

"That award was pretty much made for you," Jordyn says from behind me.

If there was one person in the world that would vote against me getting any sort of citizenship award, it would be her. She's seen the worst of me.

"Thank you," I say, and then because I don't want the conversation to end there I add quickly, "What's up with you and Tyler?"

She smiles, and that kind of says everything.

"You're not nervous anymore, then."

"Hell yeah, I'm still nervous." We both laugh, but mine gets caught in my throat when I spot Mekhi coming out of the auditorium.

My body is instantly on fire. I open my second bottled water and start gulping it down.

Reese joins our gawking. She's a little less covert than

me and Jordyn. "Damn, Autumn. Slow down. It's like you invented thirst or something. Is that his dad?"

"No. His dad wouldn't be here." Then I look a little closer at the man standing next to him. They remind me of me and my mom. One an older, more confident version of the other. "Maybe."

I'm happy for Mekhi if it is, but also a little sad he didn't keep his promise to tell me if he talked to his parents. Even if he believes I'd hurt him again, he can't question whether I'd be a good friend and listener. I've been that for him. If I hadn't kissed him, I'd be that right now.

Slightly behind him are his mother and sister. They catch me staring. Taj waves and taps Mekhi. Before he can catch me, I pull my phone out of my gown as if I'm getting a call. It's off, but I discreetly turn it on and swipe anyway until it comes to life.

It vibrates in my hand. I have an email.

From Mercer.

"What's wrong?" Reese says to me, and then looks at Jordyn. "Why does she keep reading the comments?"

If not for my shock at the subject line of the email, I would smile at Reese and Jordyn readying to gang up on me again.

From: Admissions, Mercer School of Business, Great Lakes University

To: Autumn Reeves

Subject: Congratulations

That's all I can read before I let go of my phone and cover my mouth with both hands. OMG. My parents want to go to dinner, but after that I'm going to respond to the email and tell Mercer that while I feel like I have the right to hold them to whatever this email says, they've been hacked. For real this time.

Reese screams. Loud enough that my ears ring. She smothers me in a hug and starts jumping up and down until I'm jumping with her. She has my phone. She's read the same thing I have.

"You. Got. In," she says in rhythm with our jump.

Then another pair of arms goes around me and then another that I know belongs to my mom because I smell her perfume and Baby's little voice is screaming as loud as she can.

Then I hear my dad, reading the entire email aloud to anyone who'll listen.

Dear Autumn:

Congratulations! On behalf of Mercer School of Business, Great Lakes University, it is my pleasure to offer you acceptance to our upcoming class for January. As a first-year student beginning midyear, you'll have the opportunity to get acquainted with the campus, meet your advisor, and register for classes over winter break.

Your gap semester is an opportunity to continue to grow as a Mercer student. Our most ambitious midyear students often use the fall semester to pursue other interests and endeavors, including studying abroad, volunteering, and gaining valuable experience in their chosen field of study.

We are excited to offer you this opportunity and would like you to accept or decline this acceptance as soon as possible. If you choose to become a student at Mercer, a more detailed packet with housing, financial aid, and tuition information, along with an invitation to visit campus, will be forthcoming.

Sincerely,
Valerie Ferrer
Dean of Admissions
Mercer School of Business, Great Lakes University

Leave it to Mercer to give me exactly what I want, but on their timetable. I don't even care when I start. I'm in.

Later that night, when I'm all swaddled and reading the email from Mercer for the thousandth time, I get a text.

It's the one word again. *Congratulations.*

This time, instead of the numbness of disbelief at seeing the word, I get butterflies. They make me throw all my blankets off and smile into my pillow. I've been wanting to talk to Mekhi for days. I have paragraphs and paragraphs to tell him, but his text is just one word. A friendly word, so I keep it simple.

Autumn: Thank you. I can't believe it.

Since I have no idea what will happen if I bring up his dad, I don't. Bringing up old promises doesn't feel like the thing to do in our fragile situation. But I want to know. I want Mekhi to want to tell me what's been going on with him.

Mekhi: Believe it. You deserve it.

Yes, as conversations go, it's my turn to speak, but I don't know what to say. After his dad, the next thing that comes to mind is telling him how good he looked today and that I wish I could see him right now. And do these texts mean he's not mad at me anymore? After the fake promposal debacle, I figured he'd want to go back to the way we were before. He'd stay in his corner, and I'd stay in mine.

Maybe we still will. It's one text. Not even a whole conversation.

Mekhi: ●●●

I sit up in bed and wait. Maybe it *is* going to be a whole conversation?

Please don't let it be one of those situations where he forgets to close the app and leaves his cursor blinking in the text box for me to stress over all night. Please let there be more.

Mekhi: Having a late dessert with my dad. Alone.

Wait. Okay. He's going to tell *me* about his father. I don't know if he's telling me because he promised he'd let me know, or if he's telling me because I'm the person he wants to talk to about it. Either way, I can't think of a better ending to this night.

I can't be any happier for him.

Autumn: Thank you for telling me, but aren't you supposed to be talking to him?

Mekhi: I'm in the bathroom.

Autumn: 👀 You're texting me from a urinal???

Mekhi: There's a men's parlor.

Autumn: Oh. Y'all fancy.

Mekhi: He's trying to be. Doesn't change anything. I can't fake it. Not even for Mercer.

> **Autumn:** Don't. Just tell him the truth. Tell him what you're thinking.

Mekhi: I can't do that either.

> **Autumn:** You have to try. At least once.

Mekhi: I have. Plenty of times.

I lie back onto my pillows.

I am probably one of the last people who should be telling him to spill his guts even when there's a chance he could be hurt. At the same time, if I'm the only person he's going to talk to about this, I have to say the thing that will make him consider *and* disregard the source. I have to convince him to do what's best for him.

> **Mekhi:** He's found me. Have to go.

Even though it's probably too late, I tell him what I most want him to know.

> **Autumn:** You're worth the risk it takes to say what you feel.

Chapter Thirty-Five

By the time Reese gets to my house, my mom has taken roughly two hundred pictures of me, but she's still game for more. I'm not mad. I'm loving my look too.

"Y'all out here making a statement." She claps her hands in excitement. "Reese, you have to give me your mom's information so I can pass these pictures on. They're turning out so nice."

Reese wears a slip of a dress with spaghetti straps and a high slit, perfect for someone with legs as long as hers.

Our backyard is the perfect backdrop for this kind of thing. It doesn't take a lot for Mom to make everything look semiprofessional. Baby is in some of the pictures because she won't stop whining until we let her. But Mom has dressed her up too. She looks like she fits right in.

After Mom does her official ones, we take some to post of us together. We've both already posted plenty of ourselves alone. Every time I put something up, I resist the urge to go through my feed and check for Mekhi. I can't imagine him dressed up, but of course he would look perfect, and if I were to see him, I'd miss him. I don't want my night to be melancholy like that. I want it to be happy and carefree.

"Dinner, prom, and then an afterparty, right?" Dad reiterates for the fifth time tonight.

We all give an affirmative answer.

"Who has the address to the party?"

"Dad, I told you it's over by the school. All you have to do is check my phone location anyway."

"Maybe I want to do a drive-by before you even get there," he says.

"I have the exact address, Mr. Reeves." Reese walks over to my dad and pulls up a map. "My mom asked the same."

"She'll be fine, honey. Call if any plans change, Autumn." Mom makes eye contact with Reese. She's probably checking to see if Reese's eyelashes are a strip or singles because they're fabulous, and also inhumanly long. Reese doesn't seem to notice too much before she finishes giving my dad the information and goes back to her own world.

"You ready?" I ask.

"Hmm. We don't have to hurry. My uncle won't let them give our table away, we're good."

"You sure? We don't need a prom night horror story." I try to look over her shoulder to see what on her phone has her so captivated, but she instinctively body-blocks me.

"There's no need for anyone to break a heel trying to get there. That's all I'm saying," Reese says. "I need to go to the bathroom anyway."

Before she moves, she texts feverishly on her phone and stuffs it in her purse.

Not wanting my feet to get tired before we even get to dinner, I slide my shoes off and wait in the front hall for her to do her business. It's the perfect time to catch up on posts, especially ones from PROMposal Queen clients. Jordyn looks beautiful, but there's stress on her face. I hope she's okay. Somehow, even though we refused to do the promposal, Skyla and Ryan are hand in hand. And of course, Will and Margo, the couple that started it all, look gorgeous.

Has Mekhi seen all this? What does he think about it?

That thought makes me want to check and see if he's posted anything. Maybe it's better if I see him via pictures before I see him in real life. I can get the initial ache over with privately and look unbothered when I'm in his face.

AJ posted from a barbershop earlier, but all I got of Mekhi was his chuckle in the background. I love that chuckle. It makes me appreciate when I get a real laugh from him that much more.

I look up to see Reese staring at me suspiciously from down the hall. "Are you repeatedly watching AJ's post?"

"No," I say defensively.

The look on her face says she's not buying my cover.

Letting my shoulders slump, I cave.

"Yes, I'm repeatedly watching AJ's post. I know I'm pouring salt in my own wound, but I thought Mekhi might get in touch with me or something today."

He hasn't given me all the details, but he's texted me about conversations he's had with both of his parents. They've made him feel less guilty about accepting help from his father. And as it turns out, that was a good thing. The committee for the scholarship he wanted put out a short list last week, and he isn't on it.

She rolls her eyes as if my pining annoys her. "Let's go. Tonight is about to be everything. No matter what."

I yell goodbye to my parents, slip my shoes back on, and follow her to the limo, where the driver gets out and opens the door for us.

"I'm already connected, and the playlist is set." Reese pulls out her phone and music blares from the limo's speakers.

In the middle of me recording a video of us scream-rapping one of our favorite songs of the school year, Reese stops and looks at her phone as intently as she did earlier.

I open my clutch for gum. What's inside catches me

off guard. I take out a small square packet and hold it up between two fingers.

"What the hell is this?"

"A condom." Reese narrows an eye, obviously confused by my confusion.

"I know what it is technically, I'm saying what"—I empty the contents of the tiny purse onto the leather seat—"what are five of them doing in my purse?"

Reese laughs.

"Did you do this?"

"I wouldn't have snuck them in your purse, I would've handed them to you. Maybe your mom?"

"My mom?" I say in horror at first, and then, after a little more thought, "My mom. Maybe, but why do it all on the sly and what would make her think there's even a one percent chance I'll have the opportunity to use these?"

"No idea." Reese shrugs. "Wishful thinking?"

Over the intercom, Reese tells the driver we need to go to Unique Foods, which is way out of the way and will make us later than late for our reservation.

"I was just thinking. We need to get postprom treats so we don't have to stop before the party."

I'm hungry. Starving. But at this point, I'm open to anything that prolongs the time leading up to my seeing Mekhi.

Between checking out prom posts, we bring a new energy to almost every song that comes up on the perfectly crafted playlist. By the time we get to Unique Foods, I've already had a night's worth of fun. The driver drops us off at the door and explains that we should wait for him there when we come out.

I take every step very carefully, not sure if me, these heels, and this flooring are a good match. Equally scared, Reese latches onto me.

We head to the gum and candy aisle singing the last song that played in the car.

"Why don't you be in charge of the chips? You know how picky you are." She's deep into a message again.

"Don't go too far, though. I'm not trying to play hide-and-seek in these shoes."

She nods, and when I round the corner, there's whispering and shushing and I think the click-clack of her shoes behind me, but every time I turn around it stops and nobody's there. I step slowly into the chip aisle, reminding myself to consider Reese's taste buds when I make my selections.

I start at the top and scan the shelves from left to right. My eyes settle on the display of the first bag of jalapeño chips Mekhi was convinced would restore my faith in potato chip manufacturers. I get butterflies seeing them and thinking about that first moment we connected on something. Yeah, it was chips, but it was a moment. Some of the butterflies are sad, and some of them are happy.

I only want to be happy tonight, so I shift my focus when something else catches my eye.

A bag of chips called Autumn's Perfect Jalapeño.

I laugh to myself. Universe, stop playing.

I grab the bag and turn it over to see where they're made and read whatever little story or anecdote the brand is sharing about how their chips came to be, but I get caught up on the Nutrition Facts box.

Serving Size: 1
Cute 100% Date Value*
Fun 100% Date Value*
Kissability 100% Date Value*
Potentiality 100% Date Value*
Risky 100% Date Value*

* The % Date Value shows what percentage of your
requirements I provide. It is based only on what
you want. Even though not everyone has such
high standards for a prom date, the % Date Value
can help you determine if I'm high or low in what is
needed to ensure a special night.

Autumn, will you go to prom with me?

I read it and read it and read it, afraid that if my eyes drift somewhere else my requirements will be replaced by actual edible ingredients and this'll be a joke I've played on myself. When I trust it, I look behind me.

And he's there. Tapping his fingers nervously on his pockets and wearing a smile I will never get used to seeing directed at me. There's enough in that look to inspire every promposal forever.

There's only one thing to do. I can't go up on my tiptoes any more than I already am in my heels, so I grab the lapel of his suit jacket and put everything I want him to know into a kiss. And I want him to know a lot.

His lips are soft and needy, and their pressure against mine assures me he's not going to push me away this time. As if to leave no doubt, he wraps his arms around my waist, pressing us together.

When someone clears their throat and we pull apart, he chuckles at me and I'm grinning so wide, laughter bubbling up in my own chest. I straighten his tie since I'm pretty sure I'm the reason it's crooked. That's when I realize we match. Still not able to find my words, I look up at him for an explanation.

"Jordyn hooked me up with Kamia. She made a tie for me out of the same material as your dress so we could coordinate." He nods toward the end of the aisle. Jordyn is there, with Tyler and a few of his friends that she probably had to drag here. Reese's and Mekhi's friends are on the other end.

I can hardly believe that after everything, Mekhi put all this together for me. *We* inspired all this.

"You look so good," I say, finally.

He laughs and ducks his head like he's embarrassed.

"So do you. I saw you walking in, and I felt like I should rethink my strategy. I wanted it to pass all your tests."

"Everything is perfect. It couldn't make sense for anybody but us." I give him a stern look. "But the chips better be on point."

"I can't promise that. They're from a party supply company. Answer me before you taste them. Just in case," he says. "Yes or no. Will you go to prom with me?"

"*Yes.*" I kiss him again.

"Here," a voice says next to us. It's AJ holding a box with a corsage in it.

"Sorry. I don't have anything for you."

AJ shows me his other hand. "We got everything covered. Don't worry."

Mekhi puts the corsage on my wrist, and after several failed attempts, to my surprise, Jordyn comes up from behind me to pin the boutonniere on him for me. Something occurs to me as she does.

"Does my mom know about this?"

"Yeah. We didn't want her wondering where the limo was taking you if she checked," Jordyn says. "Why? Did she give it away?"

My face heats with embarrassment. "No. Not exactly. I'll have to explain it to you later."

"My uncle can't ask them to hold a table all night on prom night, y'all. Let's go."

I grab Mekhi's hand. He's coming with me. That's the only thing I'm sure about tonight. And honestly, not knowing what else might happen is the magic of it all.

Acknowledgments

Thank God.

Thanks to my parents for loving me, and for showing me the path of least resistance but always allowing me to go my own way. To my husband for supporting my dreams without question, never doubting me even when you have no clue what I'm talking about, and laughing with me until it hurts. To my son for keeping me on my grind by being so hard to impress. I will always remember the look on your face when I said I'd finally sold a book. I'm aiming for that look all the time now. To my daughter for your endless encouragement, for sharing your beautiful light with me, and for never letting me forget that I still have a lot to learn (and for being so eager to teach me, lol).

Huge thanks to my agent Natalie Lakosil. Not just for selling my books but for helping me lean into my strengths and what I love to write. Thanks to my editor, Ruqayyah Daud, for wanting to see Black girls in love on the page as much as I do, and for loving and understanding Autumn.

And to everyone at Little, Brown Books for Young Readers who believed in this book and had a hand in making it a real thing: I know there are many of you, and I am forever grateful.

Thanks to my Spartan crew, Gavina, Nicki, and Phyre, for still being with me all these years later, and for always listening, laughing, and being down for anything. You get me even when you don't get me, and hopefully you know how much that means. To Sophina for being a great example of walking in faith and refusing to settle. And to my cousin Dwan for always seeing something worthy in me even when I don't see it in myself.

To Louise Harrison for helping teenage me find my voice, and for telling me it was perfect as is. I wish I could've shared this with you.

Lastly, to anyone over the years who took the time to read my words and offer support, critique, and/or encouragement: I truly appreciate you.

Y'all. We did this! It actually happened. To many more dreams come true for each of us!